THE GARBAGE BAG GIRL

CAROL KNUTH

Dream Swept Publishing

This book is a work of fiction, inspired by true events. Names of characters and places are fictional.

The Garbage Bag Girl. Copyright © 2012 by Carol Knuth

First paperback edition

ISBN 0985924306
ISBN 978-0-9859243-0-0

Printed in the United States of America

*To my husband, children, grandchildren,
and the rest of my family and friends that have inspired within me
the courage to dream...*

CHAPTER ONE

Screams pierced the ears of fourteen-year-old Emma Snow as she stood on the sagging wooden porch of her Aunt Vicki and Uncle Walter's home. The screams had come from her sixteen-year-old cousin Abby, and Emma's seventeen-year-old sister Katie. Horrified, they watched as Cody, Emma's fourteen-year-old cousin, fell to the floor of the uncovered porch, flat on his back—out cold. His face was illuminated eerily white by a light on a utility pole.

Emma rushed to his side and dropped to her knees. Bending over his body, she pressed her hand to his chest and felt the racing of his heart.

"Oh my God!" Emma sobbed, as she looked down at the gaunt, still body.

Gently, she placed the palm of her hand onto the side of his cold face, feeling the sharp angle of his cheekbone. Cody was perilously thin from lack of food, and treated more as slave labor than a son by his father and stepmother. Emma moved her hand to the back of his head—kneading her fingers across his scalp feeling for sticky blood caused by the fall to the hard surface of the porch. Cody had been home from the hospital for just a few days—recovering from a ruptured appendix—and now...*this.*

She heard the tattered screen door slam behind her, and knew it was her Uncle Walter storming back into the small one-story house. Walter was a field hand for one of the farmers in town, and he and his family—along with the newest occupants, Emma and her two older sisters, Katie, and Amy—lived in a small two-bedroom house located in the middle of the fields, five miles from town. Katie said the house had probably been built during sharecropper days, so the teens in the house referred to the run-down house, crammed with two adults and six children, as a shack, which was what it looked like with its sagging wooden porch, plywood floors and roughly added on bedrooms.

Cody's father, Walter, was the reason he now lay unconscious on the chicken shit and cat shit covered porch. He had punched his son so hard it had knocked him out—it had been the terms of their agreement. If Cody allowed his father to punch him, he would be allowed to see his girlfriend the next night.

Cody's stepmother, Vicki, had grounded Cody from his usual Saturday night date with his girlfriend, although there had been no violation of any of her quirky, inconsistent rules. No, she had grounded him simply because she enjoyed making him miserable. Devastated, Cody, with tears in his eyes, had begged Vicki not to take the one thing that meant so much from him—a few hours with his fifteen-year-old girlfriend. Most Saturday nights, Cody's stepmother drove him the twenty-minute drive to his girl-friend's, parents' home, where he was allowed to spend a few short hours pretending to be like other teenagers. It was a place where he was treated like a human being—safe from the torment of his monster of a stepmother.

Earlier in the day as Katie, Abby, and Emma, had watched, Cody had stood in the middle of the living room, with tears in his eyes, and begged Vicki not to ground him, promising to do anything she asked of him. Emma had watched as her Aunt Vicki looked at Cody. Vicki's eyes had twinkled as the grin on her pudgy face spread wider, and her belly jiggled as an evil giggle hissed out of her sounding like air escaping from a tire. Vicki was as fat, as Cody was thin—as if she gobbled up all the food in the house just so he would starve—anything to make her stepson miserable.

When Walter arrived home several hours later, reeking of alcohol, he had offered Cody an out. Walter had stated, *Cody, if you let me punch you, just one time, you got yer date.*

One time? Cody had asked. That had been a half hour ago. Emma had watched the exchange between Cody and her uncle, a tall man, at least six foot two, and aged beyond his years by years of heavy drinking. Emma wasn't sure how old Walter was but calculated his age to be in his early forties, although he looked as if he were in his mid-fifties. Walter always had a dirty, disheveled look about him, even early in the day before he cracked open his first beer. He always seemed to be somewhere else, lost somewhere in his mind, even before he began stumbling in a drunken stupor about the large yard, or as he roamed aimlessly throughout the house. His hairy beer belly always seemed to be poking through whatever stained shirt he chose to wear for the day, the front held together with a few randomly stitched buttons. Cody was much shorter than his father was, barely five foot eight, with hair bleached almost white from hours of working in the sun. Emma couldn't believe her ears when she had listened to her uncle's offer to Cody, wondering if the people she was living with had finally toppled off the edge of sanity.

Cody groaned and slowly raised his hand to his face, hiding his expression. He struggled to sit up as Emma crouched next to him.

"Cody. Cody, are you okay?" Emma asked softly.

He pulled away from her and stumbled to his feet. Emma, looking up, saw tears wetting his cheeks, and rose to her feet as he ripped open the screen door and disappeared inside. The three girls stood looking at each other for a moment not sure what to do.

Emma was the youngest of the five teenagers living in the house, and at five foot four, was the tallest, by several inches, of the girls. She had a distinct look, different from the other five children, with golden light brown hair, deep green eyes, the shade of an oak leaf in mid-summer, a dark complexion, easily bronzed by the sun, and a small nose, the one feature similar to her two older sisters, Katie, and Amy. Katie, Emma's oldest sister, was the oldest of the teens living in the house, had a fair complexion, with brown eyes the color of weak coffee, and short hair a few shades darker than the color of her eyes and was petite, several inches shorter than Emma was. Abby, one year younger than Katie, was Walter's oldest child, and the tiniest sixteen-year-old, Emma had ever met before, barely five feet tall. Everything about Abby was petite. She had light blonde hair like her brother Cody, and like Cody, had eyes the shade of a blue cornflower, and a fair complexion, easily burned if she stayed in the sun for too long. Amy was one year older than Emma was—fifteen—her other older sister. She was the spirited one of the bunch, had blonde hair many shades darker than Abby's hair color, cool gray eyes, with just enough blue to add warmth, and was fair skinned like the rest of the family. Amy was taller than Katie by an inch but shorter than Emma by almost two inches.

Katie, Abby, and Emma heard shouting inside the house. Emma grasped the metal door and tugged, pulling it wide as Abby grabbed hold. Emma walked across the plywood kitchen floor, her tennis shoes echoing in the small room. Almost to the door leading to the living room, Emma glanced at the large silver milk machine sitting next to an old white refrigerator against the far side of the kitchen. Emma had never known a family that drank so much milk that they had to buy a huge machine like one you'd find in a restaurant, and still they never made it to the next week's delivery before running out. She skirted the small metal kitchen table and walked through a doorway leading to the living room in search of her cousin. Scanning the smoke-filled room, she realized he must have gone to the back of the house, to the room he shared with his eight-year-old sister, April, a quiet little girl, with dark brown hair. Emma glanced at the occupants in the living room, her uncle, and her obese aunt with food staining her tight top. Emma was still in awe that the woman didn't pop the sides off chairs when she squeezed into them. As she walked to the center of the room, Abby and Katie brushed past her, walking toward the back of the house.

Emma paused and glanced over at her uncle as he leaned forward in his gold colored, high backed chair, dragging on a cigarette. He reached up a hand and tugged his sweat-stained, green ball cap off, then scratched his balding head as he looked over at his wife seeing her through blood shot eyes. Scowling, Emma continued to the next room of the house, the room she shared with Katie, Abby, and Amy. She walked through the dark room, and kept walking onto the next room—her aunt, and uncle's bedroom—then further still toward the light in Cody's room. As she walked in the dark, a room's length from his bedroom, she saw Cody walk passed the doorway.

Abby and Katie rushed toward her, blocking out the light that had been guiding her way, and shouted, "Cody jumped out of his window, right through the screen! Just jumped right *through* the screen! He said he's runnin' to town."

Emma stopped as the two girls ran by her and stared after them. Light from Cody's bedroom washed over her as she glanced toward his abandoned room, then turning, she stared through the dark toward the light of the living room, and raised voices.

Nervously, Emma walked slowly back through the dark rooms, watching as Amy ran passed the living room door toward the kitchen. Emma stopped and stood in the doorway, darkness to her back and bright light blinding her eyes as Walter and her sister Amy entered the living room shouting at each other. She watched and listened to what had become her life over the last six months.

As Emma leaned against the doorjamb, she reflected over the last year of her life, thinking, *so far social services has done a piss poor job of saving my sisters and me.* Eight months earlier, on a cold February day, Emma and her two older sisters had been removed from their father's home because of abuse and neglect. She and her oldest sister, Katie, had been placed in separate homes with relatives, and Amy had been placed in a foster home in a town twenty minutes away. Then at the end of May, after the school year had ended, the three sisters had been moved down south to live with their Uncle Walter, Aunt Vicki, cousins, sixteen-year-old Abby, eight-year-old April, and fourteen-year-old Cody, a family they had met only the December before. They had loaded their belongings into Vicki's beat up station wagon, then she had driven them two-hours south, passed endless cornfields, to their home, a one-story house outside a small southern Indiana farming town. Emma had thought once saved from her dad, her life would be like the other kids in her class, whatever that was. She wasn't exactly sure what everyone's life was like, just knew it couldn't be this.

Emma watched as Walter stumbled out of the living room as Amy followed close behind, shouting something about him being a *bastard.* The room was empty now, except for smoke wafting in lazy circles in the light. Shoving her hands in her jeans pockets, Emma looked toward the kitchen, and cringed when she heard a loud bang, probably a cabinet door or something being thrown across the room, she considered—maybe a chair.

Emma heard her aunt's annoying voice from the other room, shriek, "Amy—Amy! Get back in here!"

She heard another bang, and then heard Vicki shriek, "Walter— you leave that girl alone!"

Emma jumped back as Amy and Walter crashed through the kitchen door to the plywood floor of the living room. Walter straddled the small body of his niece, Amy, holding her down as she struggled beneath him.

Carefully, Emma maneuvered around her uncle and her sister as they punched and shouted at each other.

"Stop!" Emma shouted. "Walter, let her up! Get off her!"

"I'm done with her mouth," Walter slurred, as he wrapped his large hands around Amy's neck.

Amy thrashed about beneath her six foot two uncle. She kicked her feet up trying to dislodge him, balled her hands into fists, and punched his face.

Walter's hands squeezed Amy's neck. Her screams became raspy and her face turned red.

He shrieked like a man gone mad, "You fuckin' bitch! You stupid fuckin' whore! I'm gonna kill your mother fuckin' ass!"

"Get *off* her!" Emma screamed. "Stop! Walter, stop!"

Emma jumped on top of her uncle's back and tried to pull him off her sister, but she couldn't budge him. As she pounded on his back and pulled on his shoulders, his hands continued to squeeze Amy's throat. Emma's hands hurt from punching her uncle, and her throat was raw from shouting.

Walter reared back like a bucking bronco and threw Emma off his back. She fell with a thud to the hard wooden floor cracking the back of her head and bruising her bony spine, as he rose clumsily to his feet and then stumbled toward the kitchen.

Emma rolled onto her side, and then got to her knees as she heard the screen door slam shut and knew it was Walter storming out of the house. Crawling over to where Amy was still lying on the floor, Emma tried to brush the hair aside that had fallen onto her sister's face to see if she was okay.

Amy swatted Emma's hand away.

"Amy—Are you okay?" Emma cried.

She looked at the marks on her sister's throat made by her uncle's hands.

"Amy—*Amy*." Emma's eyes clouded with tears, not knowing what to do. "Are you okay?" Emma asked, beginning to panic. Emotions swirled inside Emma—anger at her aunt and uncle—fear at what her uncle might do next—despair as she wondered how they were going to get out of the mess they were in.

Amy rolled over onto her side as she clutched her throat, coughed, and scowled up into Emma's concerned face.

Staring down at her sister, Emma whispered, "We have to leave. We can't stay here anymore."

Struggling to her feet, Amy rasped, "No. I'm not leaving. I'm not leaving, Jarod!"

Amy stumbled toward the kitchen leaving Emma, still kneeling, staring after her.

Emma slumped her shoulders and stared at the floor, her thoughts racing. She had to get out of there. It was as bad at her uncle's house as it had been at her dad's house, just in different ways.

CHAPTER TWO

Slowly, Emma walked through the dark rooms of the house—away from the shouting in the kitchen—toward the room at the opposite end of the house—to Cody's bedroom. She found Katie sitting on his bed watching him as shirt-less, he paced back and forth across the small room, agitated like a caged animal.

Emma asked, "What's going on? Cody, I thought you left. Abby said you ran to town."

"I'm going," he said, as he looked down at the floor and continued to walk back and forth across the room. "I'm goin' now!" he shouted. He looked up at her with a wild expression in his eyes. "I'm goin' to the cops. That son of a bitch is goin' to jail!"

Nervously, Emma looked over at her oldest sister, noticing her neatly combed dark brown hair, and wire rimmed glasses with thick lenses.

Emma wondered if Cody meant what he had just said, or was it talk, like they all talked from time to time about leaving their uncle's loony shack house. It was always just talk—Emma was tired of talk.

Looking at Cody, determined, Emma announced, "I'm coming with you."

Cody looked at her in surprise, with an expression that meant he didn't take her statement seriously. "You can't run across the field, Emma," Cody said softly.

"Yeah I can," she said with calm intensity.

Cody looked at her gently, but she could tell he didn't think she could make it.

"I can't stay here!" Emma said, feeling as if she might burst into tears.

No one was listening to her. No one ever listened to her. For months, she had been pointing out all the craziness that was going on in the house and that it just wasn't normal, but no one seemed to care but her. She was sure that other parents weren't throwing mixed drink and beer parties for their kids and encouraging them to have sex whenever and wherever they wanted. Her aunt and uncle were such strange people. It was like living in a crazy house with her obese sex kitten of an aunt hitting on any man or boy that came near their house, and her uncle who was always stumbling drunk, doing the craziest of things. At first, their antics had been funny, but their weirdness had grown old fast. It hadn't been some welcome to their home party, because the party had lasted for the last five months. Emma wanted to be normal—live with a *normal* family.

For the first few months, after Katie, Amy and Emma had moved into their uncle's house, there had been frequent parties; the kitchen table filled with bottles of alcohol, but by mid-summer, Vicki seemed to grow bored. The parties escalated. After the alcohol began to flow, it was show time—and Walter was the main event. After Walter was sloppy drunk, Vicki's fun began as she humiliated and enraged him. During one of her parties—while Walter was in a drunken stupor—at two in the morning, cruelly, Vicki pushed him to the brink, and then had to load all the kids in the station wagon and drive into town to escape. Vicki had tormented Walter for hours and when he couldn't take anymore of her nasty insults, he stumbled out of the house. Typically, after one of Vicki's tormenting games, Walter stayed outside no longer than fifteen minutes, but when a half hour went by, Emma had gone outside to find him. She had found him stumbling along the side of the house facing the road, with a gas can clutched in his hand. As Emma followed behind him, she could see clear liquid trickling out of the can, and smelled gasoline. Not getting too close, she had asked him what he was doing, and heard his mumbled response…*He was going to burn the house down, with everyone inside.* Vicki had gone too far that night and had no choice but to take the six children away, promising she would not take them back to the house. But a few hours later, much to Emma's surprise, Vicki had pulled the station wagon, loaded with the six children, onto the gravel driveway in front of the shack-like house. Vicki had eased her heavy frame out of the car, hoisted herself onto the rickety porch, and through a crack in the front door, coaxed Walter to let them back in the house.

"They're crazy," Emma insisted. "I can't do this anymore, Cody. Your dad could have killed you *or* Amy, tonight." Looking over at Katie and then back to Cody, Emma said emphatically, "I have to leave. I'm *not* staying here anymore."

Emma shifted her body in the doorway. Turning toward her oldest sister, Emma crossed her arms across her chest, and asked, "Katie, are you going with us?"

"Well—hell," Katie said sighing. "Yeah."

"Amy's not gonna go because of Jarod. I already told her we need to leave, but she won't leave her boyfriend," Emma said, worried. "She just almost gets herself killed tonight but she won't leave because of a *boy*." Emma shook her head and as nervous energy coursed through her body, she flung her right hand on her hip, and leaned into the door-jamb. "We have to go to the cops. Amy can just be as pissed off as she wants, but if she won't save herself, then *I'll* save her. I'm not letting her stay here with these crazy people," Emma insisted, as the image of her fifteen-year-old sister lying helpless beneath her uncle flashed across her mind.

Cody stood in the center of his bedroom, clenching and unclenching his hands into tight fists, his arms taught against his body. "Let's go!" he shouted, as if he were at a pep rally at school trying to inspire the crowd.

Emma didn't need any inspiration. She knew that the events over the past five months had been escalating, her uncle's actions becoming increasingly dangerous and she had no intention of bearing witness to just how far he would go. As she watched, Cody lunged toward the one window in his bedroom and pushed it open.

She stared at her cousin, noticing his scraggly hair, badly needing a trim. She glanced at his bare chest, and as the cool night air entered the room, she wondered just where the boy thought he was going in the frigid fall night with no jacket or shirt. Scanning the rest of him, she noticed his brown boots with broken laces and holes in the toes, and his jeans with holes in the knees, sagging on his hips. Her heart broke for the boy that stood before her. Why did life have to be so cruel she wondered? When did it get easier?

Cody scooped an old blue flannel shirt off the floor and shrugged his arms into it. He attempted to shove the white buttons, clinging to the shirt by threads, through the buttonholes, too large for the buttons, not noticing when the buttons slid out of the over-sized buttonholes. He turned toward Emma and extended his hand.

"Are you comin'?" he asked softly, with a pleading look in his eyes.

Determination and resolve cloaked her as she walked over to the window and peered into the blackness beyond. Placing her hand in his, she held tight as she half sat and swung her legs over the grimy window-sill. She looked down into the darkness below and hesitated—her heart pounding in her chest—and then jumped into what felt like nothingness as her eyes adjusted to the inky black that enveloped her five feet below the window. She landed in a crouched position, her hands steadying her in the tall grass. Standing, she wrapped her arms around her shoulders to warm and comfort her as she squinted into the dark trying to make out the strange shapes nearby. Her heart raced as a wave of fear washed over her as a thought struck her...what if they were caught climbing out of Cody's bedroom window by her weeble-looking evil aunt, or her stumbling drunk uncle? Squinting, Emma looked toward the edge of the house, trying to make out any movement, but there was no one there—just darkness—and silence.

Turning back toward the window, Emma watched as Cody helped Katie crawl through the window and to the ground. Katie was so tiny—so fragile. Emma watched Katie brush her jeans off as the light from Cody's bedroom glowed softly on her face, and Emma wondered, would her sister be able to run across the plowed, uneven cornfield under the cover of night. Then a thought occurred to her, would *she* be able to. God hadn't given Emma the legs or body of a runner. Last year Emma had tried out for track and she had lasted two miserable, leg aching, chest-heaving weeks before she had dropped out.

Standing together in a circle, Cody asked calmly, almost a whisper, "You ready to do this?"

Determined, Emma whispered, "Yeah."

"Well let's go," Katie insisted.

They cloaked themselves with the shadows of the yard, ducking into the ditch for a few breathless moments, waited, and watched to see if anyone would come out of the house and yell for them. As they lay in the damp, shallow ditch, no cars passed by, and no one came out of the house. It was eerily quiet as Emma held her breath.

Cody looked down at Emma and Katie. "Okay," he said quietly. "We're gonna run low as we cross the road to the field. The flood light lets out a little light over the field for a bit so we're gonna have to run low until we get farther into the field."

Looking at Emma, he asked, "You okay Em?"

Everyone knew she was afraid of the dark. Bad things seemed to come out of the dark, so many bad things…

"I'm okay," she said shakily, as she turned her head and looked out across the blackness of the plowed field wondering what was there waiting for her. The green sea of corn stalks had been plowed months ago, and as she looked across the road, it was as if she was looking into a black abyss.

"Go!" Cody hissed.

Emma sprang to her feet feeling as if she might throw up, pee her pants, or fall down in a dead faint. She was terrified that her aunt or uncle might catch them, and of running across a field that seemed to disappear into nothing. She sprinted across the road toward the nothingness.

After running a few steps on the uneven ground of the field, Emma slammed to her knees and winced as the hard clumps of dirt dug into her hands and knees. Fear spurred her on as she pushed up and propelled forward. Stumbling, she flung her hands in front of her, trying to feel her way in the vast field, her heart racing as she began to panic.

She cried out as her ankle turned over on the uneven mounds of hard dirt, but she was too terrified to stop. She ran and ran until the black closed in all around her. Panting, she tried to find her breath. Sweat trickled down her forehead and down the middle of her back. Her mouth was dry and her chest heaved from running and fear.

"Stop," Katie moaned, behind her.

Emma stumbled to a stop and turned toward Katie's voice. She squinted into the darkness, barely able to make out her sister's form half laying on the ground. Bending over, Emma placed her hands, covered with field dirt, on her knees, then licked her lips, and tried to catch her breath. She looked down at the ground, not wanting to see what was in the darkness, and shivered as she imagined something had glanced off her spine.

"I can't go on," Katie rasped. "Ohhh, I can't. I think I sprained my ankle."

Emma pushed upright and darted her eyes across the field to see if the things in the dark were coming. She walked over toward Katie's voice and looked down.

"We have to leave 'er here," Cody said, breathing heavily.

Emma's heart caught. *"What?"* she panted, looking at the outline of Cody's face. "We can't leave her here!"

The very thought of leaving Katie alone in mile after mile of field, in the middle of the night, *in the dark,* with nowhere to hide—exposed to whatever was out there—brought horrifying visions of her murder by someone or something tearing her apart as she screamed in horror and pain. Emma closed her eyes and shook her head to clear the image and sounds of Katie's imagined cries out of her mind.

"Emma," Katie said, looking up from where she sat. "Go with Cody. I'll be fine. Go! Go! Get to the police and then send someone back for me."

Emma didn't want to leave her sister alone in the middle of the massive field in the dark and thought she should stay with her. What if something happened to her—how would they find her, she worried. But she knew Katie was stubborn and wasn't going to change her mind.

"Okay," Emma exhaled. "We'll send someone back for you," wondering if the police would be able to find her in the middle of nowhere—in the black of night.

Emma thought of Katie as she stumbled forward over the field feeling as if at any moment she would fall into black nothingness. She couldn't believe she had just left her sister behind. What if the police couldn't find her, she worried—what if something was out there and got her. Fear kept her moving, as her tennis shoes stumbled on large chunks of dirt, and falling to the ground, she pushed herself back to her feet, and panting, she pressed on.

Emma looked up from the clumps of dirt that seemed to stretch endlessly before her and saw lights glimmering in the distance. Tripping over a large clod of dirt, she fell to her knees again. Grunting she pushed to her feet and stumbled toward the lights, growing slowly closer. Emma smacked her tongue on the roof of her mouth trying to create liquid, spit anything. She was so thirsty.

Finally, at the edge of town, Cody and Emma kept to the shadows of houses as they edged their way to the center of town, toward the police station. Within a block of the police station, Emma and Cody hid from the glaring light shining from the street lamps by ducking behind dumpsters. *So close, they were so close to the police station.*

Emma stood up from her crouched position behind a brown, dirty, rusty dumpster. She could see it—the police station was right across the street. Crouching, she scooted to the side of the dumpster and prepared to sprint across the street when Cody grabbed her arm and yanked her down next to him.

"Get down," he hissed. "Hide."

Emma stopped and strained her neck to look into Cody's face, pursed her lips, and prepared to ask why.

He placed his finger to his lips then gestured toward the police station, and whispered, "Over there. It's *them.*"

She snapped her head up and scanned the street as her aunt's beat up station wagon rolled slowly down the street. The car was about a half a block from where Emma and Cody were crouched, near the entrance of the police station. Her stomach churned as she ducked behind the dumpster, fearing they had been seen.

The teens waited a few breathless moments as the station wagon continued down the road, passed the police station. Emma let out the breath she had been holding, and then looked up at Cody.

Looking down into Emma's face, Cody whispered, "Let's go."

Her heart was pounding, and still crouched she sprinted across the street. Emma felt a tingling sensation creep down her spine as the glow of the streetlight followed her like a spotlight. She crossed the street, and then climbed the concrete steps of the station. Her hand touched the cold metal door handle. *They had made it.*

Emma tugged the door open. As she passed through the door, a wave of fatigue washed over her. She was safe, but there was still one more pressing issue—Katie. Looking to her right, she saw several uniformed officers sitting around a small desk. Nervously, she walked deeper into the small room where several empty desks were sitting along the wall, with Cody following close behind.

Slowly she walked toward two men in navy blue uniforms, with shiny silver badges affixed to the upper right of their shirts, standing with their hands on their hips. Glancing at the guns and handcuffs hanging from the belts wrapped around their waists, Emma stopped in front of them as they stared down at her, looking very stern. Rubbing her hands on her jeans, she tried to wipe the field dirt off, and then she ran her hand through her hair, trying to smooth the wind and sweat generated tangles. She tugged at her jean jacket realizing they must look rough after the dash through the field.

In a hoarse voice, Emma spit out, "My sister is alone in the middle of a field," gesturing toward the door. "You've got to send someone out to find her. My uncle tried to kill us, my sister, I mean. He was choking her. He wouldn't stop…" she said, her voice trailing away. Looking over at Cody, Emma pointed and said, "And he hit Cody so hard he was knocked to the floor, out cold."

The officers were quiet as they stared at her. Why weren't they saying anything, Emma worried—it was as if they hadn't heard her, so she tried again. "You have to hurry and find my sister," she said, raising her voice. By speaking louder, she hoped to convey the seriousness of the situation.

"Is that right?" one of the officers asked casually, as he looked over at the other officer. Emma noticed the strange look they exchanged.

"Well, why don't the two of you come in and tell us all about it," the shorter of the two officers said, as he looked down at Emma and Cody. "Come on in here with me," he said, as he walked down a hall, turning to look back at the two tired and dirt-covered teens. *"Come on,"* he insisted.

Emma looked at Cody and he stared back. She wondered why no one was flying out the door to save her sister, as she followed the police officer to a small bare room where he motioned for her to have a seat. Cody pulled out a chair and sat down. Emma pulled out one of the chairs around the small table, next to Cody, and stiffly sat down. Irritated, she answered the officer's questions, providing her name, her age, and again why she was wandering around town in the middle of the night. She turned to Cody when the officer asked her what her address was, unable to provide that crucial piece of information.

Damn, she thought—Justice sure moved slowly in this hick town. Feeling anxious, she wondered if the officer thought they were lying but couldn't image why. Perhaps they just didn't want their night of coffee and donuts interrupted, she considered angrily.

The officer looked over their heads toward the door and Emma turned to see what he was looking at, hoping it was Katie. No such luck—it was just the other officer. He had part of his body in the door and he was gesturing at the other officer.

"I'll be right back," Emma heard, and watched both officers leave the room.

"What's goin' on?" Emma whispered to Cody.

He shrugged his shoulders, his eyes not meeting hers. Emma had a bad feeling. Something wasn't right.

"Okay," the officer said, as he walked back into the room, his hands resting on his belt with all the gadgets. "Son, why don't you come on in the other room with me and," gesturing at Emma, "you stay in here. I'll be right back."

Swiveling in her seat, Emma watched as Cody, with slumped shoulders, walked out the door. She wondered where they were taking him and why they were taking him away. She sat in the small room with her hands clasped in her lap, and waited.

"Okay," the officer said, as he walked back into the room with a white Styrofoam cup gripped in his hand. "We found your sister. She was right where you said she'd be, in the middle of the field a few miles from your aunt and uncle's house. She's fine." He placed the cup on the table in front of Emma. Looking at the very tired, disheveled teen, he continued, "Now why don't you tell me again what happened tonight?"

Relieved they had found Katie, Emma gulped the cool water, soothing her dry, raw throat, then she repeated what she had told the officer just a half an hour before, when Cody had been seated next to her. As she retold her story, she wondered if they had taken Cody away just to separate them to see if their stories would change, kind of like the cop shows where they separated the criminals. As she looked down at the table, it was what she felt like, a criminal, as if *she* had done something wrong, even though she knew she hadn't.

The officer sat quietly across the small table as she spoke. She told him everything that happened, not just that night but also everything that had happened over the past five months. When she grew quiet, he stood and walked to the door, and with a blank expression on his face said, "Your sister will be here soon," then left her alone again.

The round clock on the wall displayed, 6:15. It was morning—and Emma's body knew she should be asleep. It had been a long night and Emma was exhausted. As her eyes drooped, she thought longingly of a soft place to lay down, a bed, couch…somewhere. Crossing her arms over her chest, she dozed, her head bobbing to her chest.

Fifteen minutes later, Emma was jarred back to her surroundings by the sound of Katie's high-pitched voice. Drowsily, she turned her head toward the door and watched as her sister, Katie, walked through the door, looking like she was in a foul mood.

Clumsily, Emma scooted back her chair and walked toward Katie.

Waiving her hand in the air, Katie dismissed whatever Emma was about to say. "I'm fine," she said sounding annoyed.

"What's going on?" Emma asked. "Where's Cody—and Amy?" Waiving her hand in the air, Emma said, "I've been sitting in here forever, alone. They took Cody to a different room. I haven't seen him since."

"I don't know what's goin' on. They asked me some questions and I told them what happened with Cody and Amy, and all the stuff that's been goin on since we've been livin' there," Katie said quietly, not looking at Emma.

"Yeah, Cody and me, we told them everything that happened tonight and all the other stuff. What do you think they'll do and *where's* Amy?" Emma asked, worried.

When Katie didn't answer, Emma asked, "What's going to happen, Katie? What's going to happen to everyone—to Abby, April, and Cody, and us?"

Katie, looked down at her hands as she sat next to her younger sister, and responded, "I don't know."

Emma hunched over the table and rested her head on her arms. Her emotions had run the gamut during the last twenty-four hours and now she was crashing, her body heavy and sluggish.

She was so tired, and as her stomach began to rumble, she realized she was starving too.

"Let's go!" the police officer shouted, as he walked briskly into the room and clapped his hands.

Exhausted, Emma didn't jump at the sharp sound. She lifted her head off the table and glanced at Katie wondering, go—go where—and where was Amy? She scooted her chair back and got to her feet, and followed Katie out of the room. As she walked into the main area of the police station, Emma was surprised to see Amy standing by the entryway, and by the look on her face, she wasn't happy to be there. She had her arms crossed over her chest with a nasty look on her face, and as Emma walked toward her, Amy looked away.

Looking the officer in the face, Emma asked, "Where are we going?"

Expecting a response, she was surprised and a little irritated when he stood looking at her, holding open the glass door to the small parking lot. She paused for a moment waiting for an answer but when she realized he wasn't going to give her one, she walked passed him and down the stairs into the crisp fall morning air. As she walked down the concrete steps attached to the side of the red brick building, Emma looked up at the squad car parked about ten feet away, noticing the front and back doors were wide open. The officer she had met earlier that night was standing on the far side, his arm propped on the passenger door. Emma looked up at the officer that had been questioning her all night as he walked by. Without saying a word, he motioned his hand at her to get into the back of the police car.

Persistently she asked, "Where're we going?" as she fixed her eyes on his.

As he rested his hand on the car door handle, he looked at her, raised his eyebrows, and said, "I'm takin' you back to *your* county. We don't need your kind here. Let *them* deal with you."

Emma felt as if she'd been slapped. *Her kind.* Just what *was* her kind, she wondered. It wasn't her fault she'd been stuck with those people. The *state* shouldn't have placed her with *those kinds* of people. Her feet felt glued to the pavement as she stared at the back of the officer's dark head as he climbed into the front of the car. She glanced over at Katie and Amy to see what their reaction was to the officer's comment but they were avoiding her eyes—they were looking straight ahead—with their jaws clenched. Emma could see the tension in their faces as Katie climbed into the back of the car. Amy stood on the opposite side of the car and motioned for her little sister to get in. Quietly, Emma slid across the soft comfortable seat, too exhausted to think, to try to figure it all out. She scooted to the center so Amy could climb in beside her. She glanced out of the rear window and wondered where Cody was. She hadn't seen him for hours. Where had they taken him, she fretted? She hadn't gotten to say goodbye. The car was silent—no siren blared—no lights flashed—no one said a word as the police car pulled away from the station in the gray of early morning.

Miles down the highway, the motion of the car began to lull the tired fourteen-year old. Her head wobbled and she closed her burning eyes as the car sped down the deserted two-lane highway.

CHAPTER THREE

Emma felt an elbow dig into her ribs, and struggled to open her eyes. She had slumped over while she slept and now Katie was digging her elbow into her side to get her to sit up. Squinting, she saw that the glaring sun had replaced the gray of the morning. Looking out the window of the squad car, Emma recognized the landscape. They were back in their own county two hours north of their aunt and uncle's home.

She whispered to Katie, "Where're they taking us?"

Sticking her bony elbow in Emma's side, Katie growled, "I don't know!"

Sighing, Emma sat up straight, making sure not to touch either of her sisters, and wondered where the police were taking them.

Exiting the highway, the car headed into town and within minutes, they pulled up in front of a large house. The officer seated in the passenger side of the car, got out of the car, and pulled Amy's door open.

"Which one of you is Amy?" he asked.

"Me," Amy responded.

"Follow me. This is where you'll be staying," he said, as he waved his hand toward the house.

So they were to be separated again, Emma realized. Amy climbed out of the car and the officer slammed the door as Emma scooted over and watched them walk up the sidewalk. She looked over at Katie and scowled at her, trying to get some type of response out of her oldest sister but only got a mouthed, "I don't know."

Leaning her head against the door, Emma watched trees and fields fly by. Katie had been dropped off in town at a foster home and now the officers were driving Emma to a foster home somewhere in the country. Her eyelids felt so heavy and her eyes burned as she fought to stay awake and she was so hungry she felt as if she might throw up all over the back seat of the car.

She must have dozed off, because when she opened her eyes the squad car was stopped in front of a rundown, fudge colored farmhouse, and one of the officers was standing by the open car door. Emma squinted up at him as the sun and the officer glared down at her.

"Come on," he said impatiently.

Tucking her hair behind her ear, she stumbled out of the car. A firework of colorful spots erupted, blurring her vision and a rushing sound flooded her ears. Grabbing the side of the car, she steadied herself and then followed the officers, already standing at the door of the house. Barely able to stay on her feet, Emma just wanted something to eat, drink and a bed or at this point, the floor would be just fine. She was exhausted.

A small woman with short dark brown hair, wearing a red plaid shirt, blue jeans, and cowboy boots, led them into the house. Emma saw the lady's mouth move but had difficulty making out the words due to the hum in her ears. She sat down at the large kitchen table and glanced around the cluttered dark room as the short lady, her new foster mother, walked the officers out of the room. Emma sniffed and wondered what the awful smell was.

Back in the kitchen now, the lady was saying something…*Hungry*; the strange lady was mouthing the word hungry. Emma shook her head up and down to indicate that yes, she was hungry. Her foster mother placed a bowl of hot pasta in front of her. Emma ate the bowl of spaghetti so fast she didn't taste it and once done, looked up at the woman sitting across from her, who was staring at her as if she had never seen a teenager covered in field dirt before.

"You wanna take a shower?" her new foster mother asked. "Then you probably wanna get some rest."

Exhaustion had reached Emma's vocal chords; all she could do was shake her head up and down. She followed the lady, her cowboy boots clomping loudly on the brown painted wooden steps, to the second floor. After her shower, a borrowed white t-shirt draped over the top half of her body, Emma followed the lady down the hall to a bedroom. The lady kept up a constant stream of chatter, but Emma wasn't listening to her, she was zoned in on the large bed in the small bedroom. Pulling the white fluffy comforter back, she climbed on top of the bed, and sank deep into the center and closed her eyes.

Hours later Emma woke to the sounds of muffled voices, and what sounded like pots and pans clanging together. Continuing to nestle down in the bed, she wondered why she was sunk so deep into the bed, and sniffed again. What the *hell* was that disgusting smell, she wondered? She had smelled that smell before…it was old people smell. Couldn't they smell it, she wondered, trying to breathe through her mouth. Emma didn't want to get out of the bed—didn't want to walk down the stairs—didn't want to be in a house with strangers. She wanted her sisters.

Emma rolled over and faced the door. As she looked across the small room, she saw the clothes she had been wearing when she had arrived, now clean and folded on a dresser. She stared at the bright flowers printed on the maroon colored peasant top she had worn the day before. It was one of her favorite tops, but she suspected it would soon be going into the trash, associated with this time in her life.

Sniffing, Emma detected the smell of old people mingled with the scent of food. It had to be late evening. She had slept the entire day away, and felt as if she could go right back to sleep. Instead of closing her eyes, she grabbed hold of the edge of the mattress, pulled herself out of the deep crevice of the bed, and then stepped onto the wooden floor. Pulling on her jeans, she glanced at the relatively bare room, containing a bed, an old beat up dresser, and a few pictures hung on the walls. They were probably afraid the foster kids would steal something, she figured. After she pulled her blouse over her head, she cracked the bedroom door and peered down the empty hallway toward the bathroom, and then tiptoed down the hall.

Unable to stall any longer, Emma walked as quietly as she could down the creaky stairs, to the kitchen. The lady was there, clanging pots and pans as she cooked dinner, but now the room contained two more people, two very strange looking girls.

"Hey," the taller of the two girls called out. "My name's Margaret and this here's my younger sister, June. Say hey, June," Margaret said, looking down at the shorter girl.

"Hey," June said shyly.

"Hi," Emma responded.

"Yuh hungry," Emma's foster mother asked.

Emma shook her head, yes.

"We're havin' stew," her foster mother said.

"Hey!" Margaret exclaimed. "Yuh need a cigarette? I've got some Marlboros in my purse. It's okay," Margaret said, looking at the lady. "Isn't it mom?"

"Sure. As long as you girls stay in the kitchen," she whispered, and placed her finger to her lips as she looked toward a dark room on the opposite side of the kitchen.

"No thanks," Emma said.

"Awe come on," Margaret said, sounding disappointed.

Emma considered her new and temporary family. She looked at her foster mother, taking in her short dark brown hair, dressed like a cowgirl, and then looked at her two daughters. It was obvious to her that they were nerdy people. She herself was a nerd, so recognized her kind, but they were even worse off than she was. Apparently, they were trying to use the act of sucking on a cigarette to modify their status. Inwardly, Emma rolled her eyes. Why, she wondered, did foster families think *all* foster kids smoked? Feeling sorry for the strange looking girl and wanting to shut them up, she reached for the cigarette Margaret was extending toward her and the blue lighter. Puffing away, Emma didn't inhale. She had learned, painfully, awhile back that she didn't have what it took to smoke. She held the smoke in her mouth for an adequate amount of time then blew out, just as the other girl was doing. She wasn't really smoking either—she was just trying to be cool.

The next morning, Emma sat silently in the passenger seat of her foster mother's car as her foster mother drove her to her new school. She was thankful to be getting out of the house and away from the strange people with their cigarette issue. Emma peered through the passenger window up at the gray sky reflective of her mood, as the fall fields passed by, empty now, just like her.

It wasn't even November yet, and she was switching to a different school, the second high school of her freshman year and she wondered if the work she had done at the last high school would transfer over. Her aunt and uncle's home was two hours away, much too far for a commute she thought, so now it was a new school with new teachers, kids—another adjustment. The last school had been much smaller, accommodating a town with less than five thousand people. This school, Emma reflected as she walked through the massive glass doors, could fit five of her old school buildings within its walls. The new school was cold, impersonal, and intimidating.

Emma saw Katie and Amy as she walked into the office to be registered for her freshman classes. As she walked toward them, she noticed they had both lucked out in the clothing department. They were no longer wearing the same clothes they had on during the ride in the police car over the weekend. Emma still had on the same blouse she had worn to school Friday. Borrowing clothes from her new foster sisters hadn't been an option as they were both several sizes larger than Emma was. Her foster mother was about the same size as Emma, however, a plaid cowgirl shirt hadn't appealed to her, opting instead for her peasant top.

"How's it going?" Emma asked. "What's it like where you guys are staying?"

Katie shrugged her shoulders and said, "Not too bad."

Amy avoided Emma's eyes and just shrugged her shoulders.

"Girls!" their new caseworker shouted.

Katie, Emma, and Amy, looked over at the stern looking lady, as she motioned them over to the office.

The next few days passed uncomfortably for Emma. She hated being in the country away from her sisters, and her foster family seemed just as odd as ever. Most of Emma's time was spent lying in the sagging bed, breathing through her mouth so she wouldn't smell the old people smell. But that was nauseating because then she had old people stench in her mouth. She was now *thankful* for the evening smokes because the second they all lit up and fake smoked, it masked the stink a little. She just had to make it through the evenings, wait for the next day to arrive so she could leave the house, even if it was just to go to school. A visit was arranged for the weekend for Emma to spend the night at Katie's foster home and she couldn't wait!

The next morning, before classes started, Katie was waiting for Emma at their usual spot in the three-story lobby by the ceiling to floor windows, but Amy wasn't with her. Walking up to her oldest sister, Emma asked, "Hey. Where's Amy this morning?" expecting her to say she was sick or maybe had made a few friends and was hanging out with them.

"She ran," Katie said flatly.

"*What!?*" Emma said, stunned. "You have got to be kidding me! When—how did this happen?"

"Jarod drove up in the middle of the night last night and she snuck out of the house. She went back," Katie said.

Tears sprang to her eyes. Emma couldn't find the words to express the physical pain she felt at losing her sister again. Amy was gone.

CHAPTER FOUR

Emma was ready to blow the stench of her foster home off her, literally, as she climbed out of her foster mother's car and walked toward the small red brick ranch house. It was Friday evening and as her caseworker promised, she was spending the night with Katie at her foster home. Stepping up on the small concrete porch, Emma rang the doorbell, which was promptly opened by a petite young woman with shoulder-length strawberry blonde hair, looking to be about nineteen years-old.

"Hi!" the young woman said with a grin. "You must be Emma. I'm Sara. Well, come on in and let me take your coat."

Emma felt comfortable as she stepped into the well-lit, small living room. The glow from the lamps, at either end of the inviting looking couch, welcomed her. She handed her jean jacket to the young woman.

"Hi," Emma said with a smile. "It's nice to meet you," comfortable for the first time in months. Emma spent the evening with Katie, and one of Katie's foster sisters, Sara, watching movies and eating pizza.

The next day, sitting in the kitchen eating left over pizza, Emma glanced at the clock hanging on the wall. Soon, her foster mother would be picking her up. Her stomach began to churn as she thought about the stinky old farmhouse and strange foster family. Absently, Emma listened to Sheila, Katie's foster mother ramble away. Sheila was slightly taller than Emma was, and almost as round as she was tall, made rounder by her enormous sized breasts, which forced her to stoop forward when she walked. Her hair was a thick mane of coal black, course strands that hung below her shoulders and she had the largest teeth Emma had ever seen before, at least in a person's mouth. Emma guessed Sheila's age to be around her dad's age, thirty something. And she had a habit that would have infuriated Emma's dad…she snapped her gum, constantly. But she seemed nice.

"Sweetie, have you heard a word I've said? You just seem to be goin' off somewhere," Sheila said.

"Oh, I'm sorry," Emma, said with a sigh. "I was just thinking. My foster mother is going to pick me up soon," glancing at the clock on the kitchen wall again.

"How's it goin' at your foster family's house?" Sheila asked, raising her thick eyebrows in concern.

Examining a spot on the wooden table, Emma responded, "Oh, it's different."

Sheila threw her head back and laughed, and it dawned on Emma that her foster mother's ticks and weird mannerisms were not just apparent to her.

Smiling, Emma said, "They're just very different. Have you ever been to their house?" She wrinkled her nose, and looked across the round table, finding Sheila surprisingly easy to talk to.

"No," Sheila said with a toothy grin. "I've never been out to their house, but I know 'em."

"So…." Emma said, leaning forward in her chair, trying to coax Sheila to say more.

Squirming on her cushioned chair, Sheila responded, "*Weeellll.* She's a strange one."

I knew it!" Emma shouted, with a victorious grin. "I knew it wasn't just me! They *are* strange."

"Okay," Sheila said, snapping her gum. "Tell me what's goin' on."

"Well, if I could get beyond the stink in their house that would help," Emma said, wrinkling her nose again. "I know it sounds silly, but when I go into their house, I swear, I want to *puke*. It's awful. I don't know what it is…just—old people smell."

Sheila looked at her, and said, "Come on. You're exaggerating."

Shaking her head, Emma assured her, "I'm not. Honestly. It's gross. And not only that, I know—I know, I sound mean," she acknowledged, "but, they're weird. Rolling her eyes, she continued, "Not once have you offered me a cigarette. Not once!"

"I'm sorry," Sheila said in surprise. "Did you need one?"

Laughing out loud, Emma shouted, "No! I mean, you don't make me feel weird for being a foster kid. They do. What's up with that?" Shaking her head and rolling her eyes, Emma said, "Do they just not know what," waving her hands in the air, "we are all like? Really, we all smoke? *Come on!*"

"Oh," Sheila said with a grin. "I thought you were tellin' me you needed a smoke."

Smiling, Emma answered, "No. I know they are going out of their way to make me feel comfortable. They are making special accommodations because I am a foster kid based on what they *think* a foster kid is like, but we're not all alike. We don't *all* smoke. We're not all whores that throw our morals out when we are given the title foster kid. Some of us actually want what all other kids want and have—a family, an education, friends, and a place to belong.

Sighing, Emma picked at a spot on the table and continued, "It's not just them you know. Lots of people look at foster kids differently than regular kids. Before I was placed in a foster home, the kids at my old school treated me like all the other kids but after I moved into a foster home, kids in my grade, and even younger, laughed and pointed when I walked by them in the hall at school between classes. Younger kids were never nasty to me before I was put into a foster home. But everyone knew when it happened, when I was taken from my dad and put in a foster home—all the kids—everyone in town. My sisters and I were the *only* foster kids in town so it was a big deal. *Younger* kids at school started walking up to me, confronting me, with grins on their faces saying things to me, nasty things. They had never done that before," Emma said looking up at Sheila.

Sighing, Emma tried to shake off the bad memories as she asserted with a small smile, "And my foster family *is* weird, to me. The mom has this tic thing going on. When she gets excited about something, her head starts to twitch and snap back and forth. She did it the other night when she was talking to her girls after dinner. The more excited or stressed out she gets, the more noticeable the tic is," Emma said, simulating a jerking motion with her head. "And her girls look like turtles, and the smoking thing—I keep saying no. Really, but they just will not take no for an answer, so every night after dinner we all stand in the kitchen and fake smoke!" laughing at how ridiculous it all was.

"Well," Sheila said, waving her hand in an elaborate circle in the air. "We have plenty of room. You can stay here if you want."

Surprised, Emma looked across the table at Sheila. Living with Sheila had not occurred to Emma. As she thought about it, a smile spread across her face. She liked the idea. Not only would she be able to get away from the strange people with their stinky house, but she would at least be with one of her sisters. Glancing over at the clock, she sighed. She could do this knowing it was only for a few more days.

"Really?" Emma asked. "I could move in here with you?"

"Well, sure," Sheila said, as she popped her gum.

"How—when?" Emma asked excitedly.

"How 'bout Monday after school?" Sheila asked. "We're all meetin' after school to get your schedules straightened out. I have to be there, your foster mother will be there, and your caseworker will be there too. Just talk to your caseworker *then*. Should be simple enough."

"That *would* be perfect. I can make it through another day over there," Emma said thoughtfully, as she looked across the kitchen and twirled her long hair around her finger.

"Then it's settled," Sheila, said. "Just tell your caseworker you wanna live here and then after school you can ride home with Katie and me."

Relieved that her life finally seemed to be changing for the better, Emma smiled and sighed. When the doorbell rang, she turned toward the door the smile slipping from her lips.

"That's gotta be her, "Sheila said, getting to her feet and waddling to the living room. Emma remained in her seat, stretching the time as long as possible before she had to head back to the old people-smelling house.

"Emma," Sheila called.

Grimacing, Emma scooted her chair back and slowly walked to the living room.

"Are yuh ready?" her foster mother asked.

Offering her a small smile, Emma said, "Sure." As she looked at the lady with short dark hair, blue jeans, cowboy boots and over-sized belt buckle glinting at her, she realized she wasn't trying to be weird. Ugh. But she just felt so uncomfortable with her. In one night with Katie's foster family, she had been able to sit down and sink into a couch and watch TV, and laugh. She just could *not* do that with the stinky family, and she wasn't sure how to break it to the lady, wondering what she was going to say.

Emma's bag was already by the door. Turning toward the couch, Emma waved and softly said, "Bye," as Katie, Sara and Jessie walked toward her.

"Bye," the three girls chimed. Jessie was Sheila's daughter, even shorter than Sheila was, but unlike her mother, was thin. Jessie had made her appearance late last night after a date with her boyfriend.

Sheila grinned at Emma, popped her gum, and then said, "I'll see yuh tomorrow."

Sighing, knowing she had a plan, Emma responded, "I'll see you tomorrow at school," then shut the door behind her.

CHAPTER FIVE

Emma was nervous as she sat next to her foster mother during the drive to school. Last night was the last night she would ever have to sleep in the old people-smelling house. Thank you, she thought, as she rolled her eyes. She knew just what she was going to say to her caseworker later that afternoon. It couldn't fail. She would simply say she wanted to live with her sister. How could she say no? It made perfect sense. Of course, they would want her to live with Katie. Why they hadn't found a home big enough for Emma and her sisters really made no sense at all. So why did she feel like it was such a big deal, she wondered, as she rested her chin on her hand and watched the countryside whiz by.

After school, they were all going to meet in the guidance counselor's office, her foster mother, Katie's foster mother, their caseworker, Katie, and Emma. Her plan was to make it to the guidance counselor's office before her foster mother arrived so she could tell her caseworker she wanted to live with her sister. Then, her caseworker could let her foster mother know and she would be onto a stink-free and weirdness-free home.

The teen-crowded halls of the high school slowed Emma down as she sprinted to the counselor's office at the end of the day. She clutched her schoolbooks in her arms not taking the time to throw them in her locker, it didn't help that her last class was on the opposite side of the large school!

Shoving the door open, she saw that she was the last to arrive. *Damn*, she thought, as she tried to catch her breath. As she entered the reception area of the guidance counselors' offices, the three ladies, Emma's foster mother, wearing her typical cowgirl garb, Sheila, chomping away on her gum, and the caseworker, appearing efficient in her brown pantsuit, with an oversized bag stuffed with case files slung over her shoulder, and Katie, looked up at her.

Emma flopped onto a chair across from her sister as the guidance counselor asked the adults to join her in her office. As the two teens sat waiting, Katie flipped a page of the horror novel she had brought with her, and Emma grabbed the book she had checked out earlier in the day from the school's library and cracked it open.

Unable to focus, Emma folded a corner of a page in her book and laid it aside. She was distracted as she waited for her caseworker. She had hoped to talk to her before the meeting, but now it was going to be awkward. She had no intention of driving home with her foster mother, planning instead to go home with Sheila. Just how was she going to pull this off, she wondered?

Emma looked up when she heard the guidance counselor's voice. She walked toward the center of the lounge, talking to the other ladies about credits transferring, but Emma didn't care about credits right now.

Sitting up straight, trying to catch her caseworker's eye, Emma asked softly, "Could I talk to you for a minute?"

Standing next to her foster mother, the caseworker responded, "Sure. What's up?"

Nervously, Emma asked, "Can I talk to you *alone*?"

The caseworker glanced at the woman in jeans and cowboy boots standing next to her, and replied, "Whatever you have to say to me you can say in front of everyone."

Surprised, Emma raised her eyebrows, exhaled, and said, "Well, I'd rather just talk to you."

"Come on Emma. Just say what you have to say," the caseworker said shortly.

Emma stalled, trying to find a way out of hurting her foster mother's feelings, in front of a room filled with people. She looked at her caseworker and knew she was not going to budge. If she wanted to live with Katie, she was going to have to say so—in front of her foster mother—even if it hurt her.

"Okay," Emma said slowly, looking down at her hands. "I'd like to live with my sister."

Emma peeked up at her foster mother, catching the surprised look on her face.

Mouth gaped open, her foster mother stared, tilted her head back, and asked defensively, "Why? What's wrong with my house?"

"Oh—nothing. There's nothing wrong with your house," Emma lied.

"Then why don't you want to live with *me*?" she asked, as her head started to jerk.

This was not going well at all, Emma thought, as she looked at the three women standing in front of her. They were not making this easy for her. She didn't *want* to tell her foster mother the real reason she didn't want to live with her. Her answer had been a half-truth. She *did* want to live with her sister. It was only natural she wanted to live with Katie. They should understand that. So what was the big deal?

"No—No. There's somethin' more. I can tell," her foster mother said, as her head began to twitch more intently. Emma couldn't stop staring at her foster mother's head as it snapped back and forth.

Emma looked at Sheila for help but she just looked away.

Feeling as if she had been backed into a corner, Emma rolled her eyes, and said, "I want to live with my sister, *at least one of them*. What is so wrong with *that*? I think it's normal!"

"Come on," her foster mother insisted, as her lip curled up. She snatched her jacket off a chair and demanded of Emma, "Let's get goin'!"

Emma felt anger begin to burn inside of her as she looked at her case-worker. Why the hell couldn't the stupid woman talk to her in private? She hated that she had so obviously hurt her foster mother's feelings, and it was all her caseworkers fault. Well there was no backing down now Emma decided. She dug in and said, "No. I want to live with Katie. I'm sorry, but I *don't* want to live with you!"

Her foster mother huffed as she looked at the caseworker standing close enough to touch, and placing her hands on her hips demanded to know, "What's the *real* reason you don't wanna live with me?!"

Emma stared at her foster mother's large silver belt buckle, imprinted with a cowboy on a horse throwing a lasso in the air, and wondered, what was her problem? Why was she taking it so personally? She had known the woman less than two weeks.

Gritting her teeth in annoyance now, Emma realized she had no choice but to be honest, even if it hurt her foster mother and said, "You make me uncomfortable. I don't *smoke.* Your house *smells* and your girls are *weird!*" There, she had said it, and she felt awful.

Curling into her seat, Emma watched her foster mother jerk and squawk like a chicken, flapping her arms about in anger and then storm out of the room with her caseworker chasing after her. Scowling, Emma thought, what the hell. Shoving her hands in her coat pockets, Emma watched Katie's foster mother follow the other two women out of the office.

Emma wondered, weren't sisters supposed to live together...at least in the normal world? She was so confused and hurt as she sat quietly and waited for the adults to decide where she was going to live.

"Okay," her caseworker said, as she breezed back into the room a few minutes later. "You're going home with Sheila."

Emma looked up and saw her very grumpy caseworker, and Sheila, her new foster mother chomping away at her gum. Quietly, she climbed off her chair and followed the unhappy group, feeling suddenly uneasy.

CHAPTER SIX

The transfer from one foster home to another was relatively easy. Emma had only lived at the stinky country foster home for a few weeks; it was the fourth home and third school in less than a year. When she had run away from her aunt and uncle's home a few weeks ago, she had left behind everything she had acquired during the last ten months; clothes, books, jewelry and even the jewelry box her mother had given her. Had she known her things wouldn't be returned to her, she would have grabbed the small box and taken it with her.

Growing up, Emma had been told that her mother had left her when she just a baby, when she was two years old, and that after she had left, she had died. No one had told Emma how her mother had died, or when she had died, just that she was dead, so it had been quite a shock when her mother had shown up at her father's house for a visit last Christmas. After the initial shock had worn off, that the mother she had not seen in twelve years was still alive, her mother had another surprise for Emma and her two older sisters, Christmas gifts. She had given each of them small packages wrapped in shiny paper, and inside were white and gold jewelry boxes. At the time, Emma had been angry at her mother thinking, *as if a crummy jewelry box could make up for all the years she had been absent from their lives, all the years she had left them with their dad to endure the beatings and the touching*. Although Emma had been angry with her mother for abandoning them, the jewelry box *had* been held in her mother's hands, and she still loved the woman that cared so little about her that she had left her so very long ago.

When Emma's caseworker told her that none of her belongings would be returned to her, she had felt as if she had been punched in the stomach. She hadn't had many material possessions, but what little she'd accumulated were reflections of who she was—her memories. Her caseworker had explained that all the occupants, her aunt, uncle and her three cousins had vacated the house and they were not going back. Her things were just sitting in the empty house, even her precious jewelry box.

Ten months ago, when the police had been called to her father's home because of abuse, Emma had packed a brown paper sack with the few articles of clothing she owned, most borrowed, and the jewelry box, not even filling the sack half full. She had looked around the bedroom she had shared with her two older sisters for over ten years, at the handmade wooden Barbie house that had served as a bookcase, at her books stacked neatly inside, at items strewn across the two dressers, and sack clutched in her hand walked out the door. She hadn't known she would never step foot inside the house again, so anything not in her small sack remained behind. But this time, after running away from her aunt and uncle's house, running to the safety of the police, there had been no time to scrape together a few things into a sack.

Sheila showed Emma to the bedroom she would share, not with her sister Katie, but with Jessie, Sheila's eighteen-year-old daughter. It seemed strange not to be sharing a bedroom with her sister, Katie. They had slept in the same room almost all their lives.

Emma placed the small garbage bag containing the few items that had been purchased for her recently, underwear, bras, socks, two pair of jeans, and a few tops, onto the twin bed. Then she looked around the room at the other twin bed, at the teen type posters taped to the walls, and the two dressers placed on either side of the bedroom. Nice, she thought, as Jessie walked into their room wearing a big grin.

"Whatta yuh think?" Jessie asked. "Will this be okay for you?"

Emma smiled, nodded her head, and said, "Yeah. This'll be just fine."

She liked Jessie, with her dimpled grin and easygoing nature. Maybe, Emma considered, she would stay with this family long enough to fill up one of the dressers sitting next to the window. She hoped so. She wanted to belong somewhere.

The next few months were good ones for Emma. Her caseworker had managed to have a clothing order approved for Emma and Katie, so on several snowy Saturday afternoons they spent time at the mall sorting through the stores for the necessities that had been left behind at their aunt and uncle's house. She settled into life with her new foster family, finding she now had two *new* sisters, Jessie and Sara, and a new brother, George, Sheila's twenty-year-old son. He was a strange looking man, Emma reflected, with thick blonde scraggly hair, horse teeth like his mother, and although he was taller than Sheila, he was short for a man. During the night, he worked at a facility for special needs people, and during the day, he slept in Sheila's garage. There wasn't room for George inside the house—not enough bedrooms—so Sheila had helped him set up a twin bed in a corner of the garage—just tucked into a corner of the garage beside an old car. It seemed strange that Sheila would take in other kids when she didn't have room for her own.

Then there was Jessie, Sheila's daughter. She was a great sister, even if she was a foster sister, sharing her clothes, teaching her new ways to do her hair, providing her makeup tips, and even allowing Emma to hitch a ride each morning to school. Jessie and her friends were seniors, just like Katie, and Emma was just a freshman. Being seen in the presence of seniors was a big deal, *and* they were nice to her.

Sara, Emma's other foster sister, was Sheila's niece. She had lived with the family for several years and was every bit as generous as Jessie was, but in different ways. She was a source of big sister talk, about anything on Emma's mind, such as boys, music, school, and what seemed to take up much of her thoughts, her family. Amy wasn't all Emma thought about. Her two half-brothers, Timmy and Robby, and her half-sister, Laura, weighed heavily on her mind.

Emma's stepmother had left her father after someone had found out about the secret. She had taken Timmy, Robby and, Laura, and moved them into a small house on the other side of the small farming community where they had all lived. Her little brothers, sister, and stepmother still lived in the small community, Emma's childhood town where she had gone to school all her life, until last fall when Emma had moved down south to live with her aunt and uncle.

Not only was life at the foster home going well, but her new high school was working out too. A group of kids had accepted Emma into their group, and they were good kids, not the popular crowd with cheerleaders or jocks, or the druggies, just the regular, slightly nerdy crowd…her kind of crowd. It hadn't been that way for the past few years, not since she had become a foster kid. Since she had been moved out of her father's house, she hadn't been accepted into any group of kids, not at her childhood school of nine years, and not in the last school, the high school down south with her aunt and uncle. She could understand the exclusion from the other kids when she had lived with her aunt and uncle; she hated driving up to the shack on the school bus, having all the other kids knowing where and with whom she lived. It was embarrassing. The house, the family, it all stood out—they were the town joke—the town trash.

Life at her new high school was different, different from the last school year when she had been in eighth grade, and different from the school she attended when she and her sisters had lived with their aunt and uncle for the past five months. In Emma's mind her last year of junior high, as the senior upper classman, should have been great, the best, but it hadn't been. The kids at school had found out that Emma and her sisters had been removed from their father's home and the reason why. It wasn't long before Emma's classmates began treating her differently, they didn't want to talk to her, or hang out with her. No one called to ask her over to their house—no more sleepovers—no more party invitations were received.

Then, as so often happens when children are determined to be different from their peers, Emma was singled out, and the cruel taunts began. Switching classes during the day became a strategic mad dash to her next class as Emma tried to avoid questions, snickers, and confrontations. Emma walked quickly down the hall, passed her classmates and even under classmen. She heard the snickers, saw fingers pointing at her, and saw the sneers on the kids that had at one time been her friend's faces. She kept her head down and tried to avoid the stares, tried to block it all out, tried to blend in with the old uneven wood floor, wishing she could disappear. A few of the kids were bold, dared by their peers to maliciously confront her. They would block her way so she had to stop as they blurted out, "We know what your dad did," or they made lewd comments about the way she was dressed, or about her body, then they would scamper back to their group of friends. Emma, face burning, and head down, would stumble to her next class as laughter rang in her ears from the group that at one time included her. It was as if everyone at school, the students and even the teachers, had changed the day she had been placed in a foster home. But Emma hadn't changed. She was the same old Emma.

"Hey Tammy," Emma said with a smile, as she squeezed into the lunch line next to her new friend. "Where's Paul?" referring to Tammy's boyfriend.

Pivoting her weight, Tammy replied, "He had to stay behind in English class to talk to the teacher about a paper he needs to redo. I told him I'd *help* him with it, but he insisted he do it since there will just be more papers to do this year."

"Oh," Emma said, urging her friend forward in line. "So what're you guys doing this weekend?" knowing as freshman none of them were allowed out on actual dates, but hanging out at the bowling alley was acceptable.

"I don't know. Maybe Paul will hang out at my house. As long as my parents are home, they're okay with it," she said, rolling her eyes.

Emma knew she had a greater appreciation for rules and structure than her friends did. It was nice to pretend she was normal—like any other kid—and she pretended she agreed with Tammy to fit in.

"Yeah," she said with a sigh. "Parents."

Carrying trays filled with cheeseburgers, fries, and chocolate cake, the two girls walked to their usual table. Emma smiled at the kids, crammed onto the bench seats, the smiling faces of her new friends.

"Hey Emma!" the group chorused.

"Hey guys," she said smiling, and slid across the bench.

One of the girls leaned forward on the bench seat and asked, "Emma. Is it *true*? Are you *really* dating a senior?" with a look of awe on her face.

Chewing her French fries, Emma smiled and shook her head, *yes*.

She heard gasps amongst her girlfriends as Paul walked toward the table carrying his lunch tray, heaped with two cheeseburgers, fries, pie, and an apple.

"*Who?*" Shelly the tall brunette sitting on the other side of Emma, asked. "Who is he?" Scrunching her shoulders, she scooted closer to Emma. "What's he look like? Is he cute...tall, what? *Tell us!*" she insisted with a grin. "Give us the dirt?"

"Yeah," Tammy said, sliding over to make room for Paul. "Where'd you meet him, and why am I just *now* hearing about this?" she asked, as she cocked her head.

"Well," Emma said, taking a sip of her chocolate milk. "We just started dating, and" she stammered, "I wouldn't exactly call it dating. It was just one date to the movies." She smiled, feeling a little uneasy at being the center of attention.

"*What?!*" Tina said. "You have *already* been on a date? How did I not know this?" she asked, raising her hands, palms up in the air. "Wait a minute. You mean you went to the movies with a boy—*alone?*"

Swirling chocolate crumbs around her plate, Emma answered, "I didn't want to say anything just yet. I felt kind of silly, and yes, *alone.*" She looked up and said, "Besides, it was just *one* date." Shrugging her shoulders she continued, "He'll probably never ask me out again anyway."

"Who—Who is he?! What's his name? Do we know him?" Shelly asked excitedly.

Wondering if any of her friends knew him, Emma said, "His name's Mark Turner, and I met him through Jessie. She came home one night from a date a few weeks ago and told me he had mentioned me. He asked her if she thought I'd go out with him. She seemed to think it'd be okay, so…I said he could call me—and he did. We went out the next weekend. It wasn't a big deal. We grabbed something to eat and then went to the movies."

"No way," Shelly said, leaning her arm on the table. Leaning forward she whispered, "Did he *kiss* you?"

Embarrassed, Emma said, "Just a quick peck."

"Wow," Shelly commented. "My friend, dating a *senior.*"

"Shelly, I'm not dating him!" Laughing, Emma said, "It was *one* date," raising one finger in the air for emphasis. "The boy will probably never even call me again. I'm not exactly a senior's type you know." Wrinkling her forehead, Emma continued, "Why would he ask me out *anyway*? Why not someone his own age? Just what could we have in common?"

Emma had only gone on the date so Jessie and her friends would think she was cool. She hadn't been the least bit excited as she waited nervously on the couch Saturday night. If anything, she had felt as if she might throw up. She had no idea what she would say to him, some boy she didn't know. What did girls much older than her say to boys, much older than her? Sheila, Jessie, and Sara had been excited about her date, flitting about and making a big deal over her hair and makeup. You'd have thought they were going on the date instead of her and she kind of wished one of them would so she could stay home and watch TV.

It had been an uncomfortable evening, spent trying to be much older, and experienced than she was. The only prior experience Emma had with boys was the two boys she had dated at her aunt and uncle's house. She had dated a boy she met at the skating rink, for all of a weekend. Their dating experience had consisted of holding hands and skating in a circle around the concrete rink. They had broken up the following weekend, but it had been a worthwhile experience. He had taught her how to skate.

Sam, her only other real boyfriend had been easy to talk to because he really didn't have a lot to say, besides that, they had never actually gone out on a date. Their dates had consisted of rolling around on the skating rink floor in front of her entire family or hanging out at her aunt and uncle's house, and someone had always been around. She had never really been alone with a boy, not alone—alone.

She had met Sam at the rink too. They had dated for a few months during the summer, and then she had broken it off. He hadn't been her type—not that she knew what her type was just yet—she just knew he wasn't it. He had been friends with Amy's boyfriend. Whenever Amy's boyfriend drove out to the country to their house, he had brought Sam with him. It's not that Sam wasn't a nice boy. He was and she knew he had really liked her. But she had been only fourteen and he had hidden the fact that he was nineteen from her. He had been her first kiss. She had felt safe with him, but had known she was too young to get as serious as he wanted. He had already graduated from high school, and she, well, she was just beginning high school. She was just a kid, not ready for any meaningful relationship or commitment.

Emma looked at Tammy and asked, "Do you know Mark, or have you heard anything about him?"

Tammy was quiet for a minute, looking down at her tray of mostly eaten food and then looked up, and said, "No. No. I don't know him. I've heard the name before, but I've never heard anything bad about him." Turning her head toward her boyfriend she asked, "Paul, do you know him?"

Shaking his head, Paul said, "No. The name doesn't sound familiar."

Well, Emma thought, at least there was nothing negative about him, at least not from *her* lunch table.

CHAPTER SEVEN

"Emma," Sara said, as she peeked around the wall that separated the kitchen from the small living room. "Shelly's on the phone."

"Thanks!" Emma said with a smile, as she bounced into the kitchen and took the telephone from Sara's hand.

Pressing the white telephone to her ear, Emma asked, "Hey, what are you doing?"

Emma scooted one of the cushioned chairs away from the kitchen table and sat down, preparing for a long chitchat with, Shelly, her second best friend.

Emma was quiet for a moment as she listened to Shelly talk about cute freshman boys—giggled—then asked if she was going out with Mark over the weekend.

Emma responded, "Yeah. Mark and I are going to the movies tomorrow night. What are you doing this weekend?"

Emma listened to Shelly explain that her plans consisted of hanging out with her older brother Neal and his friends, throwing in a few unflattering comments about her brother. Typical Shelly, Emma thought with a smile.

Emma laughed and chided her friend, "He is *not*! Your brother is *not* a nerd. He's nice."

Shelly was constantly giving her brother, Neal, a hard time. Emma knew Shelly loved her brother, and the mean things she said about him were just her way of fitting in. It seemed as if most kids didn't get along with their brothers or sisters, but Shelly and Neal were unique. It was kind of cool, at least Emma thought so. Neal was a year older than Shelly and

Emma, and kind of cute, and very sweet, but he did have a way of irritating his little sister, but Emma knew he did it on purpose because he cared back.

"Hanging out with your brother and his friends—rough life Shelly," Emma said with a wistful smile.

"Oh—sure. Tell Neal I said hi," Emma said into the phone, surprised Shelly was cutting their girl talk short. Typically, when her friend called she could count on getting a meal and snack in during the conversation. The girl liked to talk which was okay because Emma loved hearing about her normal, simple life. It was like a good book.

Emma placed the handset back onto its cradle and eased her legs up onto the chair across from her wondering, now what to do. It would be hours before Mark picked her up for their date. Mr. Spock's voice drifted to Emma from the TV in the other room. Katie loved Star Trek.

Stretching her arms above her head, Emma thought to herself, she loved the show too, but she didn't have all day to sit and watch it like her sister. A few weeks ago, Katie had announced she was dropping out of school, much to Emma's surprise. Katie was one of the smartest people Emma knew, like a librarian, constantly sharing information about history, science, music, authors and even movies. She of all people shouldn't have quit school. The guidance counselor had told Katie that not all her credits would transfer over from the other two high schools so, she quit. It had been too much for Katie. She had done all the right things. It wasn't her fault her life was so screwed up and she just couldn't get a break. Katie had it tough growing up, in different ways, at times filling in as a mom for six kids, and well, just other stuff.

Star Trek it was, Emma thought, as she scooted her chair back and headed for the living room to catch the end of the program with her sister.

A half an hour later, Katie relinquished the remote to Emma and headed to her bedroom to read one of her horror novels. Emma was curled up on the couch in the living room flipping through the channels on the TV. It was quiet in the house, but for the chatter coming from the television across the room, that and the annoying noise coming from the kitchen. Katie and Emma were the only ones home, besides Sheila's twenty-year-old son, who was rummaging loudly through the kitchen cabinets.

"Hey," George said with a big grin, as he plopped down onto the couch near her feet.

"Hey," Emma sighed, annoyed that her afternoon had been disturbed.

She curled her legs tighter to give him room, not liking the feel of his body touching hers. She felt his hand stroke her calf and she glared at him, and kicked his hand away.

"Watcha doin'?" he asked.

Turning away, she looked at the TV and began flipping through the channels again. Well," she said, as if talking to a small child. "I'm watching TV," and rolled her eyes.

Leaning on her hip, pinning her beneath him, he asked, "Wanna get high?"

Panic rose in Emma as she struggled to sit up. "No," she said, staring at him and giving him her most annoyed look.

"Awe, come on," he said, as he pulled something white out of his shirt pocket.

Emma looked at what George held between his stubby fingers. She noticed a white kind of cigarette—a weird looking thing—and wrinkled her nose at the smell. She'd never seen pot before, but she had heard about it from kids at school.

"Uh—no," she snarled, and got up and walked across the room. She plopped down on the chair closest to the TV and did her best to ignore him.

He wasn't like the rest of the family. He was just *weird*, she thought. Sitting with her chin resting on the palm of her hand she stared blankly at the TV screen wondering, *were all boys so—so disgusting?*

Later that night, home before curfew, Emma leaned toward the mirror in the small bathroom as she washed the makeup off her face, thinking about her date with Mark. They'd had a nice time, cheeseburgers for dinner, and then he'd taken her to the garage he worked at after school and on weekends. He worked at an auto body shop, smelling of gasoline and paint, just like the garage at her dad's house. Then they had gone to see a movie.

As she brushed her teeth, her thoughts turned to her afternoon—George and the joint. She spit and rinsed, then grinned at herself in the mirror. Pressing her face closer to the mirror, she examined the crooked tooth on the upper right side of her mouth. She ran her tongue across her teeth, stepped back, and stared at her reflection, assessing her long golden brown hair, with bangs and sides flipped back off her face giving it a feather effect. With a heavy sigh, she slumped her shoulders. She flipped the light switch off, and walked down the hall to her bedroom, as George continued to flit through her thoughts. He made her uneasy.

Not bothering to turn the light on in her bedroom, Emma walked the few steps in the dark to her bed. She slid beneath the blankets on her bed, tugging the fuzzy blue blanket to her chin, and thought back to other times that boys and men had given her that uncomfortable feeling. Laying in the dark, her head cushioned by her pillow, Emma stared across the small room at the closet door.

Her thoughts turned to Katie. They weren't getting along very well lately. She had grown distant, although physically she was right down the hall. As Emma snuggled deeper into her pillow, she wondered how Amy was doing, and as ribbons of childhood memories made a trail through her mind, she fell asleep.

Emma jolted awake, her heart pounding. She looked across the small bedroom at the closet near her bed. Blinking the remnants of sleep away, she wondered if she'd had the nightmare again. She froze when she felt something brush her hip and a chill crept up her spine when she felt a hot breath on her neck.

Emma was dizzy with fear, but with as much power as she could in the small space, she shoved her elbow into whomever of whatever was touching her breast and heard a grunt. She jerked her body away and jumped to her feet. Breathless with fear, she spun around, and looked down at the rumpled covers and saw what had touched her while she slept. George was lying on his side in the center of the small bed, his overly large teeth seeming to glow in the dark as he grinned up at her.

Shaking as memories swirled, feeling angry, and disgusted, she hissed, "Get the *fuck* out!"

Slowly he rolled off her bed and walked toward the door. He looked back at her as if she might change her mind with a smirk titling the corners of his mouth.

"Out!" she hissed. Shaking, she crossed her arms across her chest.

After he closed the door behind him, Emma glanced across the small room toward Jessie's bed, empty, the blankets exactly as they had been when Emma had fallen asleep hours ago; then she stared down at her own empty bed and shivered.

CHAPTER EIGHT

E mma leaned back against the stoop and absorbed the warm spring sun as she listened to Shelly and Neal argue, again. She loved it at their house. It was how she had always pictured normal. She peeked at the brother and sister and noticed how similar they were. They were both tall with a muscular build, Shelly being maybe five foot eight and Neal was easily six foot. Emma watched as they wrestled in the center of the grassy yard. If she hadn't known better, Emma would have sworn they were twins, Shelly a smaller version of Neal. They had perfect facial features, hair just a shade lighter than Emma's golden light brown. Neal had nice hair, a little shaggy, just long enough to skim his collar and Shelly's hair hung down the middle of her back. Emma smiled as she wondered if they realized just how much they looked and acted like each other.

"Emma," Shelly said, as she punched Neal on the arm. "I can't believe you're going to prom!"

Swinging her legs over the side of the concrete stoop, Emma smiled and said, "I know. Can you believe it?"

Mark and Emma had been dating exclusively for three months, and a week ago, he had surprised her by asking her to go to prom with him. She and Jessie had already made a special trip to the mall to buy shoes. It was way too early for dress shopping, but they had reasoned shoes could be bought anytime. Emma had selected a brown leather high-heeled sandal that double strapped around her ankles. Hours had been spent wandering around the house breaking them in and becoming acclimated to the very tall heel so she wouldn't fall on her face when she danced, not that she knew how to dance, a minor detail.

"So, how did he ask you? What did he say?" Shelly asked, as Neal, standing behind her, rolled his eyes.

"Well," Emma said, "he just asked. We were sitting outside my house and right before I got out of the car, he asked me if I'd go to prom."

Shelly walked over and sat next to Emma on the stoop.

"*Wow*," Shelly said. "Are you doubling with one of his friends?"

"I have no idea," Emma said, wrinkling her forehead.

"You two are so dumb," Neal said.

Emma looked over at him as he stood in the center of the yard and threw a football in the air, then caught it as it tumbled toward his head.

"What?!" Emma asked. "Dumb, how?"

Neal rolled his blues eyes at her, walked over, and sat across from the girls on the opposite stoop.

Emma looked at Neal curiously. She felt comfortable with him, the way she imagined it would feel if she had an older brother. George was still on her mind. She hadn't told anyone what had been happening, about him touching her, climbing in bed with her and asking her to get high.

As Neal examined the threads of the brown football he held in his hands, Emma asked, "Neal, why are boys jerks?"

He jerked his head up and said, "What?! I'm not a jerk!"

Realizing he thought she was referring to him, Emma reassured him, "No, I don't mean you. *Other* boys. Why do they do the things they do to girls. I mean, why are they so *touchy-feely*?"

He looked across at her, and said slowly, "Well, some boys *are* jerks."

"Shelly—Neal," their mother said, as she opened the screen door. "It's about time to get going."

The three teens looked up at the pretty woman looking down at them from the porch.

Neal jumped up and threw the ball high in the air one more time and then he climbed the steps to the porch and said, "See yuh, Em."

"See yuh!" she called back with a smile.

"I gotta go," Shelly sighed. "We have to go to my grandma's for dinner," rolling her eyes.

Emma rose to her feet and stretched. "I'll see you at school Monday," thinking again how lucky Shelly was.

She walked to the sidewalk and looked over at her friend standing with her hand on the screen door, and waved as Shelly waved back.

Enjoying the time alone, Emma slowly walked back to Sheila's house. As she listened to the birds chirping, she thought, boys are jerks, just as Neal had said. *Boys are jerks…*

A half an hour later, as Emma walked down the street in front of her foster home, she saw a familiar midnight blue colored truck parked in the driveway. She slowed her pace as she walked passed it, peeking in the driver's side window. Yup, she thought, it was his truck.

Walking into the living room, even though she had seen his truck parked in the driveway, Emma was surprised to see the man with black hair, brown eyes and nose shaped like a hawks beak sitting on her foster mother's couch, quite cozy looking. He was wearing his typical womanizing outfit, blue jeans, a shirt with turquoise snaps and spit shined cowboy boots. She hadn't seen her dad in over a year and warily she stared at him wondering why he was there. She had seen him once after the last day in court, the night of the tornado…and now, here he was snuggled up next to her foster mother. Angrily, Emma thought, he had no business being in her foster home, sitting on the couch that she sat on, if anything, he should be sitting in a jail cell. The judge had listened to the evidence, had even read the confession her dad had given the court appointed therapist, but the judge had sent him home—with no time served. Katie had speculated that her dad, or grandma, must have known the judge. It was the only way to explain why a rapist was allowed to go free, but it didn't explain why he was sitting on a couch in her foster home now.

Emma couldn't stop staring at the couple on the couch. Sheila was grinning, exposing her large white front teeth and her dad kept his head down, looking at his hands. As she continued to watch them, Emma walked across the room and waited for one of them to explain his presence.

Snapping her gum, Sheila, said with a big grin, "Hey, Emma. Your dad's gonna take me to dinner tonight."

To dinner, Emma thought. How in the *hell, why in the hell* was her foster mother and her…*dad*, going to dinner. From the looks of things, noticing their knees touching, it was a dinner of a personal nature.

"Hey, Emma," her dad said, as he looked up at her with a small smile tilting his fleshy lips.

"Hey," she returned, as she plopped down onto a soft chair, confused as to why this man was in her home. Wrinkling her forehead, Emma wondered, *were they dating?* As a child, she had grown used to her dad hitting on her sister's friends. Emma watched Sheila rest her hand on his thigh, and wondered where they had met.

Without saying a word, Emma got to her feet and left Sheila, and her dad alone in the room. In disgust, she pondered where they were having dinner, knowing how their date would end. More than likely, her foster mother was going to have sex with the man that had caused her years of torment and was the reason she was now a foster kid. Rolling her eyes, she walked down the short hallway to her bedroom and quietly closed the door behind her.

Emma grew quiet over the next few weeks—uncomfortable with Sheila spending time with her dad. One Friday evening, as Emma walked by the open door of the bathroom, she saw Sheila caking on her makeup and knew it was date night. Emma didn't say anything; repulsed she continued to walk toward the sound of the TV in the living room.

Minutes later, curled into a corner of one of the couches in the living room, Emma heard a knock on the door. She scowled at Sheila as she quickly waddled through the living room to open the door for her date. Expecting to see her dad walk into the room, Emma was surprised to see someone different, a very tall thin man with lots of dark hair instead.

"Hey, Eric!" Sheila said, with an ear-to-ear grin.

Perplexed, Emma watched as Sheila teetered on her tips-toes and pressed her lips to his making a loud smacking sound. The tall man wrapped his long arm around Sheila's waist, as she tugged him close. Ugh! Emma thought…but at least it wasn't her dad.

"*Eric!*" Sheila said playfully, as he grinned down at her.

"Come on in," Sheila said, as she looked up at him coyly. She pulled on his hand and presented her new man to the occupants of the living room, Katie, Sara, and Emma, "Kids, this here's Eric." Then she introduced her foster children and Sara to her new beau.

"I'll be right back," Sheila said playfully, as she looked up at Eric and then did her best to scamper out of the living, but the effect was more of a lumber, like a mama bear running across a field.

Well, Emma thought hopefully, perhaps Sheila was done with her dad. Just how desperate must a woman be to go out with someone like that anyway? Emma examined Sheila's new guy suspiciously, as he continued to stand by the door. There was something about him, Emma couldn't quite figure it out, but something about him made her uncomfortable. She didn't know if it was his creepy navy blue sweater or the way he hunched his shoulders, but something about him reeked of weasel.

With a white sweater folded over her arm and her black over-sized purse slung over her shoulder, Sheila pranced, sort of, back into the living room.

"Ready?" she asked her new friend, as she popped her gum and grinned up at him.

Looking over at Katie, Sara, and Emma, each quietly evaluating the situation, Sheila said cheerfully, "Don't wait up!"

Oh, don't you worry, Emma thought as the door closed behind the strange pair.

CHAPTER NINE

"Emma," George called. "You ready?"

Rushing down the hall, Emma answered, "Coming!" as she slung her purse over shoulder. George had offered to give her a lift to see Mark, and she didn't want to give him time to change his mind. Mark had called a little bit ago and told her he had to cancel their Saturday night date because he'd been called into work for a few hours, but if she wanted, she could come hang out at the garage with him. It was better than sitting at home on a Saturday night, she thought.

Emma followed her foster brother out of the house to his poop brown colored Chevy Camaro parked in the driveway.

As Emma pulled the door shut behind her, she smiled at George and said, "Thanks so much for taking me down to the garage."

"No problem," George said, staring at her with a toothy grin.

The smile tilting Emma's lips upward slipped a little as she looked at George's face, his broad grin exposing his large horse looking gapped teeth, and the way he was leering at her. She was still a little creeped out by him, but she hadn't woken to find him lying next to her in the middle of the night lately. Maybe he had been drunk or something that one night, she speculated, as she watched him back out of the driveway.

Looking down into her purse, Emma dug around inside until her fingers touched the object she was looking for, her clear lip-gloss. Unscrewing the top, she looked out the window as she rolled the gloss on her lips, and realized George was driving the car in the wrong direction. He was driving the car in the opposite direction from Mark's garage. The garage Mark worked at was on the west side of town. It was the side of town with the older, more established homes with sidewalks, the town square, and the one-hundred year old courthouse towering in the center of all the cool shops. George was headed East, which led outside of town to the cornfields now waist high and the tall prairie grasses, at least fifteen minutes out of their way.

Frowning, she asked, "George, where're you going?"

Turning his head toward her, he gave her another one of his toothy grins and said, "I just need to make a stop first."

Well, she thought, he sure was driving way out of the way for his *stop.* They rode in silence for a while as Emma watched the endless corn stalks pass by.

Emma wrinkled her forehead, and looked out the window as George steered the car through the entryway of the park, wondering why they had to drive to the park first. Was he meeting someone way out here, she wondered? They passed a car parked alongside the road, and as they drove further into the park, she saw two people sitting on a picnic table. Finally, he pulled into a small deserted parking lot tucked away behind tall grasses.

Emma turned her attention back to George, and asked, "Are you meeting someone?"

She watched as he pulled a red lighter out of his shirt pocket along with one of his strange white cigarettes. She wrinkled her nose at the sharp smell.

As she continued to stare, he sparked the lighter into life and lit the joint stuck between his lips.

He held his breath and offered the joint to her.

"No," she said firmly, and unsmiling.

Still holding the joint in front of her face, he exhaled, blowing a cloud of smoke in her face and said, "Come on."

Sighing, she insisted, "George, take me to Mark."

"I will. I will," he said, as he raised the joint to his lips again. "First, get high with me."

They stared at each other in silence.

"Come on," he coaxed.

Emma considered her options. She could walk across town to Mark's garage, after of course walking through the country, hopefully not getting lost, and that was if she didn't get hit by a car or attacked by one of the crazies in the park. Her other option was to accept the joint from George. Emma looked at the joint held between George's fingers and wondered what it would feel like to be high. Emma had never seen anyone high before. She was afraid of what it would do to her, how it would make her feel, and what George could do to her while she was out of it.

"You smoke it like a cigarette," George said.

There with the smoking thing again, Emma thought. What was the deal with everyone trying to get her to smoke? She rolled her eyes knowing she couldn't smoke. Amy had already tried to teach her but she had always ended up gagging and coughing.

"I can't smoke," Emma announced, relieved she would get out of the situation with her lack of smoking ability.

"It's different from smoking a cigarette," George explained, to Emma's surprise. He was clearly not listening to her, she thought in frustrated silence as she folded her arms across her chest.

"You inhale. Then hold it. Watch me," he instructed as he sucked on the joint.

Emma watched as he held the joint between his fingers and sucked, the tip burning bright. He looked like an idiot.

He choked a little and said, as he held his breath, "Don't blow it out. Hold it in as long as you can."

Maybe if she sucked in the smoke and breathed it out real fast, it wouldn't do anything to her, she thought hopefully, knowing he wasn't going to budge until she did as he asked. She grasped the half-gone joint between her fingers and placed it between her lips, inhaling a little of the smoke, then turned her head and quickly blew the smoke against the window. She turned back to him, her cheeks puffed as she pretended to "hold it" like he had insisted and then handed it back to him.

He smiled at her, satisfied by her actions. She looked over at him as he continued to suck on the joint. He extended it toward her again but she shook her head no.

Sitting in the smoke-filled car watching him suck away on the joint, Emma evaluated how she felt. She didn't feel any different. Maybe it didn't have any impact on her.

"How do you feel?" he asked.

Relieved, she said, "Fine. I guess it doesn't affect me."

Unsmiling, he shook his head, and asked, "You ready?"

"Yes," she said, feeling as if she had just dodged a bullet of some kind. She scooted closer to the passenger door and stared out the window during the quiet twenty-minute drive to the garage. When George pulled up next to the curb outside of the garage, she said a quick "thanks" and jumped out of the car, slamming the door behind her.

"Hey," Mark said when she walked into the garage. He grabbed a dirty rag off a table and wiped his hands.

"Hey," Emma responded with a forced smile. Still thinking about what had happened with George; she wasn't in the mood to talk. A feeling had come over her, a familiar feeling of needing to get away, to run, to scrape the yuck off her. As she walked over to Mark, she noticed his gray uniform with oil, or something splattered on the front. Distracted, she gave him a quick kiss on his soft lips, and then she settled onto a chair out of the way, close enough for small talk as he stuck his head under the hood of a car. As Mark clanged away under the hood of the car, Emma continued to think about George, wondering what was wrong with the man. Snuggling deeper into the chair, Emma crossed her arms tight across her chest and stared at the light hanging near Mark's head.

Mark dropped Emma off at her foster home a few hours later, and as she walked into the living room, she noticed Sheila and her boyfriend, Eric, whispering, snuggled close on the couch. Glancing at them, Emma thought, at least it wasn't her dad sitting cozied up to Sheila. Saying hi, Emma walked back to her bedroom to drop off her purse, and then she headed toward the kitchen where Sara was sitting at the table eating a bowl of ice cream.

"Hey, Emma," Sara said with a smile. Sara pushed the chair next to her out and said, "Grab a bowl of ice cream and have a seat."

Grinning, Emma said, "I think I will. Do we have any chocolate syrup left?" She hunched over and began shoving things around in the refrigerator.

"Yeah. To the right. On the top shelf," Sara said.

"Aha! Got it!" Emma exclaimed, as she grabbed the brown bottle of syrup and squirted it in loops on the top of her vanilla ice cream. Perfect, she thought, licking her fingers.

Sitting next to Sara, Emma asked, "How long has *he* been here?"

"You mean the perv?" Sara asked with a wink. "About an hour ago."

"Are they going out?" Emma asked, wrinkling her nose.

"I don't know," Sara said, as she licked her spoon.

Rolling her eyes, Emma confided in Sarah, "He gives me the creeps."

"You and me both!" Sara said, scooting her chair back and placing her bowl in the sink. "TV?" she asked, looking back at the fifteen-year-old girl scraping the bottom of her white bowl.

"Sure." Emma didn't really want to sit in the living room with the love birds, but it was better than hanging out in her bedroom for the rest of the evening.

Sara walked to the powder blue, low-backed couch, on the far wall and Emma followed. It was the prime TV watching spot in the room. A giant, ornate gold colored frame holding a picture of lilac, and pink flowers was placed above the couch and on either side were heavy end tables adorned with cream and blue colored lacy doilies. Sheila and Eric were snuggled up on the brown and blue flowered couch on the opposite wall, placed in front of the bay window overlooking the front yard and street. Emma glanced over at them as she heard Sheila giggle. Eric's tall body was almost obscuring Sheila from view as he leaned over her, and whispered something that caused her to squeal.

Gross, Emma thought.

Curled up at opposite ends of the couch, Emma and Sara watched the sitcom on TV, periodically glancing over at the rated R scene unfolding on the couch next to them.

"Okay!" Sara said, looking down the couch at Emma. "I'm off to bed. You're on your own!"

"No. Not yet," Emma begged, with a don't leave me expression on her face.

Shaking the wrinkles out of her baggy shorts, Sara said, "Night everyone."

Sighing, Emma watched Sara walk out of the room, and then glanced at the couple on the couch. Why, she wondered, weren't they leaving, or at least going go Sheila's bedroom, as they so obviously needed to.

"Night, sweetie," Sheila said.

"Night," Eric said in a distracted tone.

"Eric, you ready to go out?" Sheila asked, to Emma's relief.

"Whenever you're ready sugar," the tall man with bad posture responded.

"I'm gonna go get ready. Emma, you keep Eric company for me," Sheila said, as she stood up and looked down at him.

Oh yippee, Emma thought, as she looked over at the middle-aged playboy leering at her. He unfolded his lanky frame from the floral couch, stood and stretched. In two steps, he had plopped down beside Emma, leaning against her. Scowling, she pulled away as he bent over and looked up into her face. Not saying anything, she scooted further away from him as she looked at him suspiciously, noticing his dark blue button up sweater and slacks. She shivered.

"You sure are pretty," he whispered, as he scooted closer and leaned his arm on her leg.

She looked down at his arm as he slid it along her leg, his large hand squeezing her thigh, and looked up into his face. Still looking into his face, she used her forearm to shove his hand and arm away.

Not to be deterred, he continued with a sleazy smile, "I bet you have all kinds of boys after you. A pretty thing like you." His upper lip twitched as he looked at her face, his eyes travelling from her eyes to her lips.

Sliding off the couch, Emma stood up, and looking down into his grinning face thought he looked like an animal, and expected drool to drip to the floor at any moment. "Do you dance?" he asked in a soft, sickening voice.

"No," Emma answered shortly. She scowled, pivoted on her foot, and stormed toward her bedroom, passing Sheila in the short hallway.

Emma caught the happy smile on Sheila's face as she glanced up.

"Don't wait up!" Sheila giggled.

Emma shook her head as she opened her bedroom door, wondering what in the world the woman saw in her sleaze-ball of a boyfriend. And where were they going so late at night? Did anyone *really* eat dinner at 10:00 O'clock at night?

Emma brushed her left hand against the wall. Finding the light switch, she flipped on the light and closed the bedroom door behind her. Walking the two small steps to her bed, she flopped back as if she were about to make a snow angel. Lying on her back with one foot hanging over the edge of her narrow twin bed, and her arm draped across her stomach, she stared up at the white textured ceiling thinking about her new family. There were some strange goings on, that was for sure.

Lying on the bed, Emma listened to the quiet of the house. No noise. Jessie was out with her boyfriend. Katie was asleep in Sara's room and by now, and Sara was probably asleep too. George wasn't home yet. Maybe he had to go into work. Everyone in the house had to work to help Sheila pay the bills, except for Emma and Katie. Jessie worked at a restaurant on weekends and Sara worked somewhere too. Emma wasn't sure where.

The day had started okay, Emma thought, but as the afternoon had worn on, weird just seemed to keep happening. She got off the bed and changed into a t-shirt and then quietly, so as not to wake Sara or Katie; she opened the door and headed down the dark hallway to the bathroom to finish getting ready for bed.

Curled under the blankets on her narrow twin bed in her dark bedroom, Emma hoped tomorrow would be a better day and closing her eyes, she fell into a familiar nightmare.

Emma's eyelids twitched and her head jerked as she lay on her bed in her foster home, but in her dream, she was somewhere else. Emma could hear the footsteps, closer as she stopped mid-run and snapped her head back and forth looking for a place to hide. She darted to the right, between what looked like giant bolts of fabric secured to the scuffed, dark brown wooden floor. As she ran, wispy pieces of pastel colored cloth caught at her arms and brushed her cheek. Her heart was pounding in her ears so loud she feared whoever was trying to catch her would hear. She was panting from running and fear, as sweat trickled down her face. Her hair was soaked and matted to her cheeks and neck.

She could feel him closer now. She could hear him, his breath so close she could smell him. She stopped again, frantically looking for somewhere to hide but as she spun in a circle, she could see only color, and cloth, everywhere the color. She looked up, up as high and as far as she could see, up toward the heavens. No matter how far and how fast she ran, she couldn't get out of the forest of flowing fabric. As the faint breeze blew, the wisps of gauzy fabric, like the sheer scarves women wore on their heads to keep their hair neat on a windy day, blurred together.

Emma caught a sheer baby blue fabric as it lifted in the breeze feeling the softness, looking at how delicate it was. A magical breeze blew through the fabric forest, but it had no impact on her hot sweat-soaked body. She turned her head, looking back the way she had run moments before. Colors of sheer blue, varying shades of green, orange, red, and yellow were lifting slowly, hypnotically up in the air. The colors swirled toward Emma, and as she looked down at a soft yellow, it caressed her hand. Her head snapped up as the sound of pounding footsteps became louder, and she sprinted to the right, past another bolt of blue.

Emma gasped and struggled to free herself from the nightmare, her eyelids snapping open. Heart racing, she looked across the room, trying to remember where she was, which home she was at. Tears pricked her eyes as she remembered the nightmare, a recurring dream for many years. She felt a chill and grasped the covers in her hands, pulling them toward her chin and wondered, as she always did, what the dream meant. She could still see the colors imprinted on her mind; feel the breeze on her skin, and the scent of the man that had been chasing her lingered in the air.

She sucked in her breath as she felt an arm pull her back, and a warm body pressed against her cold clammy one. A hand trailed from her waist down her leg. Emma was wide awake now, but felt as if she were still trapped in the nightmare, and pushed against whoever was behind her. Then she heard his voice.

"Awe, come on," George said gruffly in her ear.

"Dammit!" Emma hissed. "Get the *fuck* out of my bed. Stop!" She tried to wiggle away as he wrapped his arm tighter around her waist and tugged her back against him.

She felt as if she were smothering as he held her tight against him. Panicking, she leveraged a foot on the side of the bed and as her muscles screamed, she tore away from him. Spinning around, she leaned forward and said, "Get out!" to his grinning white face that seemed to glow in the dark of the room.

Looking up at her, his ankles crossed, he said roughly, "Awe…Come on."

Angrily, she clenched her hands, leaned forward, and hissed, "Get out!" then leaned even closer and quickly pushed at his chest as hard as she could, then jumped back from the bed as he toppled to the floor.

With a grunt, he climbed to his feet.

Emma looked across the dark room at the sleeping form of her foster sister and wondered how Jessie could possibly sleep through the noise two feet from her.

George, no longer smiling, looked through the dark at Emma's face as she raised her arm and pointed to the door and hissed, "Out!"

She shut the door behind him, then walked back to her bed and sat down on the edge, crossed her arms and stared at the closed door wondering if he'd come back. After awhile, she scooted onto her bed, fluffed the pillow at the head of the bed, and sat watching the door as she shook in anger and disgust.

CHAPTER TEN

The first thing Emma saw when she opened her eyes was her white pillow laying on the floor near her outstretched arm. Stretching, she grabbed the pillow with her fingertips, and then sat cross-legged at the head of the bed. Groaning in discomfort, she reached her arms toward the ceiling trying to ease the dull throb out of her back from falling asleep sitting up. Slowly she lowered her arms as she heard raised voices outside her bedroom. Emma pulled the pillow toward her chest and wrapped her arms around it, tucking her legs close to her body as she listened to George and Sheila shouting in the hall. She heard Sheila yell something about a job, and then George's voice shout in response, "It's not true!"

Emma squirmed on her bed, and hoped they took their argument to a different part of the house so she could make it down the hall to the bathroom. Her bladder was about to explode. For a few more agonizing minutes, she sat on her bed straining her ears. Finally,…silence.

Cautiously, she opened her bedroom door, just a crack, and peeked down the now empty hall. She tiptoed to the small bathroom on the right side at the end of the hallway. Standing with her hand on the doorknob, she craned her neck listening to the shouting coming from the kitchen. Yup, it was Sheila and George. Turning the lock on the knob, she flipped on the overhead fan to block out the shouting, and then rushed to the toilet, hiked up her t-shirt, pulled down her underwear, and sighing in relief, sat down.

Sitting on the toilet, with fuzzy pink covering the bowl, her elbow on her bare knee, Emma wondered what her foster mother and foster brother were arguing about so loudly and so *early* in the day.

After she washed her hands, she turned off the fan and stood with her hand on the doorknob for a moment listening. Still shouting, she thought. Slowly she cracked the door and saw the door to Sara's bedroom open. She leaped across the hall, trying to avoid the shouting, clanging, and banging of dishes and cabinets in the kitchen.

Sara was sitting cross-legged in the middle of her double bed, flipping the pages of a magazine as Emma walked across the small room and sat at the end of the bed.

"What's going on?" Emma whispered.

Sara looked up and gestured to the door, instructing, "Shut the door."

Emma slid off the bed and stretched her arm to close the door, shutting out some of the noise. Looking back at Sara, Emma shrugged her shoulders and shook her head, quietly conveying she knew something was very wrong, she just didn't know what that something was. Sitting back down on the edge of Sara's bed, Emma waited for her foster sister to explain what George had done for Sheila to be so mad at him.

"George got fired," Sara said in a serious tone.

Wrinkling her forehead, Emma said, "Well lots of people get fired. Why's Sheila yelling at him about it? He can get another job." Even as she said the words, Emma knew George's job was important to Sheila. Her foster mom wasn't married and each of her kids, and even Sara, had to contribute to the household bills. George losing his job was a big deal.

Shrugging her shoulders, Sara said, "I don't know. Must have something to do with why he lost his job."

Scrunching her forehead, Emma asked, "Well, why'd he lose his job?"

"Don't know. I woke up to the shouting, just like you," Sara said.

"I'm starving," Emma said, placing her hand on her stomach. "I hope they get out of the kitchen soon."

"Go on in there and get something to eat. They won't care," Sara insisted.

"I don't want to go in *there!*" Emma said.

As her stomach growled again, she said thoughtfully, "Maybe I'll just grab a Pop-Tart real quick."

Standing up, Emma walked to the door and opened it. She hesitated and looked at Sara and said with a grimace, "Here I go," and walked out the door.

Glancing at the two occupants in the kitchen, Emma walked to the cabinet where she knew she would find the box of Pop-Tarts and quickly grabbed a package. The air was crackling with tension as Emma walked quickly to the living room where Katie was watching TV. Emma curled up at the end of the blue couch and devoured her Pop-Tart. Holding the empty package, Emma realized she had a different problem; she needed something to wash the dry pastry down her throat. Rolling her eyes, she unfolded her body and rose from the couch. Walking into the kitchen, Emma was in time for the new round of arguing between Sheila and George.

"I told you I didn't do anything!" George yelled.

"You need to learn to keep your dick in your pants!" she yelled back.

Emma turned on the faucet and filled up her glass half way. Half way was plenty for now, she thought, and headed to her bedroom planning to hide out in her room and read the book Katie had loaned her.

A few hours later, Emma looked up from her book to see Sara standing in the doorway of her bedroom.

"Hey," Sara said in her typical cheerful voice. "Eric's making dinner for Sheila, and he's invited all of us to go too. I think he's going to cook out on the grill at his mom's house."

Groaning, Emma folded back a corner of a page to save her place in the book she had been reading for the last three hours and rested it against her chest. Emma estimated Eric to be at least in his early forties and he still lived at home with his mother. A grown man that wore sweaters and still lived with his mother, Emma thought, and rolled her eyes. Cheeseburgers, she considered. She supposed she could endure Sheila's weird boyfriend for a few hours for a well-cooked cheeseburger on the grill.

Half an hour later, as Emma took a bite out of her cheesy burger loaded with mustard, Eric walked across the yard and sat down next to her, spatula still in his hand, and asked, "How's that burger?"

Scooting over, burger in one hand and paper plate in the other, Emma mumbled, "Good."

"Yeah, nothing like a good burger. Is there?" he grinned, scooting closer.

Emma looked at his slacks covered knees, now touching her bare ones. Shifting on the concrete seat, Emma moved her knees out of his reach.

"So how's it been goin'?" he asked with a grin, she noticed, as she looked up into his face. The man just weirded her out, she thought, taking in his slouched posture. Did the man *ever* stand or sit up straight?

Swallowing the bite she had been chewing, she answered, "Fine."

Emma felt crowded as the tall gangly man with dark hair hunched over her.

"Are you still goin' out with that boy?" he asked his grin not so broad now.

"You mean…*Mark*?" Emma asked. "And yes," she asserted firmly, as she ran her tongue across her teeth to dislodge the soft bread now clinging to her front teeth, kind of like soggy dough braces.

"You know," he said softly. "We ought to hang out some time."

Emma looked up at the middle-aged man suspiciously wondering just what *hanging out* with him might entail. Looking back down at her plate of half-eaten food, she rolled her eyes wishing he'd go bother one of the other girls. Annoyed, her appetite ruined, Emma thought, fat chance she would ever hang out with Sheila's pervert boyfriend. She looked across the yard at Sheila, Sara, and Katie, the other guests at the cookout, and wished they'd hurry up and finish eating so they could leave.

Emma ignored whatever it was Eric was blabbering about, hoping he'd get the hint that she wanted him to go away. She assumed he finally got the message because after awhile he gave up trying to talk to her, and loped across the yard and slumped next to Sheila. Emma watched them. He looked like a crane, the way his tall thin body hunched over.

Shivering, she laid her paper plate next to her and crossed her legs and arms, swatting at the occasional fly and mosquito. Emma watched as Sara walked across the thick green grass toward her.

"Hey, girl," she said with a warm smile. "What are you doing over here all by yourself?"

Offering her foster sister a small smile she answered, "Oh, just trying to stay out of the way."

"I saw perv' boy talking to you," Sara said, as she sat down next to Emma.

Looking down at the ground, Emma shook her head up and down and said, "He is so weird, Sara. He *creeps* me out. There's just something about him."

"Yeah. I know. Me too," Sara agreed softly.

Finally, Eric led the way across the yard through the dark of night to his car and they all piled in. Emma was squashed between Sara and Katie in the back seat for the duration of the ten-minute drive to Sheila's house.

Quietly, Emma walked behind the group of chattering women and Eric, as they walked toward the front door when Eric turned suddenly and blocked her path. Emma watched as Sheila, Sara, and Katie continued to walk toward the house, up the step then slip inside and shut the screen door behind them leaving her alone with the tall, hunched man.

"Hey," he said, grinning down at her.

Silently, she looked up at him, wondering why he was detaining her from entering the safety and bright lights of her home. Emma continued to stare in disgust at the man, noticing how he jingled his keys in his pocket and shifted his feet.

With nervous energy, he said, "You sure are pretty."

She shifted her weight, placed her hand on her hip, stared up into his face, and rolled her eyes as dramatically as she could without popping the deep green balls with black centers from their sockets. She noticed that he was practically hopping in front of her in some sort of bird dance.

Wiping the drool from the corners of his mouth, he said slowly, "I bet you're a *real* good dancer."

A chill crept up Emma's spine as she tried to see around him to the house. No one was coming outside, or calling them into the house.

"I should take you dancing sometime," he bubbled.

She stood in front of him trying to understand what he meant. Surely, the old man wasn't asking her out on a date. He knew she was in high school and that she was only a freshman. He was a sick asshole, she thought as she glanced toward the house again, seeing light peeking between the cracks of the curtain hanging over the large living room window. Looking down at the grass, she noticed the shades of green and black, made by the darkness of night. She examined the grass around her, as his voice kept up a steady hum, trying not to hear. As if she were about to paint a picture on canvas, Emma studied a thin line of grass that stood out from all the other blades, and clumps in the yard. A sliver of golden light from a gap in the curtained living room window played on the grass beneath her feet. Emma tried not to hear what Eric was saying but as he bent lower toward her face, it was impossible to block out his next words. He leaned in toward her and grabbed her by the elbow. She looked at his hand, and then up into his face.

"They've got these places in Indianapolis where real pretty girls dance for money," he said in a raspy voice.

He paused for a minute and grinned at her, his upper lip quivering. Emma couldn't seem to find her voice. All she could do was stare at his beady little eyes, his large downturned nose, and the white spittle caked at the corners of his mouth.

As pretty as you are," he said, leering, his mouth so close she gagged on the sour smell of his breath. "You could make some *real* good money. We could meet somewhere…away from the house. You know, so no one would find out about it."

Emma sensed his mood changing, could feel the energy building as he gripped her arm tighter and his words became sharper.

"I'd drive you over to Indianapolis so you could dance. As pretty as you are…," he said.

Emma's mouth went dry and her throat burned, as if she were about to vomit as she watched Eric's eyes travel from her lips down her body, to her breasts, then down to her legs.

He licked his lips, grabbed at the front of his pants, and said gruffly, "You'd make *real* good money."

Emma shook his hand off her arm and took a step to the right, intending to walk around him, but he moved with her and said, "I'd have to hold onto the money so no one found it, of course." In a rush he continued, "You wouldn't have to take *all* your clothes off, if you didn't want to."

Emma, her path blocked, glanced up into his face as he said, "Some Saturday night you could pretend to go on a date, but instead I'd take you to dance." Grinning slyly, he continued, "As pretty as you are, lots of guys would wanna watch you dance."

Why wasn't anyone coming outside, she wondered frantically, as she glanced toward the house again. She looked over Eric's right shoulder, toward the front door. She knew he was watching her face and would block her way again if she tried to go around him. *How was she going to get in the house?* Glancing to the right, she knew he'd think she would try to go around the right side of his body, as she saw his body shift with the direction of her eyes. She considered, maybe she could fool him into thinking she was going to walk around him on his right side, but as he moved to stop her, she would run the other way. Emma placed her weight on her right foot, and saw him step to the right. Quickly, she pivoted on her left foot and sprinted around the left side of his body toward the house, as a tingly sensation crept up her spine. As she ran, she felt invisible fingers reach toward her, trying to pull her back to him.

Heart pounding, Emma yanked the door to the house open and stumbled into the living room. As she slammed the door behind her, she looked to her right and saw Sheila, Sara, and Katie sitting on the couches laughing and talking. Their voices sounded loud to her ears but their words were muffled. They were laughing and talking as if nothing had just happened outside. Feeling very much alone, and isolated in a house filled with people, Emma turned away and continued onto her bedroom at the opposite end of the small house. Shutting her bedroom door behind her, she walked over and sat on the edge of her bed. It seemed she couldn't get away from it, the hands, and the bad things.

Stretching out on the twin bed, Emma felt something poking her back. Rolling onto her side, she grabbed the book she had been reading that afternoon. Clutching the book to her chest, she curled into a ball and stared across the dark room, as tears trickled from the corners of her eyes. She thought about her sister Amy, wondering where she was…and if she was okay.

The next afternoon, as Emma sat surrounded by her friends at their usual table in the school cafeteria, she was distracted.

"Em," Tammy said, for the third time. "Earth to Em."

"Huh?!" Emma said in surprise. She'd been deep in thought about a conversation she'd had with Mark before school that morning, that and she was still thinking about her strange weekend. Mark and Emma had met that morning, before first period had started, as they did on most mornings. She loved the few minutes shared with Mark before school started, but this morning had been different. He had cancelled their date for prom, telling her something had come up but he promised they would go to dinner or something the night of prom. The weekend crap was bleeding into her week, she thought sourly.

Emma offered her friend an insincere, small smile. Then sighing, she announced to the table crammed with her friends, "I'm not going to prom."

"*What?!* Tammy said in a surprised tone.

Looking down at her tray, Emma concentrated on the pattern she was making with her fork in her applesauce before answering. Feeling the stares from her friends, she said, "Something came up. We can't go."

There was silence at the table as everyone looked at Emma, not sure what to say.

"Well," Shelly said. "You wouldn't have had any fun without us anyway!"

"Yeah," the rest of the group chorused.

Knowing they were trying to cheer her up, Emma said, "You're right."

Emma, not wanting to make her friends uncomfortable, finished her lunch and departed for her afternoon PE class. Sighing, Emma walked toward the girl's locker room. She hated PE. It wasn't the class participation she hated; it was the stripping down and showering after the class that she dreaded. Emma was a lock the door kind of girl when dressing. She had never been comfortable displaying her body to anyone, not even to her sisters.

At her last high school, they were supposed to take showers after PE, but Emma had always managed to stall long enough after class to get out of it. At this school, it wasn't like that. Each day, after whatever sports activity they participated in, Ms. Hobson, the white haired PE teacher, made all the girls walk down a narrow hallway, and open their towels, exposing their naked bodies to her ogling eyes. Disgusted and embarrassed, Emma wondered, was it so important they shower that the teacher needed to see them naked. It was a procession line. All the girls had to line up, walk single file, then stop, and open their towel. Then the PE teacher, dressed in one of her snappy polyester sweat suits, would wave her hand letting them know they could close their towel, and walk back to the locker area to get dressed. Emma didn't see the point. The girls at school said it had always been that way. They thought the PE teacher was a lesbian and seeing their naked young bodies was the highlight of her day.

The rest of the week passed slowly without incident, spent doing homework, and time on the phone in the evening with Mark or Shelly. Even her nights were uneventful. Lately, she had been free from her recurring nightmare and hadn't woken in the middle of the night to find George lying next to her. Even so, Emma had an uneasy feeling.

CHAPTER ELEVEN

"Emma," Sara said.

Turning her head toward the open bedroom door and Sara's voice, Emma responded with a smile, "I'm coming." Jessie was taking her to meet Mark at the garage. Another Saturday night hanging out with him at work, Emma thought. Oh, well, it was better than sitting home watching TV, and listening to George and Sheila argue. It seemed like that's all they did now that he wasn't working.

Grabbing her purse off the bed, Emma rushed to the door as Sara whispered, "Jessie can't take you. She was called into work. George said he'd take you though."

With her hand on the doorknob, Emma glanced up at Sara's face. George, she grimaced. Her shoulders slumped a little and offering Sara a small smile, she said quietly, "Okay. Thanks," and followed her down the hall.

"Ready?" George grinned, holding the front door open.

Emma looked at George's toothy grin and walked by him out the door, making sure not to brush up against him. Once in the car, Emma plopped her purse on her lap and looked straight ahead. She did not intend to take her eyes off the road this time. She wanted to make sure he didn't take any wrong turns.

Ten minutes later, almost to the garage, George pulled into the parking lot of a gas station, on the far side of the lot. Looking at him sternly, Emma asked, "George, what are you doing?"

Raising his hands in the air as if warding off a blow, he said, "I just have to run in and get something. I'll be right back," and quickly got out of the car and ran across the lot.

Annoyed, Emma looked straight ahead, out the windshield. A few seconds later, she snapped her head in the direction of the driver side door, as she heard it creak open. George must have literally run into the gas station and then right back out. Good, she thought, irritated. Now he could take her to Mark. She looked across the seat at him when he didn't start the car and watched as he flicked a metal silver lighter, holding the flame to the tip of the joint he was grasping between his lips.

She cocked her head at him, and demanded, "George, drive me to Mark."

"Just for a minute," he sputtered, flinging the joint at her.

"No," she said angrily, as she stared across the seat at him.

He continued to hold the joint in front of her, blowing smoke in her face.

"Come on. Then I'll take you to Mark," George insisted.

Scowling at him, she took the joint from between his fingers, and knowing it had no impact on her, placed it to her lips sucked in. She turned her head toward the passenger window, and blew the smoke out quickly, then handed it back.

"There," she said. "Can we go now?" irritated that he had tricked her.

"In a minute," he said, then inhaled deeply and handed it back to her.

Still feeling clear headed, Emma took the joint from him again, thinking it would hurry the process up if she were agreeable. She handed the joint back to George, then blew the smoke at the window and continued to stare out the window, hoping to convey the message that she was done.

What seemed like a long time later, Emma heard the sound of George's voice. He was calling her name, but his voice sounded as if it were coming from a great distance away. She turned her head toward him, but it seemed as if her movements had slowed down. Finally, her eyes made contact with his grinning face. His smile, with his unusually large teeth, seemed to stretch across his face in a cartoon character kind of way. He leaned toward her as she watched, his hand coming toward her, slowly. He touched her shoulder, and then her hand. He trailed a finger down the length of her hand and then to her lap. As if in slow motion, Emma bent her head down, and looked at her leg. She saw his hand rubbing her thigh, but she didn't feel anything. She just saw it—she was numb. Was she dreaming, she wondered. Slowly, Emma looked around the inside of the car. It had grown dark, and fuzzy, and then she began to panic.

"Take me to Mark," she heard her voice say. "Take me to Mark, now! Now!"

Emma looked at George, his face too close. He had scooted closer while she had been examining the inside of the fuzzy car. How had he gotten so close to her, she wondered. How had he moved without her seeing him? What else could he do without her knowing, with her mind in such a foggy state?

"George," Emma said, as she pushed at his chest.

His hand closed over hers, holding it against him.

"Take me to Mark," she said, turning her face trying to avoid him as he leaned closer. "Take me to Mark!" she shouted.

"Okay. Okay," George said, as he let go of her hand and scooted back over to his side of the car. He looked over at her and then turned the key in the ignition.

Her head felt fuzzy, and she felt as if she might vomit as they pulled out of the parking lot. Pressing her head against cool window, she felt dizzy and disoriented. The car had barely rolled to a stop in front of the garage, when Emma opened the door and almost fell out. Catching herself, she stood on the sidewalk in front of the garage where Mark worked. Emma noticed that all the everyday noises were muffled, even the sound of the cars passing by were barely audible. As Emma watched, she thought it seemed as if everything was in slow motion, and the colors of the world seemed to have lost their luster, now washed out in shades of gray. Walking toward the garage, Emma couldn't seem to get her feet to move fast enough. Slow, everything was moving so slowly.

Finally, her fingers touched the cool metal door handle to the garage. Like everything else, the door seemed to have changed. She struggled to pull the heavier than usual door open. Emma breathed a sigh of relief when she saw Mark standing by a car, wiping his hands on a rag.

He looked up as she entered the garage, and disoriented, she walked over to him.

"Are you okay?" he asked in a muffled voice.

Slowly, she shook her head up and down.

Placing his hands on her upper arms, the oily rag still held in one hand, he gently walked her over to a metal chair, and instructed her to sit down. He stood in front of her for a moment, and then walked to a car with its hood open and a light hanging inside. Emma watched as he stuck his head under the hood of the car.

Emma, with her hands tucked beneath her legs, sat for what seemed to her to be a very long time. She seemed to be having difficulty with time concept, hearing, and movement, but eventually the sounds in the garage became sharper. The sound of the music coming from the radio on a table became louder and crisper, and the fog in her brain dispelled.

When Emma's world righted itself—her mind clear enough to communicate—she walked over to the car Mark was working on and leaned her hip against it. Mark looked up at her. Alone in the garage, as Mark leaned against the car with a serious expression lining his face, he listened as Emma explained what had happened with George an hour before.

Her voice raspy from talking non-stop for a half an hour, she said, "I didn't know what to do. He wouldn't bring me to you, unless..." Emma's words trailed away as Mark grabbed her hand in his and pulled her gently into his arms smoothing her hair, and stroking her back.

"Are you okay now?" he asked in a concerned voice.

Pressing her cheek into his shoulder, she said softly, "Yeah."

Pulling away, he leaned in, kissed her lips softly, and then said, "I just have a few more things I need to do, then we can hang out. Okay?" He smiled down at the petite young girl, with her jacket pulled tight around her.

At ease, feeling safe, Emma smiled up at Mark. He had such a kind face, she thought as her eyes traveled from his slightly curly dark brown hair, to his brownish-green, large eyes, to a not too big or small nose, perfect lips, her eyes lingering for a moment, then continued their journey to the rest of him. At six-foot two, he had a muscular, yet lean build. He didn't look like he pumped iron, more like someone that ran track she thought, glancing down at his long legs. She walked back to the metal chair and flipped through a magazine she found on the nearby table, cluttered with pop cans and an ashtray.

Clapping his hands, Mark said, "Finally! I'm done. You hungry?"

Her stomach had been growling for the past fifteen minutes but she hadn't wanted to say anything.

"I'm starving!" she said.

She took the hand he held before her, uncurled from the chair, and walked to the door with him. Scooting onto the white upholstered seat of Mark's baby blue Chevy Chevelle convertible, tired, Emma leaned her head back against the white headrest. As she watched the lights from the buildings and the streetlights flash by, she thought about the last month of her life—George—Eric…Amy. She felt as if a sweater of sadness were wrapped around her shoulders.

Parked in their usual spot near Mark's house, Emma and Mark ate their fast food sandwiches while sitting in the back of his car. After their sandwiches were eaten and the wrappers crumpled into the "to-go" sack, "Mark and Emma talked about school. Graduation was weighing on his mind lately and his plans after that. He was still not sure what he wanted to do with his life—go to the two-year local college, or the university or just work.

Then, as on most of their dates, his hand stroked hers and somehow she found herself in his strong arms, their lips pressed firmly together as his wet tongue tickled and teased hers. She felt safe within the circle of his arms, not like when she woke and felt George's hands grabbing her, or when her dad had grabbed her when she was a little girl. Mark's hands were different; they caressed gently, and teased in a very pleasant way. No boy had ever made her feel that way before—tingly. With Mark, there was no battle of wills—Emma holding tight to keep her pants up as he struggled to pull them off. It wasn't like when she was a little girl. He knew—he knew she wasn't ready.

Emma looked up, trying to see the stars through the fogged up window. Realizing it was getting late, she began to squirm. It was time to get home. Breathing heavily, Mark sat up and leaned against the back of the seat so Emma could scoot into a seated position and tug her blouse back down.

A half hour later, Emma pressed the palm of her hand to Mark's face and kissed his lips gently goodnight, then climbed out of the car and walked toward her foster home, as he drove away down the street. She climbed the one concrete step and swung open the door of Sheila's house, and saw the glow of the TV in the living room. Glancing across the room, she saw Katie seated on one of the couches looking toward the TV, biting into a piece of pizza.

Quietly, Emma walked across the small room and then down the hall to her bedroom. Not bothering to turn on the light, she kicked off her shoes and dropped her purse and jacket on the floor next to her bed. Then she walked back to the living room and curled up at the end of the couch near Katie. She felt vulnerable, like a little girl and needed to be close to her big sister. Laying her head on the small, round, soft throw pillow, she stared blankly at the colorful images on the screen of the TV, and as a tear trickled down her cheek, she thought about Amy.

"Katie," Emma said.

"What?" Katie asked, in a muffled voice.

"Do you ever think about Amy?" Emma asked.

"Sure," Katie grunted.

"I wonder how she's doing," Emma said softly.

"I'm sure she's fine," Katie said. "Now be quiet. I'm tryin' to watch my show."

Emma did as Katie instructed. She was quiet, but she continued to think about her other big sister. Amy, so beautiful, just like a cheerleader, she thought as she sniffed. Life hadn't turned out at all as she had imagined. In her imaginings, Katie, Amy, and Emma, were supposed to be living with a family that loved them—maybe with a nice little dog—the kind that didn't bite. They were supposed to be a *normal* family now, living together like all the other kids did with their brothers and sisters. But they weren't. Amy was living somewhere else, and she hadn't seen her in months.

Climbing off the couch, Emma drug her feet to her bedroom. Not bothering to turn on the light, or change her clothes, she crawled under the blankets. With tears drying on her cheeks, Emma fell into an uneasy sleep. Blue wisps of fabric caught at her in her dream and sweat trickled down her face. Her heart pounding, she ran from the sounds of the footsteps, closer now…

CHAPTER TWELVE

"You look beautiful," Emma beamed, as a grinning Jessie twirled in a circle showing off her prom dress. A little wistfully, Emma admired Jessie's new dress. It was a beautiful floor length gown, made out of a gauzy flowing fabric. Whenever Jessie moved, it flowed out behind her. The pattern of sprinkled blue flowers on the dress picked up the blue in Jessie's eyes. Jessie's boyfriend Daryl, waited patiently in the entryway as Sheila, Emma, Sara, and Katie marveled at how beautiful she was one last time, then she glided toward her date, handsome in his baby blue colored tuxedo.

Standing on the small concrete porch, Emma waved to Jessie and shouted, "Have fun!" then closed the door behind her. As Emma walked to the bathroom to apply her makeup for her date with Mark, she thought about the comments she had made the other day to her friends during lunch. She had lied when she said she didn't want to go to the prom. She *had* wanted to buy a beautiful dress, get dressed up, and play Cinderella for an evening. Sighing, she looked at her reflection in the small mirror over the bathroom sink, and wondered, instead of dancing, while dressed in a beautiful gown, in a room filled with hundreds of other teens, what she and Mark would be doing tonight.

Emma decided to wear the brown strappy sandals she had bought for prom. No point in letting them go to waste she thought, as she buckled them around her ankles. She took extra time dressing and primping in front of the mirror, thinking Mark would probably have something special planned to make up for breaking their prom plans. She had bought a brightly colored top that hung off one shoulder that she now adjusted as she looked in the mirror one last time. It looked perfect with her new dark navy colored jeans and high-heeled sandals. Well, she thought, she may not be going to prom, but she was still going to look darned cute!

"Emma!" Sara shouted from the living room. "Mark's here!"

Rushing back to her bedroom, Emma grabbed her purse off her bed, and then walked quickly back down the hall. Smiling, she walked around the corner into the living room and noticed Mark's very casual outfit. Shifting her eyebrows upwards, Emma realized she was overdressed. She had thought that maybe they would go out to a nice dinner, just as they would have if they had gone to prom. Sheila had even extended her curfew beyond midnight since all the other kids would be out late. Prom nights were magical, with the girls dressed up in their gowns, the boys in their tuxedos, the flowers, and dinner and dancing. She might not actually be going to the hall with the other kids tonight, but in Emma's mind...tonight, it was prom everywhere.

Emma glanced over the roof of the car as Mark opened his door. He didn't seem to be in a very festive mood, she noticed. She wondered if he was disappointed that they weren't going to prom, just as she was. This would have been his last, as a senior. Not saying a word, Emma slid onto her seat and closed her door.

Frowning, but still not saying anything, Emma climbed out of the car a few minutes later when Mark pulled the car up in front of his house. Maybe he just needed to pick something up, she considered, as she followed behind him up the driveway. The driveway was empty of his parent's over-sized car and his little brother's car too.

"I'll be back in a minute," Mark said, throwing his keys in a dish on a table by the door. "Have a seat."

Emma flopped onto the couch in the small dimly lit living room, dark but for the glow of one small lamp. Looking around, Emma took in the brown and blue colors of the room. It was so quiet, Emma noticed. No TV or even a stereo played in the background. She was used to noise and light. It was so dark in here, she thought as she scooted back onto the couch.

Mark walked back into the room and asked, "You want something to drink?"

"Sure," Emma said with a small smile, noticing that he had lost his long sleeved, button up shirt on the way out of the living room, now even more casual in a short sleeved, light brown printed t-shirt. So, she thought, the evening was becoming more and more casual. She watched as the glow from the light from the refrigerator illuminated his unsmiling face. He walked back to her and handed her a can of pop, and then sat down next to her.

As Mark picked up the remote and clicked on the TV, Emma thought, finally noise.

Looking up at him as he slung his arm across her shoulders, Emma gave him a small smile and asked, "Are you okay?"

"Yeah," he said, as he looked at her upturned face.

He leaned toward her, lowering his face to hers and kissed her lips softly. Raising his head, he looked into her eyes, and Emma's slightly parted, moist lips. Emma looked up into his face, at the gentleness she saw in his eyes.

Pulling her closer to him, Mark turned his attention back to the TV, and changed the channel as Emma snuggled in under his arm. An evening in, she thought a little disappointed. It was Emma's freshman year of high school, and Mark's senior year, so she understood his mood. He was disappointed not to be going to prom. For Emma, there would be other proms, but for Mark, this would have been his last one.

She felt his fingers stroke the softness of her upper arm, and then he kissed the top of her head. Placing the tips of his fingers beneath her chin, he tilted her face up to look into his eyes, and then slowly he leaned toward her, as she parted her lips in expectancy. His lips were warm against hers, warm, gentle, and firm. He tickled her upper lip with his moist tongue.

Emma allowed Mark to lay her back on the couch as he ran his hands down the length of her body as she, not sure what to do with her hands, held onto his shoulders. She sensed an urgency in him that she hadn't noticed in the past, as the pressure from his lips grew more intense and his tongue sought deeper. Her back arched as his fingertips stroked her breast through her top, and then slowly he ran his hand back down to her waist, resting for a second on her hip.

Breath ragged, Mark slowly pulled away and stood, extending his hand toward her. Emma reached for his hand and allowed him to pull her from the couch to her feet. Her hand tucked in his; Emma followed him down the dark hallway.

Standing in the doorway of his bedroom, seeing his personal space for the first time, she looked with interest at the things that were clues to who this boy was. The room was washed in soft light from one small lamp on the far side of the bedroom. She looked curiously at the objects in the room that reflected the personality of its owner, at the light colored brown dresser and the collection of trophies strewn across its top. A chair was placed in front of a small desk, just waiting for the owner to hunch over studying, and then she glanced at the unmade bed. A sheet and blanket, tangled together, were at the foot of the bed.

As she continued to stand in the doorway, trying to learn more about who he was, he sat on the edge of the bed. His features looked haunted, as the blue glow of the light darkened his features. He held his hand out to her. Emma left the doorway and walked over to the bed, and sat next to him.

Fingers from one hand tangled in Emma's hair as Mark wrapped his other arm around her waist, pressing his hand to her back. He pulled her tight against his body and explored her lips with his. As he leaned against her, the weight of his body pressed her back against the pillows at the head of the bed.

He caressed the soft skin of her cheekbone with his fingertips and Emma felt his other hand reach down between them, felt, and heard the snap on her jeans pop open. Her hand shot down between their bodies. Pressing her hand firmly over his, she pulled her head back and looked up into his eyes, just inches from her own. Then slowly, still looking down into her eyes, he brushed her hand aside and slowly unzipped her jeans.

He pulled her jeans down over her hips, and threw them off the bed. Briefly, she felt the coolness of the air, wanting to cover herself with the blanket at the foot of the bed, but he pressed his full weight on top of her, warming her. His lips on hers, she felt him wiggle out of his jeans, kicking them the rest of the way off, and in a smooth, continuous motion, he slid her silky bikini underwear down over her hips, and off. He placed a knee between her legs, and then his hips were between her thighs. She looked up into his face and then, as she felt a hot searing pain, she squeezed her eyes shut tight. It didn't last long. When he was done, he climbed off her and quickly left the room as she lay hurting in the center of the bed.

It had happened so quickly. She had never even considered, thought, or dreamed of what it might be like to do *that* with Mark, and now it was over. She felt cold—detached—and it had hurt. It had felt as if knives had been stabbing deep inside her. How was it possible to feel so alone while being so close to someone, Emma wondered as she rolled onto her side, and then slowly sat up. Looking back where she had lain only moments before, she saw the blood. She wasn't sure what she was supposed to do next. When Mark didn't come back into the room, she plucked her underwear and jeans off the floor where they had been carelessly thrown, and shrugged into them. Walking to the doorway, she looked down the dark hallway, toward the living room, and then across the hall to what she hoped was a bathroom.

Tiptoeing across the hall, she felt along the wall for a light switch and finding it, flicked it on, bathing the room in bright light. Closing the door and locking it behind her, she pulled her jeans and underwear down and squatted over the toilet. She winced with the burning pain she felt when she peed. When she looked down at the toilet paper that she had wiped with, she saw blood mixed in with clear stuff. After she had cleaned herself, she found Mark standing in the living room. Thinking they would watch TV, Emma walked toward the couch but stopped when Mark said, "You ready to go?"

"Okay," she said softly with a slight frown, and wondered where he meant by, go.

It was quiet in the car as Emma looked out the window. She recognized the route. He was driving her back home. It wasn't even ten O'clock on prom night and she was going home. Not bothering to get out of the car, Mark leaned over and gave Emma a quick kiss on the cheek and said, "Night."

"Night," Emma said softly, feeling confused, and dirty as she stumbled out of the car. She wanted to get in the house, take a shower, go to bed, and forget what had just happened. As she walked toward the house she thought about love—sex—relationships. Before tonight, she hadn't dwelled on having sex with a boy; hadn't thought it would happen so soon. She really didn't know what she had expected it would be like, she just knew what she had seen on TV, heard from kids at school, and all the bad things she had witnessed and been subjected to as a child. She knew it was what people did. There must be some reason people did it—made love—that's what people called it—but what she had just done with Mark hadn't felt very loving. It had been cold, painful, and dirty. She felt raw, exposed, and right now, she just wanted to hide away from the world. Emma pulled open the door to her foster home and stepped inside. The beautiful night, hours ago so filled with excitement and high expectation, had ended ugly. She *felt* ugly.

CHAPTER THIRTEEN

Then next morning, Emma lay in bed longer than usual. She was soar and bruised from the night before, and felt more alone than ever. Holding her blankets bunched up to her chest as if they were a baby doll, she tried to comfort herself as tears streamed down her cheeks. She missed Amy. Everything was wrong...so very wrong, she thought.

Later that afternoon, Emma walked from the telephone hanging on the kitchen wall back to the couch, for the fifth time. She had been trying to call Mark off and on all day, but his mom, in a strange voice, sounding like a broken record said he was out. *Out,* Emma wondered irritably. *Out where?* It must be a full moon, Emma thought in annoyance as she uncurled from the couch and huffed back to her bedroom trying to escape the raised voices. Sheila and George had been going at it off and on all day and she was in no mood for their crap today.

Emma closed her bedroom door behind her. Grabbing the book she had borrowed from Katie off the floor, she flopped onto her stomach and flipped to the page she had folded back to mark her spot. Emma had found sometimes the only way she could escape life was to go too far off places in a book, and that's what she needed to do now. She wanted to be anywhere but in the foster home with the man that climbed into bed with her at night and touched her while she slept, and the older man that wanted her to do things for money, and the shouting.

Hours later, distracted, Emma looked up from her book. George and Sheila were arguing right outside her door. She sat up on her bed and tried to hear what they were shouting about. Rolling over onto her back, she clasped her hands behind her head, crossed her ankles, and listened to the shouting as it became softer. She placed her open book on the bed, bound side up, and walked to the door. Opening it, she peeked into the hall and seeing it empty, walked toward Sara's room and knocked on the closed door.

"Come in!" Sara's voice called.

Closing the door softly behind her, Emma wrinkled her nose, and asked, "What are they yelling about now?"

"Same thing—but now I know *why* he got fired," Sara said all knowing.

"Why?" Emma asked, her eyes growing larger as she rushed across the small room to sit on the edge of the bed.

Sara sat up and folded her legs under her saying, "Well, just like I thought. It wasn't *losing* his job that was the bad part. Uh-Uh," Sara said shaking her head from side to side. "Losing his job's not *really* the bad part. It's *why* he lost his job that's got her so mad."

"What *happened*?" Emma asked impatiently.

"Well," Sara said as she leaned closer to Emma, her arms propped on her knees. "They're saying he got one of the residents pregnant."

Shocked, Emma gasped, *"What?!* You're kidding. No way!" Emma stared at Sara in disbelief. Her mind wandered for a moment as she pictured George wandering the halls of the state-run facility for the disabled in the middle of the night.

"How do you know this?" Emma asked. "Did George tell you?" curious to how that conversation must have gone.

"Hell no!" Sara exclaimed. "I have a friend whose sister works there. She heard about it a few days ago." Grimacing, Sara flicked her wrist and said, "He didn't tell anyone. Are you *kidding*?"

Emma was having a difficult time understanding. "So… Sheila knows? Did George *tell* her?"

Sara laughed, "Oh, *hell* no! Sheila knows someone that works there too. And she ran into that someone last night and *she* told her."

"Damn. Who—who was it he got pregnant?" Emma asked.

"It was a young girl. I think she was about sixteen-years-old. She's disabled of course." Waving her hand in the air as if she were shooing away a fly, Sara continued, "That's why she lives there, but she's *really* disabled. She can't walk or talk or anything. He had sex with a girl that could barely move, let alone consent."

"What?! So—*What?!*" Emma wrinkled her forehead, shocked by what she was hearing. When Sara said George had lost his job, she would never have guessed this would be the reason why. People in the real world didn't *rape* people at work and especially her foster brother. How was it possible Emma wondered, to be in another foster home with such bad things going on? Weren't these people screened at all, she wondered in amazement.

Emma heaved a disgusted sigh and looked at the white wall behind Sara, shaking her head as she thought about the other night, waking up to find George next to her in bed. She hadn't really thought about that night, even when it was happening. It was more of a reactionary thing. Avoiding men's hands had been a part of her life since she was a little girl. Whenever it happened, she didn't think much about it, during those times her brain was too busy trying to figure out how to get out of the situation. When some strange man is grabbing your breast or trying to get your pants off, you don't have the time-luxury of mentally sorting it all out. She was too busy being in escape mode, but as Emma sat on Sara's bed, she had the time, and she realized that what George had done to that girl was what he intended to do to her, and she shivered in repulsion.

"So what's going to happen to him?" Emma asked.

Shrugging her shoulders, Sara said, "Guess they'll investigate some more. Sheila's really mad. He just keeps denying it."

Emma hunched her shoulders as her thoughts spun. What was wrong with men in the world she wondered? Everywhere she went—just more of the same.

Pressing her hand to her heart, Emma looked down at the paisley pattern on the quilted comforter and thought—a rapist—George might be a rapist. A rapist had touched her while she slept in her bed. How could she feel safe in the house knowing what he had done to the young disabled girl, and had intended to do to her?

Later that evening, still unable to contact Mark, Emma decided to call one of his friends. Mark had three best guy friends that she had gotten to know fairly well. Tony was his best friend, a short boy with shiny brown hair that hung to his shoulders. He seemed nice enough, but he had beady little brown eyes that were always flitting around as if he had something on his mind. He was the same age as Mark, and the smart one in the group—going away to college after senior year. Then there was Shane, he didn't really stand out. He was quiet with short blonde hair and he had a girlfriend so he didn't hang around as much. Andy was the youngest of Mark's best friends, a junior in high school, and the comedian of the group. He was tall, had cute dimples, and a thick head of messy blonde hair. She felt comfortable with him. His eyes didn't dart around as if he was up to something and he always seemed relaxed, which put her at ease.

Her first pick was to call Tony, but when no one answered the telephone at his house, she called Andy. *Finally*, she thought as she heard Andy's voice say "hello."

"Hey, Andy," Emma said, relieved he was home. It wasn't like Mark not to return her calls and she was getting worried.

"Oh—Hi, Em," Andy said shortly.

Emma wrinkled her brow when she heard the discomfort in his tone. Andy was the easy going, funny guy in the group, but he didn't sound like his usual funny self.

"Andy, have you heard from Mark today? I've been trying to call him since this morning," Emma said.

"Yeah. I saw him this morning when he came by my house," he said briskly.

"Did he mention me?" she asked uncomfortably, as she thought about last night. After what happened last night, she couldn't believe Mark hadn't called her. Instead, she was beginning to get the feeling he had been avoiding her all day.

"Yeah. He did," Andy said.

There was a pause as Emma waited for Andy to continue.

"Oh man, Emma," Andy groaned. "Emma, he doesn't want to see you anymore. You were a bet," he blurted out in a rush.

The brown table blurred. Tears burned her eyes as she stared down at the table, not blinking. She couldn't breathe. She felt her lips go numb and a buzzing roared in her ears. Surely, she hadn't heard him right, she thought.

"I'm sorry?" she whispered into the telephone. "What did you say?"

"Em," he said softly. "I didn't wanna be the one to tell you."

Emma knew it was true. Andy was never serious and he wasn't joking around now. A bet. She had been a bet.

"A bet?" she whispered into the telephone. Humiliated, she hunched over the table as she clutched her stomach trying to ease the sharp needle-like stabbing in her gut.

"Yeah," he said. "We all know."

"We all…?" she asked, horrified that someone else might know what happened between her and Mark.

"All the guys. Mark told us about it this morning," Andy, said, sounding embarrassed for her.

Emma put her forehead in the palm of her hand, feeling as if she might throw up.

"Em, the guy's an *asshole*," Andy said angrily.

An asshole, Emma thought, not knowing whether to cry or scream. The room seemed to spin as she absorbed what Andy had just told her; she had been nothing to Mark. She had been nothing but a *bet*. They had dated exclusively for almost six months and—nothing—just—*nothing*—she had meant nothing. She hurt. It felt as if her insides were ripping apart—that someone would do that to her, take something so precious from her—because of a bet.

"Andy," she whispered through her tears. "I have to go now," and pulled the phone away from her ear.

"Em!" Andy shouted.

Pulling the phone back to her ear, she responded, her voice sounding far away, muffled to her ears, "Yeah?"

"I'll call you a little later. Okay?" Andy said.

Thinking he was lying, just like everyone else in her life, she said, not very convincingly, "Sure," then hung up the phone.

Slowly, Emma walked back to her bedroom. She didn't hear the canned laughter coming from the TV, or Katie and Sara laughing along with the characters. All Emma heard was a rushing sound, as if a giant wave were pounding over her head, taking her under.

Feeling nothing, numb to the elements of the world, Emma crawled to the center of her bed, grabbed her pillow, hugged it tight to her chest, and curled into a tight ball. She stared across the room, not seeing, not… anything. Her vision blurred as the tears came, still she stared, not blinking, trying not to think…not to feel, but the pain came and the tears streamed down her cheeks as sobs burst from deep within.

Emotionally exhausted, Emma woke to Sara's voice, and hands shaking her hours later. "Em. Em. Andy's on the phone."

Emma craned her neck, and squinted as her eyes adjusted to the dark room. She stared at Sara, slowly coming out of her deep sleep. *Andy, she had said Andy was on the phone.* Sitting up, she rubbed her eyes. He called, she thought. She hadn't really thought he'd call.

"Hello," she said her voice husky and thick from the tears she had shed.

"Hey, Em. How you doing?" Andy asked.

Pulling out a cushioned kitchen chair, Emma sat down and lied, "I'm okay. I didn't really think you'd call."

After the talk they had earlier in the day, Emma didn't trust anyone. Leaning her chin on the palm of her hand, she clutched the telephone in the other. As Andy talked, Emma listened absently, her thoughts drifting back over her life... all the things, all the bad people. What had she been thinking, she wondered. Why did she think her life would ever change, just because some old foster lady had said it would? Well, she had been wrong, Emma realized as she tried to focus on what Andy was saying.

"Do you want to go out some time, Em?" Andy asked.

Closing her eyes in amazement, Emma wondered, why would he ask her that? Shaking her head, Emma said into the telephone, "Andy— thanks—really. But that is such a bad idea." Emma didn't think she'd ever be able to trust a person—a boy—especially one of Mark's friends, ever again.

"Oh. No, Em," Andy reassured her. "Friends. Just go out to get something to eat, as friends. Or, maybe we could hang out at the pool this summer. We were friends, Em. I still want to be your friend. What Mark did was shitty. He's an *asshole*. I'm *not* an asshole, Em. We're not all assholes."

"Really?" she said, not caring that she might hurt his feelings.

"No, Em. I'm sorry for what he did to you, but you can't think we're all like that. We're not," he insisted.

Emma wanted so badly to believe in someone and in something, but at that moment, she just couldn't but said, "Okay. We can hang out sometime. Andy, I've got to go. I'll see you at school tomorrow." She didn't really have to go, and she knew he knew she didn't have to get off the phone; she was just done for the day, done with boys, done with people in general.

"I'll see you tomorrow, Em," he said firmly.

Hanging up the phone, Emma thought, yeah, sure he would. She walked to the refrigerator, determined to gorge on left over pizza. It was surprisingly quiet in the house, Emma noticed as she moved the gallon milk jug out of the way, spotting the plastic bowl crammed full with sausage and extra cheese pizza. Carrying the container to the counter, she speculated that Sheila was on a date, and Jessie was probably at work. Katie was probably in her room reading a book or sleeping and Sara was watching TV. She wasn't sure where George was. She was just thankful he wasn't home. She didn't think she could handle the creep right now.

Grasping the counter, Emma steadied herself as a sob escaped her lips, and shook her head slowly from side to side. She closed her eyes for a moment and took a deep breath as a tear slipped from beneath her lashes and slowly rolled down her cheek. Opening her eyes, she cleared her throat, and sniffed as she looked across the small kitchen toward the window over the sink.

CHAPTER FOURTEEN

"Hey," Andy said, a grin deepening his already noticeable dimples. He loped up to Emma who was lying on the concrete patio at the community pool, shielding her eyes from the bright sun.

"Hey!" she said grinning up at him. Leaning on her elbows, one leg bent, she checked him out, her eyes travelling from his dimpled grin, to his ripped abs and navy blue swim trunks.

Flopping down onto his towel, he showered the golden-haired girl, clad in a bright yellow string bikini, with cool water from the pool, and in shock, she cried out, "EEK!"

Over a month had passed since Emma had given herself to Mark and then discovered she had been nothing more than a bet. He had used her; taken something from her—something special that she could never get back. Mark had never bothered to return her phone calls, and one day Emma had run into one of his friends who told her Mark was seeing someone else, a girl from his graduating class.

Since the day Emma found out that she had been nothing more than a senior boy's sex bet, Andy had proven to be true to his words, not all boys were alike. He had become a good friend to Emma, her best friend. They had become inseparable, spending most of their time on weekends and evenings at his parent's home across town. His family owned a three-story home in an older, established neighborhood. When Emma stood and looked up at the house from the street, it seemed a little scary, imposing with what seemed like endless rooms. It was big enough to get lost in. It wasn't like Sheila's small house where Emma could hear someone shouting or talking on the phone in the kitchen while she was in her bedroom down the hall. Andy's dad worked for a computer company and his mom was a stay-at-home mom. He had a sister, Emma's age, and a nine-year-old little brother. It was a normal family...*normal.*

During the week, Andy worked in the fields, which was preferable to him because he hated the idea of working in the fast food industry. He couldn't stand the thought of being cooped up inside some air conditioned building all day flipping burgers or steaming in front of a fry vat. After sloshing through soggy fields, field dirt still caked to him, Andy would make a quick stop to pick up Emma at the end of his workday. She would hang out in his family's cluttered living room while he showered.

On the weekends, he cleaned horse stalls for a friend of his family and Emma would hang around the smelly horse stable as he raked up manure and made goofy faces at her. Andy was fun and lived life passionately, with a grin on his dimpled face, and helped Emma learn how to smile and laugh from deep within her soul. When she was with Andy, she felt alive.

Several weeks into their friendship, while sitting on the yellow metal chairs in the back yard of his parent's house, Andy had asked Emma if she wanted to get high. With a silly grin, he had pulled a joint out of the front pocket of his shorts and held it up so she could see it. It was similar to the one George had months before. Andy hadn't pressured her; she wasn't trapped in a car and when she had responded, "no," he hadn't tried to change her mind. But in time, Emma did smoke a joint with Andy, not the entire thing, and just a few drags. It became an infrequent routine for them during the hot summer evenings, sometimes sitting in Andy's backyard, or even in front of Emma's foster home. He never tried to force her or trick her into doing anything. It wasn't like when George had tried to get her high so he could take advantage of her. With George, she had done what she had to do at the time to avoid a volatile situation, but with Andy, it was different. Emma trusted her sweet blonde-headed, dimpled friend, with the easy grin. She knew he would never hurt her.

Mid-summer, things began to change. Instead of smoking half a joint on a weekend night, Andy began carrying entire baggies crammed full of the dried weed, and papers to go with it. The half-smoked joint, saving some for another day, was replaced with a pipe. He even gave Emma a green and silver colored one. Emma knew Andy was weighed down by his father's expectations, the shouting matches between them growing more frequent, and that was why the sudden baggies full of pot. While high, he could push away his troubles, at least for a little while.

The carefree days of summer were ending, and as the new school year approached, Emma sensed an ever-growing change in Andy. He grew quiet and pensive. She knew it was because of the pressure his father was placing on him to be more serious. He would be entering his senior year of high school and then onto college. Andy was more like his mom, light-hearted and carefree, nothing like his dad. Emma couldn't remember if she had ever seen the tall, balding man in the business suit with a smile cracking his face. She knew he was the reason for Andy's change in attitude, for his dark side.

One rainy evening, as Andy raked straw back into a stall, Emma sat perched on the old, weathered wooden stool in the corner, out of the way, watching his progress. Emma felt sticky in the oppressively muggy air. Andy had opened the doors at either end of the building to stir the air, but it wasn't reaching her corner of the barn-like building. He had been working steadily for a few hours as she helped in whatever way she could, sweeping, straightening, and when she ran out of useful things to do, she picked up the raggedy magazine she had read several times before. Emma had read almost the entire magazine, again, when she heard the storage door creak open. Looking up from the article she almost had memorized, she saw Andy put the rake away, and then walk over to a cabinet she had never noticed before. He began riffling through it.

"Andy," she shouted over booming thunder. "What're you looking for?"

Emma could see from her position halfway across the room that he was shoving small, clear vials of what looked like medicine, the type nurses used for inoculations, aside. It was medicine for the horses, she realized. Surprised the cabinet wasn't locked, Emma wondered what he was looking for. Since he wasn't responsible for taking care of the horses, she reflected, he had no business being in the cabinet.

"Oh, I'm just looking," he said absently.

He continued to move small bottles back and forth, as if he were searching for something specific. Emma watched him take one of the small clear bottles out of the cabinet, and then as thunder crashed and lightening lit up the sky, he tied a stretchy material around his upper arm.

"What are *doing*?" In shock, Emma jumped off the stool and rushed over to stand next to him.

He held one piece of the band in one hand and the other in his mouth as he looked down at her.

"Andy!" Emma yelled, as she looked down at the syringe in his hand, pointed toward the vein his arm.

"I'm just going to try a little," he muffled, speaking with the wrap in his mouth.

"Why?!" She asked, beginning to feel hysterical. She looked into his sweet face and wondered what was happening to him. Shaking her head, not believing he would really inject some strange substance into his vein, she asked, "Andy. What are you *doing*? You could *die* doing that." She wanted to pull the needle out of his hand but was afraid to do so. She was afraid if she grabbed it, he would wrestle it away and either stab her with it, or jab it into him.

Wrinkling her forehead and with tears in her eyes, she put her fingers lightly on his arm and pleaded, as she looked up into his eyes, "Please don't."

Smiling his now very familiar smile, dimples lighting up his handsome face, he said reassuringly, "Don't worry. I'll be alright."

"Please," she pleaded. Her heart was pounding. She didn't know what to do, couldn't believe he was seriously considering sticking a needle into his arm.

For a moment, he looked down into her eyes, and then before she could respond, he quickly stuck the needle in his vein. Emma inhaled sharply, scared of what was about to happen. She could hear the blood pounding in her ears as he pushed on the syringe. She stepped back, not knowing what to expect and watched his face.

"Okay, Em," he said. "We have to get you home."

Home, she thought. And leave him here?

"I'm not leaving you here," Emma insisted, as lightening lit up the dark stable.

"Em, I'm fine," he said, the smile gone now.

"No!" she shouted over the thunder. "I'm not leaving until I'm sure you're okay."

He sat down and hunched on a stool as Emma knelt down and looked up into his face. He looked fine, she thought. Maybe he didn't really do it. Maybe he had just pretended.

After a half an hour had passed, Emma let him take her home. The worst of the storm was over. All that remained was a steady, cleansing rain.

Over the next few weeks, the vision of Andy plunging a needle into his vein haunted her. The happy boy she had spent the summer with seemed to fade away. It was still his face and his body, but the goofy grin, and life seemed to have died. They began spending less and less time together and eventually, he stopped calling all together. When school resumed after summer break, she heard a rumor that he had had been sent away to military school.

CHAPTER FIFTEEN

Snuggled into the corner of the couch, Emma tried to ignore the raised voices coming from the kitchen. Ever since George had been accused of raping and impregnating a girl at his job, life at Sheila's home had changed. Laughing had all but stopped, replaced by stomach churning tension and short tempers. George had found another job, at a garage, but for some reason money was still tight, and Emma suspected something else was wrong, but didn't know what it was.

Loud noise—things being slammed around—shouting in the house had Emma on edge, so she kept to herself as much as possible. It was too familiar, too similar to the years spent living with her dad, never knowing when a fist or hand was going to lash out at her.

Emma felt as if a dark cloak had wrapped around her. She was preoccupied during most of her waking hours, missing her sister Amy, and thinking about the bad things; the years spent living at her dad's house, and what the others, Mark, George and Eric, had done to her. So much sadness. She couldn't shake the heavy weight of the dark cloak from her shoulders. Sleep provided no respite from her thoughts as more nights than not, she woke, heart pounding, damp from sweat as she tried to escape whoever or whatever chased her in her dreams.

Sitting at the kitchen table alone, eating a bowl of cold cereal, Emma rolled her eyes as she listened to the argument taking place in the next room. Sheila had been tearing into everyone for the last few days. She had broken up with her boyfriend, the pervert, weeks ago and had been entertaining a new guy. Katie said he was some important official in town, a lot older than Sheila was. She had hit the jackpot of boyfriends. Typically, dating a new boyfriend made Sheila happy, but for some reason, she was one very unhappy lady.

It was one of those days. Everyone had made Sheila's shit list. She had yelled at Katie about something, then Sara, then Jessie, and now it was George's turn. Sara had made her escape about an hour ago, saying something about meeting a friend for lunch, and Jessie had left for work a half an hour ago, although her shift at the restaurant didn't start for another two hours.

Emma figured George was the one Sheila had been mad at all along, but was just now getting around to him. Emma wondered what had happened with the rape investigation, but hadn't asked anyone about it. She hadn't woken to find him in bed next to her in awhile, so she figured he must be someone else's problem.

PMS was making Emma just a wee bit less tolerant of the household crap today, that and life crap in general. Amy had visited a few weeks ago, and Emma had gone into an even deeper missing her funk. She missed her, and life just *sucked*. Nothing had turned out right. It wasn't supposed to be this way. Sisters were supposed to be together, *in one home.*

Emma had kept to herself over the last few weeks, not in the mood to try anymore. What was the point, she stewed. Things never worked out— homes never worked out. Life wasn't like one the funny books or even the mystery books she liked to read. Life really wasn't much of a mystery, she realized, where the gang looked for all the clues, and then reported their findings to the police, and in the end, the bad guys were put away.

Emma paused, mid-crunchy chew when she heard Sheila scream the name *Amy*, then the word *whore* all in the same sentence. Sitting up straighter in her chair, she strained her ears. She wanted to know what this woman was saying about her sister, absent and unable to defend herself.

Forcing the mouthful of cereal down her throat, Emma pushed her chair back and stood, inhaling a deep breath. What, she wondered, gave that woman the right to call a girl she barely knew, a whore? She didn't *know* Amy. Amy wasn't there to defend herself, but Emma was. As she walked to the living room she thought, *the nerve of the woman with her dysfunctional family calling her sister a whore.* She really needed to get her family in order before she started bashing someone else. Emma thought back over the months, the times when she had woken in the middle of the night to find George lying next to her groping her, and the times he had tried to get her to get high with him, probably so he could put the moves on her. Deep in thought, Emma bent her head, and crammed her hands in her pockets, her heart pumping in anger. She thought back to the night Sheila's ex-boyfriend had tried to convince her to strip for him, and who knew what else. Emma stopped at the edge of the living room and looked across the room at Sheila standing by the window, popping her gum, and flailing her hands about as she continued to talk about Amy. As she listened to her foster mother's shrieking voice, something inside of Emma burst.

The events of the past year boiled over, and Emma shouted, "She's not a whore! My sister's not a whore!"

The room became quiet as Katie, George, and Sheila turned to look at Emma. It was as if the room held its breath. Sheila popped her gum and stared at Emma, and breathlessly, Emma stared back.

Emma couldn't believe she had just shouted at her foster mother, it wasn't that she was looking for a fight, she wasn't. She was just so tired of the yelling, the horrible men trying to touch her, and all the mean-ness in the world. She just couldn't take it anymore. Standing her ground, Emma watched the corners of Sheila's lips turn up exposing her horse teeth.

"What's that you're *sayin'*?" Sheila asked as she snapped her gum.

"I said Amy's not a whore. I'm sick of you calling her a whore! You don't know her!" Emma insisted.

"Listen here. You don't have any room to talk. You and your pot smoking," Sheila said, her jaw working overtime on her gum.

Emma laughed angrily. "Pot. *Pot!* Let me tell you a few things. You think your family is so great. Your twenty-year-old son is a pothead! My *God!* I can't count the times he tried to get me high, and did *finally.* So we have him to thank for that." Emma stared at Sheila, watching her reaction but too angry to stop herself. Sheila stopped chewing and pursed her lips.

"And I don't know how many times I have woken up in the middle of the night to find your son *groping* me! I had to knock him out of bed to get him away from me. If that wasn't bad enough, I had to deal with your perverted ex-boyfriend, hitting on me. Remember the cookout at his mom's house? You know, when you all left me out in the yard alone with him—he tried to talk me into being a stripper. He's nasty!" Emma shouted.

Something flickered across Sheila's face.

Not taking her eyes off the short, obese woman, Emma continued flatly, "Your disgusting boyfriend used to tell me I'd be a great dancer. He said to me, 'I could hook you up in Indianapolis at one of the clubs.' He wanted me to meet him somewhere so he could drive me over. He said I should pretend I was going on a date so you'd never know." Nodding her head, Emma said, "So you go on all you want about my sister being a whore, but you, *you* have way bigger problems."

"You liar," Sheila hissed, red faced. "You fucking cunt."

Knowing she had passed the point of no return, Emma wrinkled her forehead and said, "I'm not lying. You're standing there bad mouthing my sister, but for months now, I've had to deal with those two sick assholes. You have no right, no *right* to call my sister a whore!"

Before she had time to react, Emma found herself lying on the floor— the wind knocked out of her—pinned beneath Sheila's massive weight. Trapped beneath her, Emma gasped for air.

Sheila screamed, "George, hold her down! I'm gonna kill the bitch!"

George didn't move from his position by the floral couch, he just continued to stand nearby and watch as his mother tried to squeeze the life out of his foster sister.

Sheila snapped. Screaming and straddling Emma, Sheila squeezed her hands around her neck, fingers applying pressure to the hollow in the young girl's throat as Emma coughed, gagged, and struggled for air. Staring down into Emma's red swollen face, tears streaming down her cheeks from the pressure on her throat, Sheila let loose the pent up rage she had bottled up since she her son had been accused of rape.

As Emma fought for air, she struggled beneath her foster mother, trying to kick her feet between them and when that didn't work, she tried to buck her off. She couldn't budge her. She couldn't breathe. The pressure and pain from Sheila's hands and fingernails digging into her throat was excruciating. Just when Emma thought for sure she was going to pass out from lack of air, and maybe never wake up again, Sheila removed her hands from her throat and stopped screaming. Emma inhaled deep ragged breathes and grabbed her neck, and in exhaustion stopped struggling. Closing her eyes, Emma rubbed her throat and flinched as she felt a stinging pain on her face, and heard Sheila screaming again. Emma balled her hands and raised them to her face trying to shield her eyes, nose, and mouth from Sheila's fists.

With renewed energy, Emma began kicking and rocking, trying to dislodge her foster mother's body. Worn out, Sheila rolled off Emma, but continued her screaming tirade. Emma scrambled to her feet and ran to the phone hanging on the wall in the kitchen. Gingerly, she felt her swollen tender cheek and cringed in pain. Shakily, Emma dialed her caseworker's office telephone number. She was done with this crazy place. Wrapping the cord around her finger, nervously Emma listened to the rings. She was just about to hang up the phone when she heard Ben, her caseworker, say, "Hello." Hysterically, Emma told him what had happened and made him promise to come right over and take her out of the home.

Crossing her arms over her chest, cautiously Emma walked back into the living room where Katie was still sitting curled on the couch and George and Sheila were standing, waiting for her.

"Ben, will be here in a few minutes," Emma said shakily.

Emma was met by no response, but for the popping of Sheila's gum.

Forty minutes later, about twenty minutes longer than Emma had expected there was a knock on the door and Emma ran to open it. It was Ben. Emma shoved him out the door, and stepped out with him onto the concrete porch.

Looking at her red swollen cheek, Ben touched it lightly and asked, "What happened?"

In a rush, Emma repeated what she had told him on the telephone. "I heard Sheila calling my sister, Amy, a whore. I'm sick of it! She has no right to make comments about her. It's not even true," she said flailing her arms wildly.

"I know. I know," he said raising his hand. "After that, what happened?"

"Well, I just told her, I told her what her son and her boyfriend—ex-boyfriend, had done to me," Emma said.

"And," Ben asked impatiently.

Exhaling, Emma put her hands on her hips and told him the rest. "I told Sheila about her son. She called me a pothead and I told her George got me high the first time and that I wake up in the middle of the night to find him groping me. And that I knock him out of my bed to get him away from me. He's *sick*. Have you heard why he lost his last job?"

Ben raised his eyebrows.

"Then I told her about Eric, you know, her ex-boyfriend, how he was hitting on me and tried to talk me into going to Indianapolis with him to some strip club, and *strip*." Raising her voice she said, "I'm sick of it! I want out of here. Find me a new home, *now*! You can't make me stay here!"

"What about, Katie?" Ben asked. Do I need to talk to her? Does she want to move to?"

Emma stopped short, surprised by the question. Why, she wondered, was her caseworker asking her about Katie? She wasn't the adult—the expert of abuse by foster parent. He was!

Exasperated she said, "*I don't know*."

"Well where was she when all this was going on?" Ben asked shortly.

Flinging her hand in the air, Emma said, "In the house—the living room."

Sighing, he said, "Fine. I'll talk to her too."

Placing his hands on his hips, looking annoyed, he said, "Alright, alright. Emma you need to know. There just are no long-term foster homes, none right now. Temporary homes, yes, but I have no where to put you."

Staring at him with her mouth open, Emma waited to hear his solution.

"Emma, do you understand what I'm telling you?" Ben asked.

"Yeah. There are no long-term foster homes so you're going to take me to a short-term home," she answered.

Sighing, he ran his hand across his face in exasperation.

"A group home. I could put you in a group home. It's all I have right now," Ben said.

"What?!" she hissed. "What are you talking about? What *group home*?"

"There's a home, a group home." He raised his hand in the air, and gave her a stern look as she began to protest, then continued. "I don't have anywhere to put you. The group home is in a county near here."

The man was talking crazy, Emma thought. Group home—*Group home!* She had watched a movie about a group home. She knew *all* she needed to know about group homes and there was no way she was going to one. They would eat her alive in there. According to the movie, they did bad things to nice, soft girls like her. He couldn't be serious, she thought. What was *wrong* with everyone? She wasn't a criminal so why were they trying to treat her like one. She had done nothing wrong. It was the same old thing; she was being punished for what others had done to her. Cover it all up, that's what they did. Then send the kids onto the next mess. Maybe it *was* because there was a foster home shortage, Emma speculated, maybe that's why they never helped the kids and never did anything to the foster parents. No one ever listened to her, and this time it was pissing her off!

Emma examined her caseworker—younger than all her previous caseworkers—fresh out of college. He had sandy blonde colored hair, and dressed as if he was on his way to hang out with his college buddies, in blue jeans and a t-shirt. He could have been mistaken for one of the guys in her high school with his clean-shaven baby face. He had absolutely no idea what he was doing as a caseworker. He was just a kid himself.

"I tell you what. I'm going on a boating trip this weekend. Let's just deal with this when I get back," Ben said.

Emma couldn't believe her ears. *Was the man nuts? Stay here for the weekend?*

"No! *No!* I can't stay here. After what just happened, with what *has* been happening. How can you just leave me here?" Emma asked in shock. She was still shaken from being beaten by her foster mother and now— she felt as if she was in an alternate universe. This can't be happening she thought, as she stared at Ben.

Ben slumped his shoulders and shifted his feet looking up at the gray sky. Placing his hands on his hips, he looked down at the young girl in frustration.

"Emma, I don't have time for this. Just stick it out for the weekend and then I'll find a place for you," Ben insisted.

Emma felt beaten, knowing he wasn't going to budge. She was going to have to stay for an entire weekend with a woman that had just beaten her, strangled her, and stated she wanted to kill her. More of the same, Emma thought. No one was going to protect her.

"Fine. Just find a home for me, and do not put me in a group home. Ben, do you know what goes on in those places? I don't belong there. I'm not a *criminal*. I'm not the problem here," Emma insisted.

Emma could tell by the look on his face that he was relieved to have the little problem solved, for now, so he could go on his weekend boating trip. She certainly wouldn't want to mess up his plans, she thought sarcastically.

"I'll find you a home," he promised. "And I will put a note in your case file that you should not be placed in the group home. Emma, I'll find you a home. I promise. Just get through the weekend, okay?"

"Okay," Emma said quietly.

"I need to talk to Sheila," he said.

Ben followed Emma into the house.

Ignoring Sheila, George, and Katie, Emma escaped to her bedroom. Ben was her caseworker, Emma thought, let him tell her soon to be ex-foster mother that she was leaving. Let him confront her about what had been going on. She was done with the situation.

Emma spent the weekend sequestered in her bedroom only coming out to eat and use the bathroom. She passed the time reading an old paper-back mystery, dozing often, and packing her few belongings back in her suitcase, a black garbage bag. She wanted to be ready to leave the minute Ben arrived after school Monday.

Monday crawled by. Emma spent most of the day at school distracted, glancing at the clocks hung high on the walls in her classrooms. Sighing as she sat in science class that afternoon, she rested her chin on the palm of her hand and wondered, would there ever be a home for her, with a family that would love her, and want her—and not hurt her?

When Emma arrived home from school Monday afternoon, she went straight to her bedroom to wait for Ben. She had expected to find him waiting for her when she got home. He must be running late, she thought. As Emma sat on the edge of the twin bed waiting for Ben, she felt empty. She was leaving another place, another home. It hadn't been great, but she had wanted it to work out. She just wanted to belong. Onto the unknown again, she reflected, but this time she'd be going on alone—no Katie, and no Amy. The afternoon light began to fade. Tired, Emma curled up on her bed and waited.

The sound of the telephone ringing woke her. Emma was pushing herself into a seated position when Sheila stuck her head into her room.

With a satisfied look on her face, and a pop of her gum, Sheila snapped, "Ben's not comin'. They're sendin' over a different caseworker. Seems Ben was in an accident over the weekend. He jumped out of a boat head first, and now he's paralyzed from the neck down. You just might end up in that kid's home after all." Sneering, Sheila walked out of the bedroom with Emma staring after her, her mouth hanging open as she absorbed what Sheila had just said. Ben had been in an accident. Not coming—Paralyzed—New caseworker.

CHAPTER SIXTEEN

Tanya, the new caseworker, the fifth in the last year and a half, had arrived within the hour. Emma sized up the thirty-something brunette wondering which category she would fall into, incompetent, bitch, or perhaps she would actually be like Brian, two caseworkers ago, and actually care. Emma hadn't known it at the time, but Brian hadn't been the run-of-the-mill caseworker. He made himself available for Emma and her sisters whenever they needed him. Of course, at the time Emma had been a foster newbie, a relatively new foster kid. It had been before all the weird had begun at Sheila's house.

Emma soon caught on to the constant rotation of caseworkers. They were never around for very long, not long enough to get to know her. After Brian, Emma didn't bother getting too close to any of her caseworkers. What would be the point, she thought—just one more person leaving her, letting her down.

As she looked at Tanya, Emma noticed she wasn't very smiley. The initial evaluation, Emma thought, was that Tanya was the bitch type of caseworker. She seemed to know her stuff as a caseworker, but she didn't seem overly caring. Yup—bitch.

Emma had lived with Sheila's family for the past nine months and could still remember the day she had arrived, filled with hope that she might become a part of their family—belong. There were no long goodbyes when Emma left Sheila's home. Katie had decided to stay with Sheila and her family, so Emma was now on her own, leaving the last of her biological family behind.

The older brunette and the teen were quiet on the short drive across town, and fifteen minutes later Tanya pulled up in front of two-story brick house.

"Okay, Emma," Tanya said. "This is it."

Emma looked up at the two story red brick house, with concrete pillars standing guard on either side of the front door then turned toward her caseworker as she heard her say, "This is just a temporary placement until we can find a permanent home for you."

Wrinkling her brow, Emma wondered, what was the point in getting to know these people if she'd be moving somewhere else soon? She hated change, new people, and new routines. Emma had developed a three-month rule. It took at least three months for her to get comfortable in a new home. If she could just make it through three months then she knew she would begin feeling comfortable. It always worked that way, but now she knew she'd have to go through at least two more, three-month rules. Assuming she'd be at this home that long.

Opening the manila file folder, she held in her hands, Tanya said, "This is the Matthews family. He's a doctor, practicing at the hospital just down the road—in his fifties—jogs every day." Flipping a page, Tanya continued, "Mr. Matthews is on the board at the hospital. *Mrs.* Matthews is a stay-at-home mom—a homemaker. They have one biological daughter, Judy. She's a junior in high school, and they have an adopted daughter named Camille. She's a freshman in high school."

Closing the file folder, Tanya looked at Emma, and demanded, "Stay out of trouble. This is just for a few weeks. Just until we can find a more permanent home for you."

Well, Emma thought, she wouldn't have to worry about her three-month rules because she wouldn't be living in her new foster home long enough to *get* comfortable, and yup, Emma thought, Tanya was in the caseworker bitch category. What was wrong with this *woman*, Emma wondered. Why was she talking to her as if she was a bad kid? Then a light bulb clicked on in the recesses of her mind. Had Sheila said something, lied about what had happened last week? That was the only answer Emma could come up with for the rudeness of her newest caseworker, otherwise, Tanya would be behaving in a more sensitive manner, wouldn't she, Emma reflected. To Emma's knowledge, Ben hadn't even filed a police report and no one had bothered to ask her about George, or Eric. There had been no, *Are you okay, or how are you doing.* Emma knew she had no say in her life, and if her caseworker really wanted to help her, wanted to know the truth, she would have asked what had happened at Sheila's house. No one had ever asked Emma any questions, not even when she was taken from her dad's home. It was as if they hadn't wanted to know what had happened to her then, or now. Whatever the reason, Emma knew she was on her own.

Unsmiling, Emma replied, "Fine."

Standing in the elegant living room, garbage bag at her feet, Emma assessed the stern looking Mrs. Matthews, her new temporary foster mother.

Emma returned Mrs. Matthews' cold greeting with one of her own, offering a sullen, "Hello."

Mrs. Matthews led the way into the kitchen where she motioned for Tanya and Emma to be seated at the small table. Sitting at the kitchen table, Mrs. Matthews reviewed the house rules with Emma. The rules were typical for any home, Emma thought, except for the one about the refrigerator. No one was allowed access to the refrigerator, which as Emma glanced over at it, realized she wouldn't be tempted to break that rule because there was a lock on the fridge that required a key to open it. Rolling her eyes, she thought, whatever.

"Okay," Mrs. Matthews said, cracking her first smile. "Let's take your picture."

Confused, Emma looked around wondering, *why.*

"We take all our foster children's pictures. Look," she said, as she handed Emma a thick photo album. "Their all in there. Every foster child that has ever been in our home."

Emma opened the book and felt nauseas as she flipped page after page, of what had to be hundreds of pictures of foster children, on display like pets, or trophies. She flipped to the last page and noticed that most were posed in the same manner, seated, hands folded, kind of like a prison picture, Emma thought.

Emma didn't want her picture taken, and didn't want to be in the stupid photo album commemorating her stay at the Mathews' foster home. She didn't want future foster children looking at her face as they flipped through the book just as she had just done. Unhappily, Emma flopped down onto the chair, as she was instructed. She allowed herself to be the latest trophy, as the Polaroid camera whirred, spitting out what would soon manifest into her image.

Heaving her garbage bag of clothes in her arms, Emma followed Mrs. Matthews to the room she would be sleeping in for the next few weeks. Emma couldn't help but be impressed by the snobby woman's home. It was like stepping into the pages of one of her books, with beautiful Persian carpets covering the floors, and elegant furniture—overstuffed—the type you looked at but never sat on. The entryway had sparkly clean windows, freshly polished banisters, and dark wood flooring, with yet another Persian rug that she tiptoed across fearful of leaving an imprint from her shoes, hoping she had no gum gunked onto the soles. Her shoes sank into the carpet as she walked up the staircase to the second floor where the bedrooms were. Mrs. Matthews wasn't very chatty, Emma noticed.

Emma continued to glance around, hoping her new foster mother wouldn't notice, figuring the woman would fear she was scoping out the place to see what she could steal. The truth was that Emma was in awe of her new foster home. Four of Sheila's houses could have fit within the walls of the Mathews' home, and even then, the elegance, the luxury…she had never spent the night in such a place. Even the foster home she had been placed at once court had concluded hadn't been this nice. Within the first five minutes of her stay in *that* foster home, the foster mother had instructed her not to touch any of her sparkly things within her beautiful cabinets…as if she would have. What was wrong with these people Emma wondered? First, the sparkly knick-knacks, and now the locked refrigerator. These people had some serious possession issues, one with sparkly things, and the other with food.

As she walked down the hall, Emma slowed her pace to better examine the paintings on the walls. She had never seen such beautiful paintings, and hung on a hall wall of all places. The paintings were not large, not like the kind you would find above a fireplace, not that Emma had lived in a home with a fireplace, but she had read about them, and she had seen them in movies and on TV. She squinted at the rich colors stroked onto the canvases.

Glancing forward, Emma picked up the pace, and watched as Mrs. Matthews disappeared into a room on the left side of the hall. Peering around the corner, Emma saw a comfortable looking bed resting against one of the walls in a room where the elegant carpet continued. Looking across to the far side of the room, she saw a door that led to another bedroom, a beautiful room with two twin beds with fluffy, frilly bedspreads. My Gosh, Emma thought, how rich were these people, remembering what the caseworker had said; Mr. Matthews was a doctor. Well, doctor's home's were very different from everyone else's, she realized.

Later that night, exhausted from months of turmoil, Emma crawled beneath the luxurious sheets, and pulled the fluffy white eyelet comforter over her shoulders, sniffed the pillow case as she sunk into it, noticing it smelled as if it had been dried on a clothes line in the fresh air. Too tired for nightmares, Emma slept soundly in the quiet house.

CHAPTER SEVENTEEN

Two weeks passed, and Emma continued to be a resident at the Mathews' home. She had met Mr. Matthews the first evening of her stay and found him to be quirky and funny, not at all what she had expected from a stuffy doctor. Her name had magically gone from Emma, to Emma—Emma. He addressed all the children living in his home, as well as all of their friends, in that manner. Emma found when her name was said twice, in quick succession, it added an air of importance, or it could have been the large man saying the name that made one feel important.

Mr. Matthews was a giant of a man, towering over everyone in the house, especially his petite wife, but it wasn't merely his physical size that had Emma seeing him in a larger than life kind of way. His unusually large, generous, and kind heart had Emma seeing him more as a hero than a foster father, or doctor. She was no one to him, but still he took time out of his evening and weekends to acknowledge her.

It was almost as if she had stepped into a modern day version of the Clever family, one with foster children, a dad that called everyone by their names twice, and a mom that was strong, enforcing rules, and keeping them all safe from the bad things. It was safe within their walls, and the safety carried her through her day at school. It was as if being a member of their family made people see her differently, almost as if they forgot she was a foster kid, or that it wasn't bad to be one.

As Emma watched the couple, Mrs. Matthews occasionally let down her guard, exposing her soft side. Emma understood. Each time Emma had to leave a foster home, it felt as if pieces of her heart were being shaved away. She speculated that it must have been the same for Mrs. Matthews. Each time one of the foster children she had in her care went away, she was left wondering, never knowing, how they were, or where they were.

At the end of the two weeks, Emma's belongings still tucked away in her bedroom, Mr. Matthews trying to convince her to jog with him each evening, and her old friends coming by to hang out, Emma felt that maybe she had found a place to belong. No boys or men tried to climb in bed with her, no one offered her drugs, no one tried to burn the house down while she was inside, and no one felt the need to offer her a cigarette. Finally, Emma was allowed to be a young girl, happy, and safe from the bad things. It had been so easy to love the Matthews family, and she began to hope they would love her back, and want to keep her. Emma still thought about her sisters a lot, especially when she lay in bed at night. There had been no contact from either one of them. She missed them and wondered if they were okay.

One Saturday afternoon, Emma sat outside her foster parent's home near the lilac bushes lining the sidewalk, talking and laughing with Shelly, Neal, and her new foster sister, Camille. Emma knew it was silly, but the sun seemed to shine brighter and warmer, the leaves on the trees seemed a deeper shade of green, and even the grass seemed lusher, cool to the skin on her feet. Life was just more vibrant, more alive—in a good way.

Laughing, Emma entered the living room, her schoolbooks under her arm and noticed her caseworker sitting beside Mrs. Matthews, with cups of coffee in their hands. Surprised, she smiled a hello. No one had told Emma that her caseworker would be visiting today.

"Emma," Mrs. Matthews said. "Come sit down with us for a minute, please."

She placed the heavy stack of books on the floral table clothed table next to her, and pulled out a wooden chair and sat down, placing her hands in her lap.

"Is everything, okay?" Emma asked nervously.

Mrs. Matthews looked down at her folded hands resting on the table, as Tanya explained the purpose of her visit. Tanya sat at the head of the small table with a manila folder open in front of her.

"We found another home for you," Tanya said coldly.

Emma felt as if the air had been knocked out of her as she glanced from Tanya to Mrs. Matthews.

"I thought, I thought was staying here," she stammered.

Closing the folder, Tanya looked at her unsmiling, and said, "Emma, you knew this was a temporary placement."

Emma looked down at her hands, remembering the conversation she had with Tanya a month ago. Yes, she thought. It was supposed to be a temporary placement, but when the two weeks had passed, she had thought—hoped—that they had changed their minds and she was going to stay, forever.

"I know that's what you said. I just thought…" Emma's voice trailed away embarrassed that she had made such a stupid mistake. Of course she wasn't staying, she realized. *What had she been thinking?* Moving, she was moving again—but—she didn't want to move again.

Mrs. Matthews continued to sit quietly, hands folded as Emma and her caseworker discussed her future, her next placement.

"So—where am I going?" Emma asked quietly.

CHAPTER EIGHTEEN

The brief days of happy were over. Emma finally got it. She was a foster kid, and no one was trying to soften the edges, pretending or offering her fake, phony hope that her life would ever be anything more than it was. It seemed as if her caseworkers had become hard, or maybe it was her, maybe she was the one that had become hard—hardened by the death of her hopes and dreams. She felt empty.

Emma felt numb as she climbed the concrete steps to her new foster home, which was exactly how she intended to remain during her stay. Another temporary home, she thought with a sigh, as she looked down at the concrete stairs and trudged behind her caseworker. No point in getting too chummy with anyone, what would be the point, she reflected. Chances were if it were a place she wanted to stay, a good home, she'd be there only a few weeks anyway. One day Tanya would arrive unannounced to pick her up and cart her off to another foster home. She wondered when it would end, when she would have a permanent place to put her clothes and her books, when she would no longer have to wonder—was today the day she'd be moving on.

Stopping short, Emma clutched her black garbage bag as Tanya rang the doorbell. You'd think they could spring for a real suitcase instead of garbage bags as often as she used the darn things, Emma thought sarcastically, rolling her eyes.

Hearing the door creak open, Emma looked up at the lady framed in the doorway. Emma had met the woman that stood before her holding the door open, her newest foster mother, Mrs. Harmon, over a year ago. Her sister Amy had been placed at the home, and Emma had spent a night with her on a rare visit with her sister. Emma remembered Amy had loved staying at the Harmons' home.

Emma thought back to that sunny spring day when Amy had taken her on a tour of her new foster home, introduced her to the town and her new friends. When Emma had arrived at the home for a visit with her sister, she had been surprised when her caseworker had stopped the car in front of what had looked to her like a Victorian mansion. She had continued to remain seated in the car waiting for her caseworker to pull forward, or turn around, lost, but she hadn't. Emma had stared up at the enormous house noticing all the various angles. A turreted room peaked high above the rest of the house and as Emma stared up at the regal structure, she had pictured Rapunzel throwing down her long hair from one of the many windows. Continuing to stare up at the house, Emma had shaken her head in wonder, in awe that the massive house was a foster home and the occupants chose to be foster parents.

When Emma had arrived at the Harmon home to visit her sister, her caseworker at the time had led the way up the stairs at the back of the house into a cozy kitchen with an inviting round wooden table and chairs with a lazy-Suzan placed in the center of the table, filled with mealtime necessities. A narrow staircase was tucked away in the back corner of the room, hidden away so effectively that Emma would not have known it was there if Amy hadn't directed her up the steep stairs. As Emma had followed Amy up the narrow curved stairwell, her sister had explained her theory that in the early 1900's, the servants of the home had used it. The main staircase, she had explained, was at the front of the house, the main entry. As Emma had climbed the steep stairs, she had imagined the servants perspiring in the heat of the day as they bustled up and down the stairs preparing the early morning and late day meals. When she had arrived at the top of the stairs, she had looked to the left toward a closed door, then to the right to what seemed to be an endless curving hallway. From her position in the hall, she could not see around the bend, but could see two doors that must have led to the kid's bedrooms. She had no idea how far the hall might go. It was such a large mysterious house, but surprisingly she had felt no fear, not as she had at her dad's house. The house Emma had lived in as a little girl had been large and quite scary, but it dwarfed in comparison to this old Victorian home.

She had been surprised that she felt completely at ease in the unique house, with all of its twists, turns, and hidden nooks. Amy had shown her the room that she had been sharing with her foster sister, and then she completed the tour of the house. They hadn't gone back down the servant's stairs, instead, she had led Emma down the curved hallway that seemed to go on endlessly but did eventually end at the top of a grand staircase.

When Emma was in eighth grade, a year and a half ago, she had lived in the Armstrong foster home, in her hometown. They had a grand staircase in their home too, however as she had stood at the top of the Harmons' staircase, overlooking their foyer, she had redefined grand. She had estimated that five people could walk side by side, quite comfortably down the white plush carpeted stairs that curved toward the large open foyer. As Emma walked down the stairs, she imagined she was one of the ladies of the home from years past, dressed in a fancy party dress, white gloves clutched in her hand, the other on the slick railing, as she glided down the stairs, ready for an evening with her friends.

The home had seemed to be in stark contrast to Mrs. Harmon's casual appearance. Emma had pictured a much more casual environment, a smaller house, unpretentious in an old neighborhood. While she did live in an older neighborhood, she had by far the largest house for blocks. Growing up, Emma had wondered about the people that lived in the big fancy houses and there she had been, standing inside of one with her sister. Her previous notions about those types of people had changed as she had realized that if there were others like the Harmons' that lived in fine homes, and chose to take care of kids like them, then they were really just people, regular people, that just lived in bigger houses than some. Amy had continued the tour, ending up in the basement where Emma had first met Mr. Harmon. The basement had been no less disappointing than the rest of the house with its maze of rooms. Mr. Harmon had been in a room with a couch and pool table, hanging twinkle lights. It had looked as if it would be a fun place for a party.

Amy had said the parents let the kids have parties sometimes, but they were always there to make sure it didn't get out of hand. She had thought what lucky kids they were. Mr. Harmon had chatted away with Emma, smiling as if they were old friends.

Now, as Emma followed Tanya into the familiar house, she realized that things were different. Much had happened since last she had been inside the walls of the fancy house with her sister. She was no longer the wide-eyed, hope-filled little girl. The world had been cruel to her, and her expectations had changed, gone from believing in fairy tales to believing in more of the same, at least for girls like her, foster girls.

Audrey, Emma's newest foster mother, led the way to the kitchen where Emma knew the lazy-Suzan would be in the center of the table ready for the evening meal. Audrey motioned to be seated at the round wooden kitchen table, offering pop or coffee, then lit up a cigarette, knowing better than to offer one to Emma. Emma plopped her black garbage bag at her feet and sat silently as the two women talked. Emma did her best to tune them out, not wanting to become invested in the situation. She had no intention of being sucked in again.

The house was quiet, besides the buzzing of the two women's voices as Emma sipped her cold can of pop. Emma was grateful that Audrey didn't try to be fakely friendly to her. It was a refreshing change. Audrey didn't look at her, or try to draw her into their conversation, which was how Emma wanted it. She just wanted to be left alone. Listening to the buzzing of their voices, Emma wished the women would shut up so she could be taken to wherever it was her newest foster mother was going to stick her in her mammoth sized house. Slumping in her seat, Emma reflected, as large as their house was, all the foster kids in town could have lived there with her. But as far as Emma knew, she was the only one. Emma swirled her finger in the moisture on the table created by her chilled pop can, and realized she hadn't met a single other foster kid at school, hadn't even heard of any.

A few cups of coffee and several cigarettes later, and the caseworker left. Alone now with Audrey, Emma followed her up the servants stairs to what would be her new bedroom. Emma's room was to be at the top of the servant's stairs, on the left side of the hall, isolated from the rest of the bedrooms around the bend. Being the only foster child residing at the Harmon home, Emma had the pick of the two double beds in her room to sleep on. She placed her black plastic garbage bag next to her bed of choice, the one by the window and dresser out of the line of the door, should she ever choose to open it. Next, Emma followed behind Audrey as she took her on a tour of the entire house. It was a quiet tour as Emma wasn't in the mood for idle chitchat; she had run out of things to say. Emma walked the same path she had a year and half earlier, down the upstairs hallway, passed the black and white bathroom with the toilet with the soft cushioned toilet seat, and newspaper looking wallpaper. Next, they walked down the curved hall, passed the other elegant bedrooms. Then onto the wide staircase fit for the chick in the movie, Gone with the Wind, as most certainly several hooped skirts could fit side by side, as they glided down the carpeted stairs.

Quiet consumed Emma throughout the rest of her day, and not knowing quite what to do, she lay on her bed thinking, wondering what her sisters were doing. Life seemed to be a constant maze of change, Emma thought, as ankles crossed, she stared up at the white ceiling. Never, it seemed, could she seem to catch her breath. She knew her current foster home was just another temporary home and soon she would be moving on again.

Emma had wondered if the quiet she had experienced on her first day was a fluke, but was pleasantly surprised when her quiet days continued. Mrs. Harmon was active at the department of children services and her husband worked, doing what, Emma was not sure. Their two children were grown and living on their own. Emma was the only foster child in their care, so on most days after school, Emma was left to herself. She didn't care. She *wanted* to be left alone. The house was beautiful, so she didn't mind wandering the rooms, watching TV, or napping in her room with the window open allowing a breeze to blow the curtains.

Emma fought within herself not to get too comfortable at her peaceful new home. She knew the drill, on any one day she could come home to find Tanya's car parked in front of the house, and then she'd be moving on. Even knowing, Emma began to find herself playing pretend as she wandered the house. She felt safe in her comfortable bedroom, and loved lingering in her private black and white bathroom enjoying long baths in the claw foot bathtub at night. She pretended that she belonged there. It was her home.

As the days passed, Emma developed a comfortable routine of walking to school in the morning, then at the end of most days, she'd walk back to the Harmons' home alone, watching as other kids ran by, laughing, and goofing off. She walked slowly, in no hurry, with no place she needed to be, no schedule and no routine, until dinnertime. Sometimes Emma would take a detour through the park near the Harmons' house. She'd sit on one of the benches that surrounded the fountain placed in the center of the park as it sprayed high in the air, then just as quickly crashed back into the pool of itself. She allowed the sounds and sights of the water to sooth her, and sometimes sat and watched for more than half of an hour. Dinner wasn't until six. Plenty of time to do nothing. Then she'd continue down the curving sidewalk, passed the table of pot smoking teens, onto her foster home only a few blocks away.

Emma loved dinnertime, and sometimes, one or both of the Harmon's kids would be seated at the dinner table when Emma, keeping a close eye on the clock, hurried into the kitchen. The Harmons' had a long-standing dinner game they played each night. Emma had been introduced to the game the night she had visited when Amy had lived with them. Emma hadn't forgotten the game, even after a year and a half had passed, and only playing it once. On her first night as the Harmons' foster daughter, at dinner, Emma had been surprised to see everyone at the table place their finger to their nose. They were still playing the game. The Harmons' grown children explained it was a family dinner game their parents had begun when they were small children. The object of the game was to wait until all those joining the family for dinner were seated at the table, and then everyone was to place their finger to the side of their nose. The person touching their nose last was the pig. It was a silly game, with no significant meaning, but it started dinner off on a fun note. It was difficult to be in a bad mood when distracted by a fun game. Emma tried never to be the last seated so she never lost the game.

Not noticing when it happened, Emma sunk into the comfort of her new digs. No one pressured her to be part of the family—no one was fake. The Harmons' knew, as Emma did, that she was just a foster kid and there was no point in pretending otherwise. She was not their daughter. She was not like them. She had grown to realize she was not, nor would she ever be, like other kids. Her dreams of one day finding a real family had been just that, a dream. There wasn't going to be a traditional happy ending for her. The very fact that her current foster family didn't lie or pretend her life was, or would be any different than it was, made it easier to relax in their home.

Mrs. Harmon asked Emma to call her by her first name, Audrey. The Mrs. was too formal she said. Audrey's son, Rick came around the house on most evenings. He was in his twenties and hung out with Mr. Harmon working on cars on sunny afternoons. Emma noticed they laughed and smiled a lot. Seemed to her, more talking went on than actual fixing of cars. Rick was nice. He didn't make her uncomfortable—didn't get too close.

The nights had been rough for Emma the first week. She'd had a tough time getting to sleep and staying asleep, plagued by nightmares. Rick had offered to loan her his small TV. It had a timer on it and as the voices and white glow from the TV lulled her to sleep each night, it would shut off at a predetermined time while she slept. With the help from the TV, Emma slept throughout the night with no nightmares of someone chasing her.

CHAPTER NINETEEN

D igging her hand into the warm bowl of freshly popped corn, Emma listened to Audrey talk. It was one of Emma's favorite topics, boys. Emma had never known an adult that wanted to talk to her, that would open up their evening just for her to watch a movie, and talk.

Emma was snuggled into her favorite overstuffed floral, very elegant chair, unaware of the warm golden light from the lamp on the small wooden table, highlighting her pretty features. Audrey was seated on the other side of the small table, on the couch, soft enough to sink into and be lulled into a nap.

Audrey looked at the young girl, so suspicious, so untrusting of everyone she met, not realizing how special she was. When Audrey looked at Emma, she saw a soft sweetness that was her strength, the very traits the young girl mistook for weakness. If only this young girl could tap into her gifts—find herself—her confidence—believe in herself, she would have the ability to do great things. She intended to help Emma see the wonderful girl she was, to banish the lies so many had instilled within her. First, it would require undoing a little of what the world had done to her.

When Emma had arrived weeks before, she had been a very different girl from the one that had visited over a year and a half ago. Something had robbed the young girl of her spirit. She didn't know what happened, she just knew the young girl that had been placed in her care, was not the same, and she intended to find that girl. Audrey had given Emma the space she knew she needed, not offering any false promises. Emma had been given a raw deal. Audrey had read Emma's case file several times, and wasn't surprised the young girl that had arrived at her home several weeks ago had been broken. She knew Emma's mother had abandoned her when she was two-years-old when her father had been in basic training, stationed at Ft. Knox, Kentucky. Her mother had taken Emma to grandparents and left her there, and then Emma's father had been released from the military so he could take care of her and her two older sisters. Within the first few years with her father, something had happened to Emma, no one was quite sure what that something had been, she had grown ill, or been abused, something, and had ended up in a foster home. The records had indicated that her mother had passed away by that time. A few months later, a four-year-old Emma was returned to her newly married father. Over the years, the home was riddled with abuse.

In the last year and half, Emma had been cycled through seven homes, this being the eighth. Audrey could understand Emma's attitude. Emma had been rescued from an abusive home and as with many foster children, she felt life would somehow become magical, her life becoming everything it hadn't been—become part of a family—belong somewhere. But this wasn't to be Emma's last stop, Audrey realized. She was licensed as a short-term foster home. The children she took in were meant to be in her home on an emergency basis or until permanent homes could be found for them. Emma couldn't stay.

Since moving into the Harmons' house, Emma had begun spending less and less time with her friends. The new school year had brought with it schedule changes. Lunch periods with her friend didn't coincide, and she didn't have classes with any of her friends. She missed joking around with her friends—missed pretending that she belonged—missed pretending she was just like every other kid. Finally, she had to admit to herself that she wasn't like the other kids. She never had been. She was a foster kid, bounced, either unwanted or abused from home to home. Trying was too much work, besides, what was the point, nothing ever worked out for Emma. It was okay, she thought. She loved her evenings with Audrey, watching TV, or movies, eating popcorn and pizza, but more than anything, Emma loved talking to Audrey. Somehow, Audrey had opened Emma up. Maybe it was just because she was the first adult that had attempted to talk to her, about important things, to *really* pay attention to her. Audrey wanted to know how she was doing and what she thought about various things.

Audrey was the first adult, for that matter, person, that Emma had shared how she felt about her family, the pain of not fitting in, and not belonging, beginning with her biological family. Emma wanted to understand why they were as they were and it hurt that no one seemed to miss her as much as she missed them. She wanted to know why it seemed that no one loved her, and wondered why she wasn't worth loving.

Audrey gave Emma a great gift, she listened to her, and she planted seeds for her future within her. She told Emma it was important to graduate from high school, even as Emma became discouraged, falling further behind her classmates. Her entire academic life Emma had been an above average student, but now she was failing. She was a sophomore, but had earned only two credits her freshman year. How, she wondered, would she ever catch up, and even if she did what would be the point. Based on how her life had gone so far, what future could she possibly hope to have? To her, it would just be more of the same, bounced from home to home, with men that touched her and no one to keep her safe from them, but herself. Emma wondered how she could keep going, wondered when the day would come that she wouldn't be able to protect herself and something really bad happened.

Much to Emma's surprise, Audrey actually talked to her about college, as if someone like her would be accepted, of course that meant she'd have to apply first. Just who was going to help her figure that one out, she wondered. If the adults in her world couldn't help her find a decent family, basic stuff as far as Emma was concerned, how was she ever to do something so far-fetched as to go to college. At one time, Emma truly would have considered college—years ago—before she had fallen far behind her class, her grades plummeting—before she was labeled as a worthless foster kid—before everyone's expectations were that she would grow up to be worthless trash. College, she thought…

Then the boy-talk. Audrey asked if there were any boys at school she liked, and of course, Emma always said no. She did not intend to be used as some bet by some sleaze ball boy again. Forget it! No—she was quite comfortable hanging out in her new home where people listened to her, talked to her, and really seemed to care about her. It was the first time she could remember where dating was not an issue. No one pressured her or tried to convince her that her world should revolve around some boy. Of course, Emma knew the boyfriend hype was well intentioned. Everyone wanted a boyfriend, it was what girls and boys did—they hooked up, but she just didn't seem to be very good at it, so why waste her time. Friends were no longer an issue either because she didn't have any. Sure, she talked to the girls in her classes and there were some very cool, nice girls in her home economics class, but they all had boyfriends and hung in a different circle than Emma…Emma being circle-less by choice now.

"No," Emma said with a grin, thinking how silly her foster mother was to ask. "There are *no* cute boys in any of my classes. They are all *dumb*."

Emma noticed Audrey's expression, knowing it meant they couldn't all be dumb. "Seriously, boys my age really are dumb. They still act as if they are in junior high. Maybe boys have changed since you were in high school," Emma allowed. "Why are they so immature—talking like babies—punching girls on the arm—talking about spit, and farts? Gross!"

Audrey laughed a deep raspy laugh.

"No," Audrey said with a smile. "It sounds like they haven't change all that much since I was in school. Give them some time. You'll see. They grow up, eventually."

Emma put her glass of pop on the end table and said, "I don't care when they grow up. I don't want anything to do with them." She wrinkled her nose and looked down into her bowl of popcorn, searching for a buttery piece.

"Just give it time," Audrey said wisely.

Emma shook her head, thinking, poor Audrey. Things were so different now days. Boys were assholes, but she wasn't about to tell her very sweet foster mother that.

"Have you thought anymore about what you want to do after you graduate from high school?" Audrey asked.

"What's the point?" Emma asked.

"What do you mean what's the point? College," Audrey insisted.

Emma knew what Audrey meant. She had been on a college kick, but really, what was the point. She was so far behind she didn't think she would be able to catch up. Never in her wildest dreams had Emma thought she'd be an academic loser, but she was. Two credits, she thought, she was a sophomore with two lousy credits. But what did it matter? What was that people said about foster kids, oh yeah, she thought, they were trash, meant nothing, and they certainly weren't going to college.

"Audrey," Emma sighed, placing her empty bowl on the carpeted floor beside her chair. "You and I both know I'm not going to college. First of all, I can't make up my credits, and secondly, I'm a foster kid. Who's going to pay for me to go to school?" Emma knew she was asking a sensible question. It wasn't likely that her father was going to pay her way. The very idea was laughable. The man had beaten and molested her. *That* had been his fatherly accountability.

"And, I wouldn't even know where to begin to get into college. It's too late for me, Audrey," Emma said discouraged.

"There must be some program that would help you," Audrey insisted.

"We'll see," Emma said unconvincingly, as she tucked her legs under her.

Emma had been with the Harmons' for over a month, the only foster child, and so far, there was no talk of moving her. She began to wonder if maybe Audrey had decided to keep her permanently. They got along great. Emma had never met anyone quite like Audrey or her family. She just fit, like a missing piece of a puzzle that fell to the floor, and when you picked it up and examined it, you knew just where it belonged and Emma belonged with Audrey and her family. She felt it.

One sunny, almost fall afternoon, Emma walked home to an empty and quiet house. She knew Mr. Harmon was still at work and Audrey was still at the family services office working on a project. Whistling a little tune she had heard on the radio, Emma skipped up the back stairs to her bedroom. Still whistling, she walked into her bedroom to deposit her schoolbooks on her bed when she noticed a strange bag on her spare bed, and then looking to the left noticed a strange girl with short blonde hair looking in her mirror hung on the wall. The girl was a little shorter than Emma was, a little heavier around the middle and upon closer examination, her hair was more strawberry blonde than blonde, and possibly a fake strawberry blonde at that. Emma squinted, and thought, the girl looked to be about the same age, maybe fifteen.

"Hey," the girl said perkily, as she spun around. "I'm Cheryl!"

Emma looked at the girl suspiciously, unsmiling, and said shortly, "Hi."

Doing her best to ignore Cheryl, Emma walked passed her toward the bed she slept on, and dumped her schoolbooks in a heap. She glanced over at the other bed, the one that was always made, no wrinkles on the bedspread and noticed its rumpled state, now loaded with clothes. Annoyed, Emma wondered what the girl was doing in her room.

"So, I'm from up north," Cheryl said in a happy voice.

"Really?" Emma commented, sitting down on the edge of her bed, looking over at what appeared to be her new roommate.

"Yeah. I've been hangin' with some guys. You know," she said with a grin.

No, Emma thought, she didn't know.

"I love truckers," Cheryl said with a sigh. "My favorite is Peterbilts. They're so hot. I've just been hangin' out for the last few months, just travellin' around. How 'bout you?"

Wrinkling her brow, Emma responded, "Truckers?"

"Yeah…truckers. Have you ever been with a trucker? Ever been in a truck? What's your favorite kind of semi-truck?" Cheryl asked.

Emma had never really given the huge trucks that blew by on the highways much of a thought. They were big, loud, and caused cars to swerve as they blew by. A favorite—she didn't have a favorite. She didn't even know the names of the trucks.

"What's a Peterbilt?" Emma asked.

Cheryl sat on the edge of the clothing covered bed, excited to discuss trucks with her new roomy. Using her hands for emphasis, she made the shape of the nose of a semi, and said, "A Peterbilt is the kind with a nose. You know, it's not boxy, or flat-nosed like some trucks."

"Oh," Emma commented. "I guess those are okay."

As Emma looked across the space between the beds she thought about semi-trucks and the scroungy old men that drove them, wondering what kind of guys Cheryl hung out with, knowing right then that they would have little in common. Cheryl was obviously into very old men, and Emma, well if she wanted to date, which she did not, it would be a boy her own age, someone that had just passed their drivers ed test within the last year or two. She shivered, repulsed by the thought of older men.

Trying to think of something to say, Emma asked, "What grade are you in?"

"I haven't been in awhile. I'm thinking of being an emancipated minor," Cheryl said.

"A *what?*" Emma asked. She had never heard the term before and as she sat across from her new roommate, it was affirmed again, they were very different.

"Emancipated minor," Cheryl said.

Emma looked at Cheryl, shrugged her shoulders, and wrinkled her brow in response.

Cheryl explained, "When you turn sixteen you can live on your own. No one gets to tell you what to do anymore. I've already been talking to my caseworker about it. When I turn sixteen, I'm out of the system. I'll get a place to live and a job, then I'll be able to do whatever I want with no adults bossing me around. *Hell*, I've been on my own for years anyway."

Emma absorbed what Cheryl had said, about being sixteen and living on her own without adults telling her what to do. It sounded crappy to Emma. She realized they wanted very different childhood experiences. Cheryl wanted to be grown up before she was an adult, and Emma just wanted to be part of a family…to be a kid. She wanted rules, school, friends, brothers, sisters, parents, and grandparents—to be a normal kid.

"Hey girls," Audrey said.

Emma and Cheryl looked toward the sound of Audrey's voice. She was standing in the doorway.

"I see you two have met," Audrey said.

Staring at her foster mother, Emma thought, yeah it would have been nice to know some stranger was moving in. Why in *this* bedroom—Why not the bedroom down the hall.

CHAPTER TWENTY

Emma sat with her legs tucked beneath her on her favorite overstuffed chair in the living room, her usual TV watching spot, and wondered where Cheryl was. Her new foster sister was from up north, so she couldn't possibly be hanging out with old friends. Emma hoped she hadn't found a new Peterbilt friend to hang out with. Emma had thought a lot about what Cheryl said about becoming an emancipated minor, but she still couldn't wrap her mind around living the life of an adult at fifteen. She hoped it was a life she would never have to experience, but she wondered, what if the county ran out of foster homes. What if the day came when Audrey didn't want her anymore? Would she have to become an emancipated minor, become an adult when she was still just a kid, she worried.

Emma glanced over at Audrey sitting at the end of the couch near her, her usual spot as they watched Wednesday night sitcoms. Audrey was a few inches taller than Emma was, with short auburn hair, and skin bronzed by the sun. Her face was beautiful, not only made so by an inner glow, but by the hint of lines that travelled her face—a journey apparent of a happy life—of a life well lived and loved.

Audrey chose that moment to look up at Emma and say, "Em, I'd like to take you out of school Friday for a visit."

A visit, Emma considered. Whom would she be visiting during a school day? All of sudden she was overcome with excitement. Amy, maybe she was going to get to see Amy!

Emma grinned broadly at her foster mother and in excited anticipation asked, "Who, who am I visiting? Is it Amy? It's Amy isn't it? Am I going to where ever she is or is she coming here?" Emma was practically bouncing in her chair in excitement at the thought of seeing her sister.

"What time will she be here?" Emma squealed.

Emma was puzzled by the serious expression on Audrey's face. The grin slipped as worry replaced her excitement. What if something had happened to one of her sisters, Emma considered.

"No, Emma. We're not going to visit Amy. I'm going to take you on a visit to a group home in the next county," Audrey said carefully.

The blood rushed to Emma's face as she stared at Audrey. A group home. What was she *talking* about, Emma wondered hysterically. *Why— Why were they taking a day off from school to go there?*

Still looking at Audrey, Emma uncurled her legs and planted her feet on the floor. "We're going where? Do you mean that place Ben told me about the day Sheila beat the shit out of me for telling her what her son and boyfriend did to me?" Emma asked shrilly.

Emma slumped forward in her chair, her elbows on her knees, stunned.

"Emma," Audrey said in a soft tone. "It's just a visit."

"Just a visit? What do you mean just a visit? Why? Why are we going there? *Why visit?* Ben told me. He put a note in my file. He *promised* not to send me there." Flipping her hand in the air, Emma said, "I knew it. It's those people isn't it? It's Sheila. She wants me away so that I won't be able to tell anyone what happened to me in her home."

It was quiet in the room as the teen stared at the much older woman, her silence demanding an answer.

Breaking the silence, Emma wailed, *"Ben promised...."*

"Emma," Audrey said calmly. "It's just a visit. I'm not leaving you there. I promise."

"Well, why take me there at all? I'm not staying in that place. Audrey, who in their right mind would stick me there?" Emma shouted. A thought occurred to Emma, and she asked, "Are you kicking me out? Are you making me leave?"

Emma stared at Audrey thinking, it was happening. She had gotten sucked in again, and now she was leaving...again! Oh my God, Emma thought. What the fuck! How could she have trusted Audrey, or anyone for that matter? No one wanted her. They would never want her...*ever.*

Exhausted, Emma stood up and said, "I'm going to bed."

"Friday, Emma. It's just a visit, I promise," Audrey said.

Emma walked away, not believing the words her foster mother, the woman that had been more of a mother than anyone else in her life, had just spoken to her.

Thursday night, Emma tossed and turned in her bed, unable to fall asleep thinking about the drive to the home the next morning. She had no idea what to expect. The only reference she had for group homes was the movie she had seen on TV. In that show a nice girl, just like her, had been sent to a home too, and within the first few days at the home she had been beaten, then held down by the other girls at the home, on the floor of a bathroom, and raped with a broom handle. No one had seen it happen and no one had heard her screams. Emma knew it had just been a movie, but she knew those things happened in real life, and knew there was no way they should be sending her to a place like that.

It had been just a little over a year and a half ago that she had been living with her dad and two older sisters, beaten, punched, and groped. Was this better, she wondered? Had her life really turned out so much better? What the fuck…? All she had wanted was to be like all the other little girls in her class, with a parent that didn't grasp handfuls of her hair and pound her head into the wall, or punch her head, or grab her when she walked by, or the other things. How fucking hard was it for the idiot adults in her life to get it right, she wondered.

"How hard was it to be wanted somewhere," she whispered, as tears of fear and loneliness slipped from beneath her lashes and fell to her pillow.

The next morning, Emma stalled as long as she could in her bathroom, her not so private bathroom now that she had to share it with Cheryl. She stared at her reflection in the oval mirror placed above the fancy white sink, taking in the dark circles and puffiness under her eyes. Gripping the sides of the sink, Emma leaned closer to the mirror and examined her face, a smallish nose turned slightly to the right from a break years ago, and then she looked into the black centers of her eyes, with gold flecks bordering her green eyes. Releasing the sink, she took a step back toward the toilet with the black and white cushioned seat.

Making sure the lid was down, she slumped onto the seat, bent forward, and pressed her face into her hands.

What if Audrey left her at *that* place today, she fretted. What if she was lying to her just as Ben her caseworker had lied? He had promised he wouldn't place her there, yet here she was, in just a few minutes that was exactly where she was going, to the children's home. It didn't make any sense to Emma. A visit—Audrey was taking her for a *visit*? No one had ever just taken her on a *visit* to a foster home—No—No. It had never been just a visit. It was a dump and go, typically with no notice. Why should she think today would be any different, she wondered. As far as she was concerned, this was it. She wasn't coming back to her comfortable home; back to the foster mother she loved.

"Are you ready?" Audrey asked, a very tired and nauseous Emma, as she walked into the kitchen.

Emma peeked up through her lashes, and not saying a word walked over to the kitchen door, letting her actions be her answer.

Silently, Emma followed Audrey out of the kitchen. As Emma walked down the steps, an intense desire to run came over her, so strong she had to force her feet to move slowly forward. Willing her body not to bolt, she gritted her teeth, and having nowhere to run anyway, she focused on the car in front of her. She raised her hand to the silver door handle, and tugged it open, then slipped onto the seat next to her foster mother. Audrey kept up a constant stream of chatter during the thirty-minute drive to the home.

During the drive, Audrey shared the history of the home. It had begun as an orphanage in the 1800's, for orphaned children from the Civil War. Over the years, the name had been changed, from orphanage to school. Emma knew her foster mother was chattering away to sooth her jagged nerves. Pressing her forehead against the cool glass window, Emma listened to the deep raspy, strangely soothing, voice of her foster mother as she told the story once again about the home as she watched the fields pass by.

"Not just anyone can be admitted to home," Audrey said. "Someone in your family has to be a veteran, and your dad was in the army so you qualify."

Emma rolled her eyes as she listened to Audrey. She knew all about her dad's service to their country. She had been two-years-old when her mother had abandoned her, left her with her grandparents. Her grandmother had convinced Emma's mother to abandon her so her dad could get out of going overseas. It had been during the Vietnam War, and her dad was in basic training in Kentucky, preparing to be shipped overseas. Frantically, he tried to find a reason to be honorably discharged, and his children had been the perfect excuse. He was no hero.

Cracking her window, Audrey said, "The school was opened around 1869, for children living in Indiana, orphaned during the Civil War. It was built on the far side of town, at that time in the country, however over the last one hundred years or so, the town has grown, creeping up to the administration building of the school. Originally, the school was self-sustaining in many ways. It was built in the country on a large piece of land surrounded by rich Indiana farmland. They had many acres sitting idle so they found a use for it by planting large gardens, growing corn, tomatoes, and potatoes. Back then, people grew most of their food instead of buying it in the stores. The land surrounding the school was even big enough to keep a few cows, chickens, and space to build stables for horses. Eventually a school was built on campus to accommodate all the children living there, from kindergarten to twelfth grade. During the 1920's they added a gym onto the school and then built a recreational center for the children. Then they added onto the gym. They built a building for an in-ground pool. They even have their own cafeteria. Oh, but one of the first buildings built, in the 1880's, was their very own private hospital.

Audrey paused and took a drag off her cigarette. Then after she had disposed of the butt through the crack in the window, she continued, "In the early days, all the kids lived in one very large, three-story, red brick building, but over the years they built cottages, separating the girls from the boys. It's truly amazing, after one hundred years, it's all still there. Your caseworker showed me all the history on the place. Hell, if I were a kid, *I'd* ask to live there. It's like a boarding school. You know the kind of place rich people send their kids."

For a few moments, it was quiet in the car. Emma assumed Audrey had run out of things to share about the home.

Audrey broke the silence—Emma rolled her eyes, as Audrey said, "In the 60's, they built new housing for the girls staying at the school. That's what we're going to look at today. Instead of stand-alone cottages, they built Y-shaped cottages. It's separate cottages, but attached. If you were to go up in an airplane and look down at the school, it would look like a Y. It gives the girls on campus more privacy, kind of like a college dorm."

Emma listened to Audrey's voice, heard her words, and the more she talked the more nervous she became. It was like listening to a social studies lecture. Why was she trying so hard to sell her on the place, Emma wondered.

Audrey stopped the car in front of a tall brick building, and as Emma looked up, she counted the layers indicating how many floors the building had, at least three, and maybe a basement that she couldn't see.

Grabbing her handbag off the seat beside her, Audrey said, "I'll be back in a few minutes. I just have to check us in."

Nodding her head in the direction of the old building, Audrey said, "It's the administration building. Just take a few minutes," and then she was gone, leaving Emma, her stomach churning, and clenching her teeth in fear of what was coming.

Emma crossed her arms stiffly across her chest worrying, what if she left her there. What if it wasn't just a visit? Glancing out of the window at the tall building, at the empty lawn, and abandoned sidewalk, an intense desire washed over her once again to run. But clenching her arms tight, and closing her eyes to shut out the world, the young girl knew there was nowhere to go. She opened her eyes when she heard the car door click open and Audrey slid across the seat, a plume of smoke from her cigarette wafting toward her.

"It's just down the road," Audrey said in her husky voice.

Moments later, Audrey drove around a bend in the road and Emma examined the building, their destination at the end of the road, a one-story blonde colored brick building, with windows dotting the sides of the Y-shaped structure. Emma furrowed her brow as she considered the strangely shaped building.

"We're here," Audrey said with forced cheerfulness.

Emma glanced over and watched Audrey put the car into park. She took a deep breath to calm her racing heart. Then she took another deep breath.

"Are you ready?" Audrey asked.

Lying, Emma nodded her head slightly up and down.

A warm breeze whipped Emma's long golden brown hair into her eyes. Tucking a strand behind her ear, Emma looked around, up the long sidewalk toward the glass door, then to the field surrounding the side of the building, and then at Audrey.

Audrey spoke to the woman behind the reception desk while Emma, hands clasped nervously in front of her, looked around the room. There were three glass doors, which she assumed led to the separate sections of the Y shaped building. It was quiet in the room, except for the hushed voices of Audrey and the woman at the desk.

"Emma," Audrey said.

"Hmm," Emma answered in surprise as she looked over at her foster mother. Emma was hyper-alert as she stared at Audrey—dressed casually in shorts and a blouse and her usual flip-flops—as if it were the last time she would ever see her. Audrey was standing on the left hand side of the reception area by one of the glass doors.

Emma walked over and stood next to Audrey and looked down a long, white linoleum floored hallway. It was deserted. She could see doors opened on either side of the hallway, equal distances apart, at quick count six on either side. Turning away, Emma glanced back toward the reception desk. She snapped her head back to the glass door when she heard muffled screams and saw figures running down the hall, shaking their hands and leaping in the air. As if they could not stop, the young girls in the hall crashed into the glass door and wall as Emma jumped back in fear and shock, but Audrey held her ground, her hand on the door handle.

She couldn't seriously think they were going in there, Emma thought hysterically, as she looked at the girls faces pressed against the pane of glass. Emma could hear what they were shouting now, muffled but legible, *Let us out! We're crazy!* The screams...the horrible screams. One girl, her skin so white Emma could make out the purple veins in her arms, her hair white as if she were an old lady, was shrieking as she slid to the floor. Tangled into her was a black girl, her hair all crazy, was banging on the window. Emma counted eight girls smashed against the door, screaming, licking the glass door, and pounding their fists.

In horror, Emma watched as Audrey slowly pulled the glass door open, the noise deafening to her ears. Her eyes wide, Emma shook her head back and forth, as she stared at Audrey.

Audrey turned and looked back at Emma. "Come on," she said calmly.

They are insane, Emma thought in a panic. As she glanced back at the girls, still beating on the door to be free, and realized they planned to stick her in a place with crazy people.

Emma backed away from the door, away from Audrey.

"I'm not going in there," she gasped.

Terrified, Emma turned quickly and rushed to the door. If she had to, she thought, she would walk all the way back to Audrey's house. She just knew there was no way, short of physically dragging her, that they were getting her past that glass door. Emma walked across the threshold into the sunlight, her heart racing, and tears of fear stinging her eyes. The warm breeze caressed her skin as she ran to Audrey's car.

Audrey caught up with the distraught teen at the car, and as Emma sobbed, tears running down her cheeks, she said, "Don't make me go in there. Take me home."

"Okay," Audrey said quietly. "Come on. Let's go home."

❧ CHAPTER TWENTY ONE ❧

Audrey and Emma were quiet on the drive home and within half an hour Audrey was pulling the car up in front of her house. When the car rolled to a stop, Emma flung the passenger door open and ran across the lawn, up the narrow staircase off the kitchen, and up to her bedroom.

Gratefully, she found her bedroom empty and flung herself across her bed, sobbing a body and soul-shattering cry. She hurt. This, this is what it had come down to? They were sending her to a horrible place, a place for children that no one loved or wanted. Emma pressed her tear streaked face into her pillow and wondered, what was so very wrong with her that no one wanted her? "Why is it so hard to love me," she sobbed, as she clutched the pillow to her face trying to muffle her anguished cries. Her body shook with the intensity of her sobs. So unwanted—so unloved—no place—never a place to belong.

Lying on her stomach, Emma wiped her nose on her pillow and then turned her face toward the window as hot tears created a trail down her cheeks and throat. Trying to shut out the searing pain of her world, Emma closed her eyes tight. Exhausted, she drifted into a fitful sleep, haunted by a figure and the sound of pounding footsteps as she ran, trying to find some place safe to hide.

Weeks had passed since the visit to the home and one afternoon after school, Emma came home to find Audrey sitting at the kitchen table smoking a cigarette, with a half full cup of coffee placed in front her. Quietly,

Emma walked through the small room, intending to continue onto her bedroom when Audrey asked her to sit down.

"Emma," Audrey said.

Sensing something was wrong, Emma sat down at the table and watched her foster mother take a drag off her brown, thin cigarette,

Audrey avoided Emma's eyes. She exhaled a cloud of smoke and picked up the red lighter that had been lying next to her flowered coffee mug and began tapping it on the wooden table.

"Emma," she began again. "Your caseworker called this afternoon. She's decided to place you at the home."

Emma slouched in her seat and stared through tear-filled eyes at her foster mother, unable to catch her breath, unable to speak.

"Em, it's a great program," Audrey said unconvincingly.

Sighing, Audrey looked into Emma's eyes and said, "It will only be for a little while. There are just no foster homes available, and my home is only a temporary foster home." Crushing her cigarette in the square, metal ashtray, already filled with cigarette butts, Audrey said softly, "Em, just a few months. You can do it. They have a great program and you'll be out in no time."

Emma's eyes welled up with tears. She sniffed, and asked, "And *then* where will I go? You just said there is nowhere to put me."

Swiping the back of her hand across her nose, Emma cried, "Ben said he wouldn't put me there. He promised. He put a note in my file. He *promised*."

Emma ran her snotty hands through her hair and then put her head in her hands, looking down at the table as large tear droplets plopped, making shiny spots onto the table.

Slowly, Audrey said, "They seem to be having a problem with your case file."   Looking up, her head still in her hands, Emma asked, "What? What are you saying? They *lost* my file?"

"No," Audrey answered. "Just parts of it. It seems some notes from your last caseworker, Ben, are missing."

Emma propped her folded her arms on the kitchen table, and then in defeat, laid her head on her arms and listened to the rhythmic voice of her foster mother.

"Emma—just a few months. Just until they can find a permanent placement, until something opens up," Audrey said. Audrey flicked the lighter and held it to another of her long cigarettes, and inhaled deeply.

"They have a program all the kids go through at the home, based on each child's needs. They have a school on campus you can go to, and a ton of activities for you to be involved in. Shoot, they even have their own pool. It's more like a boarding school, like the kind for rich kids.

Lifting her head off the table, Emma said in a dejected tone, "Audrey, you saw those girls, just like I did." Wrinkling her forehead, Emma continued, "Do you *really* think I'm going to be okay there, with *those* kinds of girls? I've seen the movies. It's nothing like a rich kid's boarding school, unless of course they rape and beat up the rich kids too." Emma shook her head in confusion over how this could be happening. How could she, she wondered, be sent to that kind of place. Ben had promised her the day they stood outside Sheila's house that he would not send her there. He would find somewhere for her, a home, a real home.

"When?" Emma asked. "When do I have to go? How long do I have?"

"The end of the week," Audrey said quietly.

Emma wiped at the fresh tears with the back of her hand as she looked across the table at Audrey. She wanted to cry out, *why don't you want me*, but couldn't. She couldn't bear to hear the response she might get. It was obvious—she wasn't her daughter. Audrey didn't love her. Emma had opened her heart, again. She hadn't meant to. It had just happened, and there she sat, her heart in tattered pieces all around her, unwanted...so unwanted.

Thursday afternoon after school, Emma grabbed an oversized black garbage bag out of the kitchen pantry and carefully folded all of her clothes and placed them in the bottom of the bag. Once done, she heaved the bag on the floor next to her bed.

"Hey," Cheryl said, as she bounced happily into the room. "What do you say we get out for awhile? Have some fun!"

Looking at her roomy, Emma shook her head as she tiredly, much too tired for a girl her age, sat down on the edge of her bed. She wasn't in the mood to be with people, and wished Cheryl would hurry along with her new guy friends so she could lie down on top of her bed and just stare off, numb, into space.

Cheryl reminded Emma of Winnie the Pooh's friend, Tigger, as she bounced over to her and grabbed her hand, and as Emma protested, pulled her to her feet.

"Come on! You have one night. *Live a little!* At this point what the fuck are they going to do to you? After tomorrow, you're going to be locked up anyway. Christ, Emma, what are you trying to prove, and to who!? Stop trying to be so good," Cheryl insisted.

Emma looked into the brown eyes of her foster sister, and thought bitterly, *she's right.* Where had doing the right thing—hoping—expecting if she tried hard enough someone would love and want to keep her—gotten her.

"Fine," Emma gritted through her teeth.

Giggling, Cheryl said, "We need to find something for you to wear," and practically skipped across the bedroom to her dresser. She yanked a couple of light colored jeans out of the third drawer.

"What do you think?" Cheryl asked, holding a pair of jeans in each hand.

Emma walked over and grasped the lighter colored of the two, a pair she had admired the many times Cheryl had worn them, between her fingers. The fabric of the jeans felt soft, evidence they had been worn often. She held them next to her, judging the length. They had a spider web pattern down each side from waist to hem, and three buttons that would draw attention to her narrow waist. Worn with her strappy heeled sandals, she'd be darned cute, she thought.

This wasn't the first time Cheryl had invited Emma to go out with her, but Emma knew they didn't hang with the same type of crowd, but for one night, Emma considered—it was just one night. Besides, who cared anymore what kind of crowd she hung out with? After tomorrow, she'd be locked up anyway. *Live a little…Why not?*

"Can I borrow these?" Emma asked, as she held the faded jeans between her fingers.

"Sure!" Cheryl said with a smile.

Looking down at the jeans, she held in her hands, Emma wondered how she was going to get Audrey to allow her to go out with Cheryl on a school night. Cheryl didn't go to school, but Emma did, and what if Audrey said no.

"Audrey's not going to let me go out tonight. I have school tomorrow," Emma said.

"No you don't. Did you forget? You're leaving tomorrow, silly," Cheryl said with a smile.

"Yeah, but I have to be packed and ready to go early in the morning," Emma said. Emma hated the idea of disappointing Audrey. Hesitantly Emma said, "I'll go ask her. Just for a few hours—I'll ask if I can go out for just a *few* hours with you."

"Oh Christ, Emma! Stop worrying what other people think. Fuck it! Let's go out. No one can do anything to you." Laughing, Cheryl added, "What's Audrey going to do, ground you?"

Still not convinced, Emma walked slowly out of the room to find Audrey. Maybe, maybe she could still convince her that she was worth keeping, Emma hoped. Maybe there was still time.

An hour later, Emma was sitting on the back of a motorcycle, speeding down the highway, with her arms wrapped tightly around the girthy waist of a big, grisly looking older man. Cheryl was on the back of another bike, grinning over at Emma, her arms wrapped around the waist of her newest love interest. Emma knew the man she was clinging to, but wondered who Cheryl's friend was and how she had met him.

Emma was seated on the back of Randall's bike. Randall had been one of Amy's friends when she had lived at the Harmons' home. Over the past few months, Randall had made it a habit to check in on Emma. At first she had thought it odd that some man fifteen years older than her would stop her as she walked home from school asking if she needed a ride, or anything at all. The first few times he had approached her she had suspiciously said no and kept on walking. Eventually, during a phone call to Amy, she had asked her about him, wondering if maybe he was an old friend of hers, and was relieved when she said yes. Amy had told her Randall had been one of her friends, a protector. He was mountain of a man and Amy trusted him—knew she could go to him if she was in trouble and Emma could trust him too. From that conversation forward, if Randall pulled his motorcycle alongside her as she walked home from school, she knew he wouldn't hurt her and many afternoons she had hitched a ride home. He had never tried to touch her or hurt her in any way.

Cheryl's boyfriend led the way, and soon turned off into a gas station where the girls dismounted and headed toward the restroom.

"What kind of beer do you girls want?" Cheryl's gangly boyfriend called after them.

Not much of an alcohol drinker, Emma shrugged, assuming all beer tasted the same and kept walking toward the restroom while her three companions were left to figure the beer quandary out for themselves.

Emma hated gas station restrooms—and this one had been no exception—it was always the same, hold your breath and get in and out as quickly as possible.

She was standing by the bike waiting for Cheryl when Randall asked, "You warm enough back there?" It was a brisk, September Indiana evening with the sun sinking below the horizon and Emma hadn't brought a jacket.

"It's a little chilly with the breeze," Emma admitted.

"Here," Randall said, as he pulled his arms out of his long sleeved brown checked shirt and handed it to her. "Put this on."

Taking the shirt in her hands, she said, "But now you'll be cold," gesturing toward his short sleeved t-shirt.

"Don't you worry about me. I've got plenty of fat to keep warm," he responded.

Emma was pulling the warm shirt around her when Emma and her friend walked toward them, with grins wrinkling their faces.

"Let's go!" Cheryl shouted.

A few minutes later, and to Emma's relief, the two motorcycles pulled into a park on the north side of town because even with Randall's shirt, she was shivering. Cheryl's friend led the way to a secluded section of the park. Dismounting from the bike, Emma rubbed her chilled arms, barely catching the can of beer Cheryl threw at her.

"Come on, Em," Cheryl shouted. "Live a little. Don't worry about what tomorrow will bring. Just be a kid," and popped the tab off her can of beer, and as Emma watched, chugged the contents.

Emma raised the cold can of beer and read the label, then tipped the can and took a sip. She grimaced, *Ugh—Gross—Why would anyone want to drink this crap?*

"Em! Chug it!" Cheryl shouted, and began to dance around with a grin.

God, Emma thought—chug it? It was difficult enough just to sip the bitter crap. She tipped it back and holding her breath, took a big gulp, and then burped hoping no one had heard her. Two beers later, Emma started checking her watch for the time. Audrey had said to be back by 9:00 and it was already 8:30.

Still looking down at her black strapped Timex watch, Emma said, "Cheryl, we have to get going. It's almost nine."

Stumbling a little, Cheryl slurred, "Come on, Em! Why you in such a hurry to get back anyway? She can't *ground* you!"

Emma began to feel anxious. She didn't want to disappoint Audrey, especially on her last night at her house.

"Oh my God, Cheryl!" Emma shrieked in surprise and anger.

Emma was wedged against Randall's bike when Cheryl shook a can of beer and sprayed it all over her.

"Beer fight!" Cheryl shouted.

Emma flung her hands to her face trying to shield her glasses from the beer squirted in her direction. She smelled the stink of beer as it dripped off her hair. Using Randall's already beer soaked shirt, she began wiping the sticky, stinky mess off.

"*Fuck*, Cheryl!" Emma shouted in anger. "I fucking smell like beer. I can't go home like *this*."

Emma wondered what Audrey would think and just how pissed off her foster mother would be at her. She would think she was drunk, which she was not. It had only been two beers, she reasoned, over several hours. Panicking, she thought, she could have snuck in the house on time, and Audrey never would have known she had drunk a beer, now…how was she going to sneak in the house reeking of alcohol!

Looking across at Randall who was standing by a picnic table watching her, Emma said, "Randall, please take me home."

"Awe, come on, Emma," Cheryl said. "Let's have some fun. Don't go home. There is no reason to go home!"

"Are you sure?" Randall asked, as he walked toward her.

"Yeah. I have to get home. I promised Audrey," Emma said.

Glancing at Cheryl as she climbed onto the back of Randall's bike, Emma asked, "Cheryl, you coming?"

"Oh Hell no!" the tipsy teen said waving her on. "The party is just starting. You go on and be a good girl and go home."

Emma held tight to Randall's waist as he pulled out of the park thinking about Cheryl's words, *be a good girl*. Her words had stung. She knew what she had meant, don't be such a goody two shoes, but Emma didn't want to disappoint Audrey. As tears stung her eyes, more from misery and less from the wind whipping her face, Emma wondered, maybe she should have stayed out later, maybe all night. Who the fuck really cared anyway, she considered. What was wrong with her, she wondered? She didn't know why she couldn't just be okay to fuck up, and have a good time like other kids. My God! They were throwing her in a home tomorrow and here she was at, she peeked at her wristwatch, 9:30 the dial read, and then realized she was a half an hour late getting home. She was still trying to prove to someone she was good enough to care about—to keep—to want…to love.

Twenty minutes later, Emma climbed off the back of Randall's motorcycle, and after handing him his shirt, took a deep breath and walked up the steps to the house planning to sneak undetected to her bedroom. So much for her plan she realized, when she walked into a house full of people. Inwardly Emma groaned. Tonight of all nights had to be when Audrey and her husband had guests over. Reeking of beer, Emma tried to walk unnoticed past several people when she heard Audrey's voice calling from the kitchen.

Emma paused, mid tiptoe. She slumped her shoulders, and sighed. Shit, she thought as she walked toward the kitchen.

"Yes?" Emma asked, as she stood in the doorway of the kitchen. Emma glanced around at the other women in the room, at the cards held in their hands, and the drinks and snacks scattered about the table.

"Do you know what time it is?" Audrey asked angrily.

"Sorry I'm late," Emma said her voice barely audible. Looking down, she hoped Audrey wouldn't notice her stringy, stinky beer soaked hair.

"What's that smell?" Audrey demanded.

Emma blurted out the beer fight story, ending with, "It wasn't my fault she threw beer on me. I barely drank any and I told her we had to get home."

"Where is she?" Audrey asked.

"I have no idea. She said she wasn't coming home tonight," Emma said, avoiding Audrey's eyes.

"Get cleaned up," Audrey said angrily. "Get in the shower downstairs. Don't try to wash the beer off in the tub."

Her feelings hurt, and embarrassed, Emma climbed the stairs to her bedroom. Audrey had never spoken to her sharply before. She knew she was late, but Cheryl was right…it was her last night.

CHAPTER TWENTY TWO

After she had showered the stinky, sticky beer off her last night, Emma had tossed and turned on her bed. She kept replaying the movie about the girl that lived in a group home over and over in her mind. The young girl—Emma estimated to be about fifteen, maybe sixteen-years-old—had stepped out of a shower, a towel wrapped securely around her body, when other girls from the home had come in and wrested her to the floor. Emma tried to think about something else, anything but group homes and the girl held down on the floor...

She thought about Sheila's foster home, Sheila's son George, and Sheila's boyfriend Eric. Emma suspected that no one knew what had happed to her in that house—Ben, her caseworker, had been the only one to see the bruises on her face. No one had wanted to listen, no one had wanted to know—it was easier to just send her away than to charge a foster mother with assault and her son with attempted rape, and Eric—Emma wasn't sure what you called what he had tried to do to her. She didn't have a name for it.

As she lay in bed, Emma's mind raced. She tried to quiet her thoughts, but wave after wave of fear crashed over her. If only she had somewhere to run—somewhere to go—if someone would just hear her.

Emma felt as if her heart was going to explode in her chest as she followed Audrey through the door that led to the reception area of the group home. She was still thinking about the movie—the shower scene— where the teen was being raped. The girl had been alone in the shower room when six girls had walked in. One stood by the door serving as a lookout while the other five wrestled her to the floor, naked but for the towel wrapped around her body. They held down her arms and spread her legs, pinning her beneath the weight of their bodies. Then the leader of the group had taken the wooden part of a broom and rammed it inside of her. Emma was terrified as she walked toward the receptionist desk, wondering if she would end up like the girl in the movie.

Standing before the desk, a few feet behind Audrey, Emma felt like she did when she hadn't eaten in awhile—or when she had been in the sun too long—dizzy. It felt as if a heavy weight were pressing on her chest. She couldn't breathe.

This time when the receptionist buzzed to unlock the glass door, there were no screaming, crazy teen-aged girls running down the hallway, and this time Emma crossed the threshold into what was called Yates Cottage. A tall blonde woman met them at the door and escorted them into the bowels of the wing of the building. Yates cottage was the intake and evaluation cottage where new girls were introduced into life at the home. During that time, Emma was to be evaluated by cottage mothers, and through daily group therapy sessions, to determine which of the other five cottages she would be best suited.

Audrey's flip-flops sounded loud to Emma's ears—the only noise in an otherwise silent building. Emma followed close behind, passing the many doors lining the long corridor. Cautiously, she peered into the open doors, expecting the crazy girls from the other day to jump out at her. *Where was everyone*, she wondered.

The corridor opened into a large room. A waist high wall was off the main walkway creating a division between the walkway and sitting space. An orange couch was butted up against the far wall centered beneath a large window. A small wooden coffee table, empty of any items that would have warmed the room, sat in front of the uncomfortable looking couch, and a chair was placed on either side of the couch. A dark brown colored wood cabinet, with glass doors, stood guard on the wall closest to the foyer, and a few green plants were sprinkled about. Emma supposed the plants were there to take the edge off the sterile feel of the room. To the right of the corridor, was another smaller hallway with a glass door set into a large glass wall. The room was dark, but Emma could still see what looked like uncomfortable orange plastic cushioned chairs with wooden arms, and a television set. Spanning the hallway, Emma saw two more doors, one open, one closed, and it was the open door they walked toward.

Audrey remained by Emma's side at the table as the cottage counselor and cottage mother explained the program and the potential duration of her stay. As Emma sat rigidly in her chair, it seemed as if the words spoken to her came from a distance, barely audible. Her mind caught the words, a year. She might be there a year. Abruptly, she interrupted the counselor.

"*A year*," she said in shock. "You intend to keep me in here for an entire *year*? No way!" Emma's voice rose as she began to panic.

"Emma," the stern looking counselor said. "It's the standard time table for a child to work the steps of the program. I don't believe we have ever had a child work the program in under that length of time." As Emma stared at the thirty-something counselor sitting across from her at the table, she thought he looked as starched and sterile as the cottage, in his crisp no nonsense suit.

Well they hadn't ever met her before, Emma thought stubbornly. She would be damned if the assholes kept her locked up for a year because of something someone had done to her.

"I'm not everyone else," Emma insisted. "I won't be here that long. Three months, maybe six and I will be out that door."

"Well, if you can work through the program in that time, you can leave," the counselor stated. "But we have to make sure there is a placement for you when you graduate from the program. There will need to be an open foster home."

Emma worried that in three months—when she anticipated graduating and leaving the home—there would still be no place for her to go. She considered her foster sister Cheryl's words—emancipated minor. She wasn't quite sure what it meant, but if at the end of three or at the very longest, six months there was no home for her, she might have to consider it as an option, and asked, "How about an emancipated minor? If no foster homes open up, is that a possibility?"

"I suppose," the counselor said. "It's something we can discuss with your caseworker as you work toward the end of the program. Of course, you would need to have a fulltime job, and an apartment. We can talk about that when the time comes. For now, let's focus on the steps and the problems that will be awarded to you. For the next month your peers, your cottage mates, and your cottage mothers will evaluate you. At the end of that time, based upon their recommendations, I will award you problems that you will need to work through. The problems can be anything from low self-esteem, easily aggravated, to drug and alcohol. One of the techniques we use to help kids know when they have stepped out of the accepted boundaries is by distributing Bring-Ups."

Emma sat back in her chair, folded her arms across her chest and wondered, Bring-Up, what the *fuck* was a Bring-Up, but remained silent as the counselor continued.

"For example," the counselor said. "If one of the girls in your cottage, or *you*, does something you are not supposed to do, such as walk away from your group, or swear, then you will be issued a Bring-Up and the matter will be discussed during the next group session. Does that make sense?" he asked, as he stared at her.

"Sure," Emma said shortly.

Looking around the white walled room, Emma began to panic. How was she going to make it locked inside these walls for a day, let alone… however long it took to get through their stupid ass program, and *why was she here*?! Tearfully, Emma looked over at Audrey and mouthed, *take me home*. Audrey placed her hand over Emma's hands.

Too soon, the meeting was over and it was time for Audrey to leave.

The cottage mother allowed Emma, tears running down her cheeks, to walk Audrey as far as the glass door. Now that she had been transferred over to the care of the home, she wasn't allowed to pass through the door to walk her foster mother to her car. For the next month, Emma was to be locked inside the walls of the Yates cottage, and if she did try to open one of the doors, an alarm would sound.

Stopping at the door, Audrey quickly stuffed an envelope in Emma's hand and then hugged her tight, as if she might never see the teen again, and Emma hung onto her, not wanting to let her go. The door closed behind Audrey. Emma stood at the glass door and watched the woman she loved like a mother walk away. She didn't move from her spot at the door even after Audrey was no longer in sight, not until she was called away by the cottage mother.

The counselor walked to his office at the far end of the hall, and the cottage mother led Emma on a tour of the cottage, first stop being the TV room she had seen through the glass door. Emma stared at the glass wall with glass door inset and realized the purpose of the windows was so cottage mothers could watch the occupants of the room. The cottage mother could easily peek at the girls in the room, which Emma thought could be a good thing, except she hated the idea of anyone watching her. Kind of creepy, she thought.

They walked back through the sitting room, and then the cottage mother, using one of the keys dangling from her large key ring, unlocked the door explaining it was the kitchen. Emma was surprised when she walked into the room; it looked like any kitchen you'd find in a house.

Standing outside the kitchen, Emma waited as the cottage mother locked the door. The kitchen, the cottage mother explained, was always locked, except on Sundays when they prepared breakfast, the only meal they ever ate in the cottage. All other meals were eaten at the dining hall on grounds, and the girls and boys in each cottage walked together as a group with their cottage. All the cottages had assigned tables.

Emma was shown to her bedroom, a room with two twin beds and two dressers—what she imagined a college dorm might look like—with a bathroom attached, shared with the occupants in the adjoining bedroom. The shower had a triangular shaped tub, and as she stared Emma realized it was missing something critical—a shower curtain, or door. Anyone could walk in and watch her shower, Emma realized in horror. *Privacy...she needed her privacy.* Shaking her head, Emma considered, she could shower with her underwear on, or cover the important stuff with a washrag, however it went, it was going to be some very quick showers. She glanced down at the small tiles on the floor and gauged the size of the room, thinking about the movie she had seen about a children's home where a girl had been raped outside of a shower. The space was too tight, she thought. There was no way anyone could pin her down in the small space.

The cottage mother walked back into the other section of the bathroom. It was another tight space, just big enough for two girls to move about. There were two large closets, one for each roommate, and a lighted desk to be used for hair and makeup.

As Emma followed the cottage mother, she listened to the long list of instructions that were thrown at her in rapid succession, "On school days, you will get up at six, get dressed, and meet in the common area ready for the day. Don't be late! The weekends are the same, except you will be allowed to sleep in until seven. You will not be allowed to lounge around in your room during the day. If you need something from your room, you need to receive permission from whichever cottage mother is on duty. We walk to the dining hall as a group for breakfast. During the weekday after breakfast, you will walk to classes on campus with your group. All activities—everywhere you go—the girls from your cottage will always accompany."

Following the cottage mother, Emma walked across the hall to a closed door. Jingling her keys, the cottage mother unlocked the door and swung it open.

"This is the cottage mother's bedroom and office," the cottage mother said. "We rotate on eight-hour shifts between all the cottages, with one adult spending the night. If you need something for a headache, cramps, a band-aid, pad or tampon, just ask the cottage mother on duty and she will get it for you. We keep everything locked up in here."

As Emma stood in the doorway of the cottage mother's room, she tried to peek around the door, curious as to what was inside. Her mind locked on the tampon comment. She was going to have to request each tampon. Ugh, she thought—could they get any more personal than knowing every time she changed her rag? As her cottage mother continued, Emma, overwhelmed, managed to maintain a mask not allowing any emotion to show.

The cottage mother explained that there were four other girls living at Yates cottage, although there was space for twelve children in each cottage. Yates was used as the intake cottage for the girls and in about a month, once they got to know her better, she'd be transferred to one of the other cottages.

Later that afternoon, Emma met the other girls she would be rooming with for the next few weeks. For an hour, they tried to pry information out of her about her past. It wasn't that she was trying to be rude, she just wasn't used to having people ask her so many questions. They couldn't seriously think she was just going to open up to a bunch of strangers, she thought. There was some serious trust earning that was going to have to happen before she cracked the lid of just who she was. That, and she intended to maintain distance while she figured the situation out. She had no intention of being beaten up or raped by any of her new cottage mates. Emma had decided before she had arrived at the home that she needed to put on a tough act. She figured if she could just keep her head down, stay out of the way, and out of trouble, she'd be on her way—to where she didn't know.

At 4:00 O'clock, Emma followed the small group of girls down the long hallway to the counselor's office for their daily group meeting. It was a small room, off another small room. The room looked as if it had been converted from one of the bedrooms into the office she now stood. Orange plastic chairs were placed side-by-side, kind of a half moon shape, facing the counselor's desk. Each of the girls grabbed a chair and sat down, and Emma sat down quickly on the nearest available chair.

Emma began to perspire, worrying that someone might ask her a question as she listened to each of the girls talk, cry, and swear, as they shared details of their lives. As each of the girls took a turn to express a thought, or pain, Emma examined them.

Emma remembered the day she had come for a visit with Audrey, the day the crazy girls had run screaming toward the glass door. There had been more girls staying at the cottage then, but since then several had been transferred to other cottages.

Emma had met her new cottage mates before group had started. They had been quite chatty, rushing to tell her about the home and sharing details about themselves and each other, as much as they could cram in a half an hour. Four girls sat scattered in the room with Emma. Her new room-mate's name was Connie. She was a strange looking girl—turtle-like—with long legs, and she leaned forward a little when she walked creating a turtle effect. She wore large plastic rimmed glasses, had long straight, brown hair, and her lips always seemed to be bright pink, but not from lipstick. The youngest girl in the group was, Chantel. Some of the girls told Emma that Chantel had lived at the home for several years, and that she had been sent home at one point, but something had gone wrong and she had been sent back to the home. Emma had thought it sad when the group explained that Chantel had arrived as a little girl, when she was eleven years old. She had just been a tiny thing, they had said. Emma's new cottage mates had told her that at one time the home had been a real rough place. The older and bigger girls used to beat up the younger kids, like Chantel, but in the intake cottage, she had been safe. She seemed happy now, Emma thought, as she noticed her almost constant dimpled smile.

Then there was Stacey, she was the girl with hair more white than blonde and a complexion so fair, Emma wondered if she ever exposed her skin to the sun. She seemed nice enough. A little different though. Emma had watched her during the hour-long meeting and noticed she moved slow…real slow, and wondered why.

Peg was the cottage mate Emma knew she'd have to watch out for, the only black girl living in the cottage. She was short but stocky, and had already had what they called a Bring-Up, in the half hour since Emma had met her. Peg was mean, and from what the girls had said, she had an older sister at one of the other cottages that was even meaner. Both Peg and her older sister had lived at the home for over a year.

Deep in thought, Emma heard someone say her name. It was the counselor.

"Emma," he said. "Do you have anything you'd like to share with the group?"

Well, Emma thought, he had clearly presented it as a question, not a demand, and she responded shortly, "No."

Emma heard a shout of voices, as the girls began talking and gesturing wildly, saying that it wasn't fair that she was allowed to sit there and hear all about their lives while she didn't have to tell them anything about herself.

"Girls," the counselor interrupted. "It's Emma's first day. She's only been here a few hours and it's all new to her. Give her a little time. She can share with the group when we meet on Monday. Until then, everyone take time to help her get acclimated. Okay?"

The girls grumbled, and to Emma's relief she dodged talking for the day. After the meeting, all the girls filed out of the room; with Emma, wondering what was next on the agenda.

"Come on girls!" the cottage mother called cheerfully. "It's time to head to the dining hall for dinner."

Emma was tired as she walked with her cottage mates to the dining hall. She hadn't slept well the night before, if at all. She looked around as she walked, listening absently to the chattering around her. Off in the distance, she saw another larger group of kids walking in the same direction and wondered if they were going to the dining hall.

Chantel walked next to Emma and filled her in on life at the home.

"That's Illinois cottage," Chantel said, motioning to the group of girls Emma had been looking at. Peg's sister lives in that cottage. That's Oglesby," she said motioning up ahead. "We all eat at the same time, even the boys." Nodding her head in the direction of the girls from Illinois cottage, Chantel said, "Everyone will be checking you out 'cause you're the new girl."

Emma could see the girls from the other cottages looking their way and wondered if Chantel was right. Were the girls looking at *her?*

The dining hall was impressive, with large tables assigned for each cottage, much larger than the cafeteria at Emma's old high school. Emma shuffled behind her cottage mates, waiting her turn in the evening meal procession line. Grabbing an orange plastic tray off the counter, she slid it along the metal bars to the various food stations, selecting her dinner.

"Take anything you want," Chantel insisted, gesturing at all the dishes cradling various types of goodies.

Emma had never seen so much food, and it all looked delicious. As Emma stared at all the various flavors of puddings, different colored Jell-O, rolls, salad, and cakes, she realized she had a problem...how she was going to choose? A girl could really pack on the pounds in this place, Emma thought. As she looked passed Chantel, she saw there was even more. Ladies with hairnets were serving hot food too, and from what she could see, there were hamburgers, pizza, chicken and some kind of pasta.

Anything—Emma considered, as she grabbed a fried crispy chicken breast, mashed potatoes and gravy, macaroni and cheese and a small dish of orange Jell-O. Grabbing a chocolate milk, Emma followed behind Chantel to the table nearest the wall-to-wall window, peeking at several tables of boys and several tables filled with girls, all looking her way, some smiling, some not, as she passed by. A few of the boys grinned and nodded as Emma walked passed their table. As Emma scanned the tables, she noticed the mix of kids: Black, White, Hispanic, Asian, and various mixes.

After dinner, the groups of children walked back to their cottages in tight clumps just as they had arrived. The first thing Emma noticed when she walked into the common room of her cottage, was the large black garbage bag placed in the center of the room—her bag—filled with all her personal belongings. Good, she thought in relief. She had wondered what she was going to wear to bed that night, what she would use to brush her teeth, and what she would use to wash her face. She walked toward the bag, intent on taking it to her room and stowing her things in her closet when her cottage mother instructed her to wait a minute.

Walking toward her, the cottage mother said, "Let me go get a marker. We need to mark all of your things."

Emma maintained a straight face as if she didn't care, as if she knew what the woman was talking about, but she did care, and she had no idea what the woman was talking about. What had she meant, *mark all her belongings*, Emma wondered, as she stared after her becoming concerned.

The tall blonde woman walked back into the common room holding a black permanent marker and a clipboard with white paper attached. Seeing the marker, Emma wondered what her cottage mother planned to do with the marker and suspected it was something she wasn't going to be too happy about. Emma had intended to take the garbage bag to her room, in private, to unpack and find a home for all her things, but as she stood next to the bag, the other girls gathered around and sat on the floor. The cottage mother knelt on the floor and asked Emma to open the bag.

You have got to be kidding; Emma thought in amazement, as she knelt on the floor and untied the plastic bag. The top of the bag opened wide and Emma sat back on her heels as she waited for the next instruction.

"Okay," the cottage mother said, as she looked down at the paper attached to the clipboard. "I need you to take all the items out of the bag so I can make an itemized list of your things. Then I need to write your name on all of your clothes."

Emma felt the blood rush to her face in embarrassment. She didn't want to take all her clothes out of the bag—underwear, bras, and everything else—in front of her cottage mother and her cottage mates sitting close by, strangers she had just met a few hours ago. As she glanced up, Emma thought the girls looked like vultures, ready to fly off with her stuff. She felt so exposed. No one was supposed to see what she wore under her clothes, but here she was, pulling item after item out of the garbage bag she had packed the night before. Carefully, Emma placed the items hidden away in the garbage bag, onto the floor in front of her cottage mother.

When Emma was in the seventh grade, her stepmother had left her father. The timing couldn't have been worse for Emma. The separation had coincided with changes Emma was going through, changes all young girls her age went through, growing in all sorts of inconvenient and horrifying places and there had been no one to buy her clothes to accommodate her growing body. She'd had to borrow clothes from one of her older sisters, who had borrowed clothes from *her* friends. When Emma had become a ward of the court, a foster child, the state had given her foster mother at the time, a voucher for clothing. After years of borrowing clothes, and going without, Emma had appreciated her new clothes, much more than most girls her age. She knew most kids took things like clothes for granted, just as she had at one time. After the state had taken her from her dad's house, she'd had very little, and when she had run away from her aunt and uncle's home, she had lost everything she had acquired.

Carefully, Emma pulled items out of the garbage bag, stacking them in categories: underwear, bras, socks, jeans, t-shirts, sweaters, shorts, and belts. Her cottage mother picked up each piece of clothing, examined it, then with the black permanent marker, and as Emma watched in horror, wrote Emma's name in the waistband of each pair of jeans, shorts, t-shirt, sweater, each pair of underwear, and on the backs of her bras. Emma picked up a pair of baby blue colored silky bikini underwear and looked at the back, near the delicate waste band. Tears burned her eyes when she saw her name in black ink, bleeding through the fabric, and she thought, *Ruined...she has ruined my things.* Disgusted, Emma glanced over at her cottage mates as they leaned forward to see what was in the bag. She felt stripped bare before the world, the privacy that was so important to her, ripped away.

Later that night, after the contents of the garbage bag were neatly re-folded, and placed in the closet assigned to her, Emma pulled the enve-lope Audrey had shoved into her hand earlier in the day out of her back jeans pocket. Emma made the most of the few moments alone while her roommate, Connie, showered. She ripped open the envelope, unfolded the single piece of paper, and read the note.

Dear Emma,

Just a note to tell you that we'll miss you and we enjoyed having you at our home. Try not to be afraid of your new home, although it's a natural thing and its O.K. to be afraid but give it and the people a chance before you make up your mind if you like it or not. Nothing is easy at first!

I know you'll be O.K. and that helps me—to let you go because you're not a bad girl or smart mouth, nor do you have a lot of problems to be worked out—so it will be easy for you.

If I can come to see you, I will. If I can write to you, I will! If after awhile you can leave for a weekend, I'll come and get you and bring you here for the weekend. (if you want me too)

Just hang in there and share with everyone – You're <u>O.K.</u>!!

If you ever need someone to talk to – Write me or call.

As Ever,
Audrey

Tears slipped down Emma's cheeks as she read the letter, then re-read it. Realizing the sound of water had stopped; Emma quickly folded the piece of paper back into its envelope and shoved it under her pillow, and then swiped her tears away. Her heart felt raw. She wanted to go home.

CHAPTER TWENTY THREE

Emma made it through the week relatively unscathed by life and the girls at the home, falling into the military style structure of the home. She decided that being away from everything and everyone familiar wasn't necessarily a bad thing.

Although Emma was sheltered from the turmoil of the outside world, the home presented its own set of challenges. Maybe it was the grumbling thunder and the lightening flashing outside the walls of Yates cottage that was making all the girls so irritable. The girls had been at each other's throats all day, and Peg seemed to be causing the worst of it. It would have been the perfect day to escape to the quiet of her bedroom, if she would have been allowed. Emma wanted to do what she had always done, run away from the noise and the yelling, but this time, locked inside the cottage walls, she was forced to watch and listen in uncomfortable silence.

Sitting at the long table used for homework, Sunday breakfast, and on most nights, letter writing, Emma looked up from the letter she was writing to Audrey and listened to the argument taking place in the hallway. Peg was having a cow about something, probably PMS, Emma reflected as she turned her attention back to her letter.

"Peg!" Connie yelled.

Good Lord, Emma thought, as she looked up to see Peg burst around the corner of the hall, the other three girls, Chantel, Connie, and Stacey, following close behind.

Emma watched as the girls continued to follow Peg down the hall, thinking, *jeez, if you'd just leave her alone maybe she'd snap out of it.* She wondered if it had dawned on any of the girls that perhaps they were a big part of Peg's problem, after all, who wanted to be followed by an angry mob?

Trying to tune them out, Emma went back to her letter.

Emma!" the cottage mother said sharply. Marge was the cottage mother on duty. She was okay as the cottage mothers went. Actually, much to Emma's surprise and relief, all the cottage mothers were cool.

Marge was short, and stocky, with collar length dark brown hair. She wore baggy jeans a lot, Emma had noticed, and rather plain shirts. She was a student at the local university studying social work, and lived in one of the buildings at the home with one of the other cottage mothers. Typically, Marge was real laid back, but right now, she was downright annoying. Emma struggled not to show just how annoyed she was, barely able to refrain from rolling her eyes, but couldn't hold back the heavy sigh.

"Emma! You need to come over here and help your group. I'm giving you a Bring-Up for not stepping in and helping. We'll address that later. For now, get in there."

What? Emma thought, unable to hold back the scowl that wrinkled her forehead. Help—*help what,* she wondered, as she looked around curiously. It looked to Emma as if they were pissing Peg off just fine on their own. What was she supposed to do she considered. Inwardly protesting, Emma pushed her chair back and walked over to the group now shouting at Peg.

Emma was at a loss, not knowing what was expected of her as she stood staring at her cottage mates. She listened to what each of the girls was saying and tried to sort out the issue. Peg was shouting and her hair looked wilder than usual as if she hadn't run her pick through it all day, and the other girls were in fight stance, leaning toward Peg. It was three against one. At least that was how it seemed to Emma and she wasn't the one with three people going at her.

"Guys!" Emma shouted, trying to be heard over the chaos.

The girls ignored Emma's soft voice as they continued to yell at each other. Emma wasn't surprised. Her voice didn't carry even in a quiet room and right now, the noise created by the four pissy teenaged girls was deafening. No one was listening to anyone—how could they—when they couldn't possibly hear over one another. Putting her two smallest fingers in her mouth, Emma blew, just as her eighth grade math teacher had taught her, and let loose an ear-piercing whistle. Shocked, the four girls looked at her.

Now that Emma had their attention, she said, "Hey guys, why don't we go sit at the table and talk about whatever is going on?" her goal being to make Peg feel less attacked so they could figure out what was wrong.

Grumbling, Peg flopped her black slippered feet over to the table and slumped onto a chair as the other girls walked over and chose seats as well, with an air of, *we got this,* which Emma seriously doubted. Emma sat at one end of the table, out of reach just in case things got ugly. She had already experienced a few of those situations, where the other girls had wrestled an angry cottage mate to the ground.

Connie sat to Peg's right, close enough to touch her arm, and led the inquisition with, "What's wrong? We know something is wrong just by the way you're acting."

"Yeah, Peg," Stacey, said. "What's going on? Is it your family? Do you miss your family?"

Emma watched as Peg put her head in her hands, and pulled at her already crazy hair.

"I told you nothing is wrong," Peg mumbled.

As Emma watched, she wondered if there was anything wrong or if the poor girl was just grouchy, and tried to jump to her rescue, as she said, "Is there something wrong, Peg? What started all this?" looking at the three girls seated near the angry teen.

Connie glared at Emma through her thick, large plastic rimmed glasses and said defensively, "She was banging things around back in her room. She's not supposed to be back there, so yeah I'd say something's wrong."

"Maybe she's just having a bad day," Emma commented. "Does there always have to be some major event going on to justify a bad mood? It happens."

Peg lifted her head up and looked at Emma.

"You weren't even there. You were in here writing your *letter* so you don't know," Connie said defensively.

"Now," Marge interrupted, "let her talk. Respect her input. You *all* have valuable information critical to the group."

No, Emma thought, she had no idea what was going on, but it seemed to her they were making matters worse by pushing Peg, literally into a corner.

"Peg," Emma asked calmly, "did something happen? Did you get a phone call or a letter or something? Or maybe you are just having a bad day or tired…?"

Looking down at her fingers, Peg answered, "I got a letter. Sometimes I just miss home, my life and my friends. I don't think I'm ever gonna get outta here."

Peg's words touched Emma's heart. She knew how the young girl felt. She missed her family too.

A half an hour later the girls had worked through what had been weighing heavily on Peg's heart and mind, and then the meeting turned to address Emma's issue.

"Girls," Marge said. "What do you think of how Emma didn't want to participate in the group's problem? If someone in the group is having a problem, it is *all* of your responsibility to help her, but I've noticed during the past few issues, Emma has chosen *not* to participate."

"Yeah, that's right, Connie chimed in. "You're no better than any of us, but you sit there like you are."

Emma squirmed uncomfortably on her seat as her cottage mates shook their heads in agreement and looked toward her end of the table. Not making eye contact with anyone, Emma listened to the girls talk about her, about how she never wanted to help anyone—remain uninvolved—as if she were some kind of princess. Emma's face was hot with embarrassment, feeling as if she were under a microscope as the teens spoke in animated tones about her shortcomings as a caring cottage mate. Thoughts careened through Emma's mind, things she wanted to share. She had lots of things she wanted to say—things that might help her cottage mates—but the words were trapped inside her. She struggled to say something, to explain, but couldn't.

As a child, survival had meant not drawing attention to her herself—being invisible—hiding her pain as best she could. It was what her dad had taught her starting at a very young age. He had beaten the reality into her that expressing her feelings—showing tears—could hurt, and it had hurt, every blow to her body had been agony. Now she didn't know how, and feared if she allowed anyone in—exposed her tender heart to anyone—she would open herself to unimaginable pain.

Emma knew she was different from the other kids just by watching them, the way they seemed to laugh so easily, and said whatever popped into their minds. It didn't seem to bother other kids as it did Emma to show anger or cry in front of people, as if it were okay to do so. She cared what people thought of her and didn't want anyone making fun of her, or using her sensitivity against her. Her experience with sensitivity had been that it was similar to a wounded animal, once kids found out you were the sensitive one in the group you became a target for their cruel fun. It hurt, even as Emma sat at the table listening to the group's comments about her, their words cut through her like a knife.

After the meeting was over, most of the girls went back to the TV room while Emma resumed writing her letter to Audrey. It was a short letter, as she struggled for something happy to share.

CHAPTER TWENTY FOUR

Nothing better to do on a rainy Sunday afternoon, Emma sat sideways, swinging her legs over the arm of one of the uncomfortable chairs in the TV room. The other girls from Yates cottage were strewn about the room. *Boring*, Emma thought, as she stared at the TV screen. There was nothing to do. No activities were planned and dinner wasn't for another two hours. She had woken up that morning bored before she rolled out of bed, wishing she had somewhere to go, something to break up the monotony.

The credits from the Sunday afternoon movie scrolled across the screen. It had had been a stupid comedy—Emma's favorite type of movie—but today it hadn't done much to improve her mood, or anyone else's she noticed as the girls stood up and started grumbling. Emma swung her legs over the arm of the chair and sat up as the other girls walked out of the dark room, made even darker by the gloomy weather. It was a windy day, and the sun was completely hidden by dark clouds. It was a blah, fall feeling kind of a day.

Emma looked up when she heard the door open, wondering which of the girls were bored enough to come back in and stare at the idiot box with her.

"Em!" Connie shouted. "Stacey's freaking out! Come on! We need you!" then she was gone.

Groaning, Emma walked slowly across the room in no hurry for the drama she knew was coming. Peace, for God's sake, why couldn't they just have some peace once in awhile, she wondered.

The sounds of screaming and shouting met Emma's ears when she opened the glass door to the hall. This time, as she paused to brace herself for the potentially long drawn out battle of wills with her cottage mates, Emma noticed the shouting seemed more frantic, more strained than usual. When she arrived at the long table near the kitchen, Emma quickly saw the problem. It was Stacey, the white haired girl with pasty skin. She looked like a wild, caged animal, as she paced back and forth, whispering something under her breath as she pound one fist into the palm of her other hand. Emma had never seen Stacey this way. A shiver ran down Emma's spine. One of the girls had told her that Stacey had some serious problems—that she flew into rages every so often—that she had schizophrenia, but Emma hadn't believed it. If anything, Stacey moved slow as a snail, strangely slow, and was always pleasant—strangely so.

Emma jumped in surprise as the seventeen-year-old girl threw a chair across the room, seemingly oblivious to the damage she could have done to one of the girls or the cottage mother. This was not some PMS, or attention-wanting situation, Emma realized.

"Emma!" Mrs. Hays, the cottage mother shouted. Emma liked Mrs. Hays. She was one of the regular cottage mothers, a very cool, black woman, married with two little kids. Like all the other cottage mothers, Mrs. Hays was very straightforward and didn't take crap from any of the girls in the home. Emma liked knowing where she stood with adults, hated the lies and manipulation that she was so accustomed to, with caseworkers, foster parents, parents…generally, most adults.

"Get in here!" Mrs. Hays said, waving frantically.

Out of reflex, Emma's hands flew to her ears as stunned, she watched Stacey throw something at the large mirror hanging on the wall behind the table in the common area. She heard and saw glass shatter and fall in jagged pieces to the floor. Snatching her hands to her sides, Emma realized someone needed to steer the group of girls away from the broken glass scattered about the floor, or someone would get hurt. Too late to move in, she watched as Stacey bent down and grabbed one of the larger of the pieces of glass.

Shit, Emma thought. Cautiously, she skirted the group leaving plenty of space between her and the shards of glass. They really needed to stop shouting at Stacey, Emma worried, as that seemed to be aggravating the situation. Standing behind a wooden chair, Emma watched and listened to Stacey whose words made no sense to her ears. It was gibberish. Everyone was shouting at the same time, Stacey was yelling nonsense, and the other girls were shouting at Stacey to put down the jagged piece of the mirror. To Emma, her cottage mates seemed to be enjoying the turmoil, perhaps a reprieve from their boring Sunday afternoon.

Emma whistled and the girls stopped shouting and stared at her just long enough for Emma to say softly, "Why don't we all sit down and talk."

Emma knew from experience that shouting made people nervous. It made *her* nervous, but when voices were brought down to a reasonable level and when given space, the feeling of being threatened, angered, and scared diminished a little, and she hoped in this case, enough to get the piece of mirror from Stacey. Emma watched as blood trickled from Stacey's hand down her arm. Then she looked up at Stacey's face and realized the girl was unaware the blade-like glass had cut into her hand, as she continued to hold tight to it.

Emma pulled out her chair and looked at Stacey encouragingly, with a small smile, and said softly, "Let's sit down."

Stacey walked around the table and pulled out a chair near Emma. Emma pretended there was nothing amiss as the bleached white looking girl, with red blood trickling a path down her arm, sat down. Emma's heart was pounding in fear, but she tried to appear outwardly calm—not wanting to upset Stacey—not sure what she might do.

"She needs a Bring-Up!" Connie yelled from the other end of the table. "She can't get away with what she just did!"

"Yeah," the girls, now seated at the table, chimed in.

Raising her hands in the air, Emma said gently, "Why don't we discuss that later," as she sensed the energy building in Stacey again. "For now, let's just talk. Let's try to *help* Stacey."

Connie scowled at Emma, and Emma turned away from her, tuning her out. Emma turned toward Stacey and hesitated for a moment as she stared at her cottage mate—so distant—still clutching the piece of mirror—not sure what to do next.

"Stacey," Emma said softly. "Stacey, are you okay? Did something happen?"

"I don't know," Stacey, slurred in a far away voice, and looked blankly at Emma.

Moving slowly, Emma placed her arms on the table. She was concerned about the sharp object Stacey held in her hand knowing at any moment she could hurt anyone of them.

"Stacey, do you think I could have that thing in your hand?" Emma asked, as she nodded her head toward Stacey's hand that held the blood stained piece of mirror.

Slowly, Stacey looked down at her hand seemingly unaware she was clutching the jagged piece of mirror. Emma watched as the disoriented girl opened her hand—not wincing from pain—not changing her expression at all. She reached her hand toward Stacey, and carefully took the piece of mirror from the palm of her hand and laid it on the far side of the table. As she continued to look at the blank expression on Stacey's face, Emma continued to talk to her in a soft soothing voice, as she would a small scared child.

Her voice barely a whisper, Emma asked, "Are you okay now?"

Stacey shook her head up and down. The teen was out of it, Emma realized in amazement. She had never seen anything like it before. It didn't seem as if she even felt the cut on her hand.

"Stacey," the cottage mother said, standing next to her chair. "Come on, let's get you cleaned up," and slowly she reached out and touched the girls arm, helping her stand. As Emma watched, Stacey shuffled slowly behind Mrs. Hays out of the room.

"Girls," Emma heard Mrs. Hays say from the hall. "Grab a broom and start sweeping up that glass, but be careful you don't cut yourself."

After helping Chantel clean up the glass, not knowing what else to do, Emma walked back to the TV room. She walked to the oversized window and stared at the gray sky, and feeling a chill, rubbed her arms. Soon it would be time to walk to the dining hall. Maybe that would improve everyone's mood, Emma hoped.

When it neared five O'clock, Emma walked back to the common area ready to get out of the cottage for a while even if it was just to the dining hall, when Mrs. Hays made an announcement. "You have a cottage mate that needs your help," Mrs. Hays said. "So tonight we'll just eat here at the cottage. I already called the dining hall. They'll make up sandwiches for us and deliver them here."

Emma wanted to roll her eyes but knew better. She'd get a Bring-Up if she did, so quietly she pulled out a chair and sat down.

When Emma came home from school the next day, the cottage mother on duty told Emma and her cottage mates that Stacey had been taken from the home. During the afternoon group meeting, the counselor explained to the girls that Stacey had problems that couldn't be handled at the home. She needed care she could get only at a hospital. The counselor tried to draw the girls into conversation about what had happened with Stacey, wanting to know how they felt. As the conversation drifted around her, Emma tried to imagine Stacey's life in a sterile hospital, dressed in a hospital gown, and wondered if they would medicate her so heavily she wouldn't be able to think, or feel. Emma cried inside for the lost girl and hoped she would be okay.

It was a somber group that entered the dining hall that night, each trying to come to terms with the loss of Stacey, and each thinking of their own pasts, presents—wondering about their own futures. The dining hall seemed quieter than usual to Emma's ears, and knew that the other cottages had been informed during their group sessions about Stacey. Emma could see the drawn expressions and emptiness in many eyes as she walked passed with her tray. So many sad and unwanted kids, Emma thought with a heavy heart.

Emma was sitting at her usual evening spot, the table in the common area writing a letter to Audrey when she heard a scream. Then she saw Peg rush out of the TV room and disappear down the hall. Emma couldn't see what was going on. She could hear shouting, and what sounded like banging on a door. Then she heard Chantel and Connie's voices yelling. Slumping her shoulders, Emma sighed. She placed her head on the table for a moment and groaned, thinking, not again. Slowly, she pushed the heavy wooden chair back and walked toward the raised voices, as Peg ran by, screaming. Then Connie ran passed shouting, "She's trying to get out of the building!"

Still emotionally drained from Stacey's collapse, Emma wasn't ready for another cottage mate issue. Slowly, Emma followed the three girls down the hall and saw Peg pounding on the glass door leading to the reception area, screaming, "Let me out!"

Marge, the cottage mother on duty, met Emma outside the room the cottage mothers used as their office and bedroom.

"What's going on?" Marge asked.

"I have no idea. I saw Peg run down the hall and now she's screaming for someone to let her out. Probably just stress from the other day with Stacey. It's got everyone shaken up," Emma answered.

As Emma watched, mid-way down the hall Connie and Chantel grabbed Peg's arms—a big mistake Emma thought, clenching her teeth. The girls were asking for even more trouble than they had. Peg was a scrappy, stocky girl, and in Emma's opinion, Connie and Chantel must have lost their minds if they thought they could physically subdue her.

Emma was proven right as Peg, looking like the hulk, flung her arms up in a massive upward motion and knocked the two girl's hands away, sending Connie into the wall and Chantel to the floor. Peg stormed toward her bedroom, with the girls scrambling after her. Before Emma could make it to the bedroom, Peg ran through her bedroom door and then toward the common room. Emma wasn't about to run laps around the cottage trying to catch Peg. She knew eventually she would tire out, and hoped it would be sooner than later.

Marge got to Peg first and said, "Stop. Peg stop! Let's just sit down and figure out what's going on."

"Tell them to leave me alone! Stop following me!" Peg shrieked, as Connie and Chantel ran around the corner from the hall where the bedrooms were located.

Marge held up her hand to hold the girls back. "Okay. But you need to talk to us. We can't help if you won't talk about what's bothering you," Marge insisted.

"I want the *fuck* out of here!" Peg wailed. "I'm sick of this place. I can't take it anymore!"

Emma pulled back a chair and sat down, hoping it would trigger the others to do the same. As usual, Connie was in confrontation mode standing close to Peg as if she was a prison guard. Emma examined Connie as she had many times before. She couldn't figure her out. She looked like such a nerd, so what in the hell was she doing in a place like this, Emma wondered. Emma hadn't noticed any major issues with the girl, just that she was an instigator looking for a fight, which was funny because any one person in the cottage could take her, even Emma. She smoked, and in Emma's opinion, it was only to appear cool. What was she doing at the home, she pondered. Whatever it was, she annoyed the hell out of Emma. She hated sharing a room with her. Connie was moving over to Grant cottage soon, and Emma couldn't wait to be rid of her.

Finally, the three girls sat down while Marge stood at the head of the table, waiting for trouble, Emma suspected. Peg was one of the physical kids in the cottage, and Emma was glad Marge was on duty. Marge was stocky and taller than Peg was, and she looked to Emma like she had played sports in high school. If Peg got out of hand, they were going to need Marge to step in.

"What's going on?" Connie demanded.

"I want out of here!" Peg insisted.

"Well you're not going anywhere, just like the rest of us until you work through the program!" Connie snarled.

"Well, what's going on?" Chantel asked with her typical compassion.

"I just don't want to be here! That's it. I want out!" Peg shouted.

Emma watched the girls, knowing she had to say something or she'd get a Bring-Up.

"Peg, this isn't like you. Talk to us," Emma said softly.

Peg looked toward her end of the table. "I just want out of *here!*" she shouted, and stood up so fast she knocked over her chair.

Connie jumped to her feet and stood next to Peg, blocking her from leaving the area.

Emma lowered her head and shook her head from side to side. Rolling her eyes, she thought, Connie, you are making everything worse.

Peg stepped back from her chair. Connie stepped with her and grabbed Peg's upper arm in a vice grip. Trying to shake her hand away, Peg twisted her body as Chantel, with a loud scraping of her chair on the linoleum floor, stood up. It happened so fast. Emma wasn't sure *how* it happened, but in the midst of Peg trying to pull away from the two girls, she was thrown to the floor. The girls were tangled under the table and chairs. Emma pushed back her chair and rushed over to the three girls. Fists were flying and feet were kicking as Emma knelt down into the mix. Emma grabbed one of Peg's fists and helped restrain her until she calmed down. Worn out, Peg's body went slack.

It was agreed there was no point in trying to draw Peg into any kind of reasonable conversation while she was in such a combative mood, and as far as Emma was concerned, Connie was just as big a problem. Marge recommended Peg spend the night in the Quiet Room. The Quiet Room was one of the bedrooms at the very end of the hall stripped of all comforts. The only object in the room was a mat, like the type you would find in a gymnasium. When someone needed the solitude and reflection the Quiet Room offered, they were stripped of everything, interaction with the other girls, no meals at the dining hall, and even their clothes were taken from them. Considered flight risks, they were issued a pair of threadbare pajamas with the initials of the school written in black ink on the waistband. The entire cottage was on lock down, unable to leave the cottage for any reason, not even allowed to go to the dining hall. Not only was the person in the Quiet Room punished, but so were her cottage mates— punishment by isolation—stuck in their cottage where nerves became even more brittle.

The next day, Emma was exhausted and irritable from her sleepless night spent listening to Peg's echoed cries from the Quiet Room. It had been too many days, too many weeks of drama. She wanted to get away from everyone, just go to her bedroom, and shut out all the noise but it wasn't allowed. As part of the group, she had to remain engaged in order to help her cottage mates whenever they had a problem. Worn out, she felt she was about to have a meltdown of her own. If only she could get away from everyone and get some sleep.

Sitting at the long table in the common room, Emma stared down at the blank piece of paper. It was another gloomy day. The sun was hidden behind gray clouds, and a blustery Indiana wind rattled the windows on the opposite side of the room. It was a backdrop noise for Peg's constant shouting. Stuck in the cottage for the day, Emma decided to use the time to write letters.

September
Dear Audrey,

I hate it here! I'm always in a bad mood, jumping on everyone for no reason. I'm getting a lot of bring ups now.

There's a girl that's been here for seven months, they sent her to the hospital the other day, and I don't think she's coming back.

Another girl has been here in the intake cottage for seven or eight months, she's never even made it out of the evaluation cottage! They locked her up in the quiet room last night, they said for maybe as long as three days!

We have group meetings at least three times a day, and I have yet to hear anyone say I belong in here. They keep asking why I'm here because I obviously don't need to be. I just need to find somewhere to live. I'd rather come back to town, and if they'd open up some foster homes I'd like to come back. Do you think my old caseworker can help me? Can I call her?

I'm sorry this letter wasn't more cheerful but this is the way I feel in my heart.

Love Always,
Em

Superintendent's Progress Notes – Emma

Emma is a shy, quiet girl who was frightened of the other girls at the time of placement. She was extremely withdrawn for the first week but gradually began to come out of her shell.

She had difficulty accepting her placement at the home. Her initial lack of involvement with the other girls created a few problems, she was considered "snobbish." As she became more comfortable in the cottage and began to participate in group activities, this problem resolved itself. However, Emma never lost that certain basic reserve that seems inherent in her personality.

CHAPTER TWENTY FIVE

After staying almost a month at Yates cottage, a permanent cottage was selected for Emma, Grant cottage. After weeks of evaluation, she was placed with the most mature group of girls on campus. Almost at full capacity, Emma was to share the cottage with ten girls and within a month, much faster than usual for her, Emma settled in and began to feel comfortable.

Emma was happy with her new roommate, Claire. She was one year older than Emma was, had long black hair, and was taller by several inches. Emma had met very few people with such an even temperament. Nothing seemed to rattle Claire. If a problem arose with one of the other girls, Claire spoke her mind, and no one tried to stop her. Maybe it was because she was always so bubbly, so when something serious or stern crossed her lips, ears perked up. Claire was the perfect roommate. She was just as consciences as Emma was in keeping their room clean and most of the time, they won the cottages cleanest room award and it was Claire and Emma that competed against the other girl cottages for the cleanest cottage award. Many weekends, Claire and Emma occupied their time stripping the long cottage hallway of wax build up. Grant was the most worn of all the girl's cottages, with old stained linoleum flooring, so it was rare that the girls won the trophy, but when they did, it made all the long hours of work worthwhile.

As Emma got to know the girls in her new cottage, she wondered why most of them were there. She was truly baffled. Connie had been transferred to Grant cottage a week before Emma and she still couldn't figure out how someone so nerdy could be sent to the home. Then there was

Connie's roommate Erin, a short, chubby young girl with the thickest glasses Emma had ever seen. Erin and Connie constantly had group meetings called on them due to their anger issues, but Emma suspected their issues were forced and fabricated so they'd fit in.

Beth was tall, stocky, and sweet. Emma knew she had no business being at the home, but was thankful she was there. Beth was a lot like Claire, skipping around the cottage all the time, borrowing earrings, and offering to loan her things. It almost *did* seem more like a boarding school instead of a children's home, at least what Emma imagined a boarding school would be like.

Megan was a short little thing who never seemed to stop grinning. Emma knew Megan had a lot of buried pain because of something that had happened to her. Megan didn't like talking about sad things even though the counselor tried to dig it out of her. Teary eyed, but still with the smile, she'd just say it was no big deal. They all knew what it was—it was a *very* big deal. Emma and the rest of her cottage mates knew no one should hurt Megan or anyone that way, especially from someone you loved and trusted.

Then there was Michelle, the oldest in the group, beautiful, with long brown hair, and a model's body and face. Everyone loved her, all the girls at Grant cottage, and their teachers. Michelle had lived at the home for a year and a half and seemed to be in no hurry to leave. She had a boyfriend on campus, and had a routine down. Emma wasn't sure why she wasn't anxious to leave the home to go back to her real life, but she knew Michelle's younger sister lived in one of the other cottages. Maybe having her sister living at the home made it easier for Michelle, Emma speculated. Michelle was Megan's roommate and their bedroom was across the hall from Emma and Claire's room.

Corey was a year younger than Emma was, and had arrived a few weeks after her. Issues with Corey's underwear had landed her a group meeting. It had been discovered that she didn't own a single pair, so a shopping trip for underwear had been arranged. She was nice enough, but Emma knew they had little in common.

Cheryl, Emma's foster sister from the Harmons' home, had been sent to the home a month after Emma. She had been assigned to Grant cottage also, and was sharing a room with Corey at the far end of the hall.

Eileen was the youngest in the group, a black girl, almost as beautiful as Michelle was. At twelve-years-old, she was already a mother to a one-year-old. Eileen was feisty, with a quick temper. Emma liked her. She was like a kid sister to all the girls in Grant cottage.

Jena was Eileen's roommate, and was also a mother. She was fourteen-years-old, and had a baby boy, who was eighteen months old. Group meetings related to Jena stemmed from her anger issues because she missed her son. It was heartbreaking for all the girls to listen to Jena, teary-eyed, talk about the little boy she missed so much. Jena was the quiet one in the group and Emma often wondered if she felt like the odd man out since she and Eileen were the only mothers in the group.

Emma appreciated various things about each of her cottage mates, like the way Eileen could run, laughing down the hall to her bedroom in pure joy, for no reason. Or when Jena made some funny crack about something, or when on the rare occasion she made some sharp comment about one of the girl's rude behavior, in a funny way. Emma knew as quiet as Jena was, she heard and saw everything.

Emma envied the freeness that her cottage mates seemed to have in showing happiness, silliness and even in exposing their angry sides. To be so free, she thought. Often Emma wondered what it would feel like to just let go.

Each morning, Emma hurried to get ready for the day not wanting to keep anyone waiting for breakfast. She was always dressed and waiting well before it was time to leave the cottage for the dining hall. After a breakfast of whatever she chose, she walked with her group to the school and waited in the brisk Indiana wind for the school bell to ring and the doors to open at the on-campus school. Once inside the warm walls of the one-hundred-year old building, Emma spent her day listening to the rickety old English teacher with the tissue tucked into her belted dress, and the middle-aged math teacher that constantly walked around the classroom looking over her shoulder as she worked.

Emma's favorite classes were health and PE. The teacher seemed to be in touch with life and most importantly, she listened as the other girls asked her questions about anything that came to mind. Unlike most adults, the petite, long blonde haired twenty-something teacher, gave them answers. She wasn't the kind of teacher Emma was used to, not the flowery, fake kind that was of no help at all. She knew better than to sugar coat or lie to the girls because in many ways the girls had experienced more trauma than many of their peers and even many adults would ever know. The topic during the afternoon class typically turned to boys and babies. Her teacher never shied away from her students questions. Instead, she made the most of the opportunity to teach the girls important things about the world, such as how to handle boys, and the difficulties of being a mother and the complexity of relationships.

CHAPTER TWENTY SIX

All eyes were on Emma during the afternoon group session. Today was her day, the day she was to tell her life story. Bert, the cottage counselor had given her three days to prepare what she would present to her cottage mates. She had never discussed her past—her life—with anyone before, at least not in detail. An off-handed comment here and there to one of her foster sisters and a foster mother had been the extent of her sharing. No one had ever asked her about her childhood before—no caseworker—no police officer…no one.

Her stomach churned as she looked at her cottage mates—all eyes on her—smiling in encouragement to begin the story of what brought her to the home.

Taking a deep breath, Emma looked down at the floor and said, "My real mom left me when I was two. She left my sisters and me with our grandparents, and then took off with some drunk. My dad was in basic training at the time.

My dad met my stepmom while he was in basic…he needed someone to take care of us. She was young, barely eighteen, just a kid herself. He drank a lot back then. He was violent. She left when I was three because he used to beat the crap out of her. She wasn't the only one he beat; he beat me too. I ended up in a foster home soon after she left. Something happened to me. There are several stories, but the most believable is that he beat me up so badly, probably because I had dared to get sick, that I almost died. I don't know who to believe. My gut tells me they are all lying or telling bits of the truth that help them sleep at night. I remember being really sick.

I remember my dad yelling at me for getting sick and then having my head beat into a wall. That was his favorite quick punishment when I made him mad. He'd grab a handful of my hair and then bash my head into a wall. Anyway…I was out of it and he wouldn't take me to the hospital…probably because he would have been arrested. My grandma finally made him take me to a doctor…not our regular doctor. Some hack. It was bad. That's what happened to my hearing, and my face was messed up—paralyzed—because of what he did, and then didn't do. When I look in a mirror, I still see that ugly little girl. Kind of his gift to me…it's always there. Then if that wasn't enough, I used to have people in my family point out the issues with my face. They'd get real close to my face and examine the damage, my droopy eye, the difference between the left and right," Emma said, as she touched the right side of her face, then let her hand drop to her lap. As if I couldn't see it without having them point it out to me."

Emma sighed and smiled bitterly. "You know what *does* make me mad? That they lie about it, and that I have to hear people *pretend* that I just happened to lose my hearing…as if there couldn't possibly be a connection to my head being slammed into a wall and all the things wrong with my face and my hearing." Clenching her jaw, Emma closed her eyes for a moment, and shook her head, and thought, *were they so stupid they really thought anyone believed their lies.*

"After that, my two older sisters and I were put in a foster home for a few months. We were returned to our dad when my stepmom went back to him." Absently, Emma waved her hand in the air and said, "She left years later, after someone told her he was sexually abusing my sister. I don't know if she knew he was sexually abusing all of us…it doesn't matter. She left.

Emma stared at a spot on the wall across the room and said, "My dad used to play this little game, kind of like the boxing or wrestling matches on TV. He would have my older sister Amy stand on one side of the room and make me stand across from her. Then he would try to make us fight, but I didn't want to fight. She would hop around and punch me on my arm, trying to get me to fight her. Then she'd knock me down and punch me in the face, with him sitting on the couch shouting, 'Punch her—Punch her.' I love my sister so I didn't fight back. He used to tell us that he was a small kid growing up and people picked on him…he just wanted to teach us to stand up for ourselves." Shaking her head, Emma said, "You don't hit people you love." Looking down at the floor, Emma insisted, "I wouldn't hit her back."

Sighing, Emma continued, "My sisters and I ended up in foster homes when my sisters told a nurse what our dad was doing. We went to court. Not much was said. No one wanted to know anything really, not the judge, or the attorneys. I guess someone talked to my sisters about my dad. I waited for someone to ask me something…but no one ever did. Anyway, he wasn't charged. He went home and my sisters and I were stuck in foster homes. We stayed with relatives for a while, in different homes—we were separated. Then we stayed at a home that was crazy with parties. My uncle tried to run over us in a pool and tried to burn the house down. I ran to the police and then we were all sent back north to more foster homes. Then more foster homes—with groping men. Then I was beaten up by a foster mother when I told her that her son kept crawling in bed with me and tried to give me drugs, that and her boyfriend was a perv. That little incident started because I was standing up for my sister," Emma said wryly. "And now I am here. That's pretty much it," Emma said, matter-of-factly, as she looked up at the counselor.

There was a hush in the room for a moment.

"So, Emma," Bert said slowly. "How do you feel about your dad and the things he did to you and your sisters?"

How did she feel about her dad—*was he kidding*, Emma thought sarcastically.

"How do I *feel* about him?" she asked. Frowning she said, "He's sick. He's an ass. He's hanging out with his teeny bopper girlfriend while I've gone from one shithole foster home to the next. He should be in jail. The only reason he isn't is because he or my grandma knew the judge or *someone* that had some influence." Shaking her head, Emma said in disgust, "Adults don't listen to kids. So far, most of the adults in my life, and that includes foster parents and caseworkers, have been a big fat disappointment."

"What about your sister, Amy?" Bert asked. How do you feel about her?"

Amy was more complicated. She loved her older sister and had spent years as a little girl following her around trying to protect her from all the bad stuff. Somehow, Emma knew that she and Amy *felt* the same, but handled the pain they felt differently. Emma had run away and hid when her family had been cruel to her, hiding her tears so she wouldn't be made fun of or beaten to toughen her up and Amy, she always seemed to be tough as nails. But Emma suspected it was her way of hiding how she really felt. Emma tried so hard to understand when her sister was mean to her, because she knew about the bad things, because the bad things happened to them all, just in different ways. But it hurt so badly to have someone you loved so much, lash out at you.

"Amy?" Emma asked, as she looked up. "I love her."

"Even when she hit you and was mean to you?" Bert asked.

It was a raw subject, one Emma did not want to discuss, and slowly she said, "Yes. It was awful what she had to deal with. I understood why she was so angry and did the things she did. I love her."

"Are you angry with her?" Bert asked carefully.

Emma felt her heart begin to pound. She was done with her life story—done talking—and said shortly, "No."

"What about your stepmother—are you angry at her?" Bert asked.

Looking across the room toward the door, Emma said distantly, beginning to shut down, "She did what she had to do to protect her children. She had done all she could for us. There was no one there to help her either."

Bert watched Emma and knew he couldn't push her too hard. She had shared enough. He knew she had something bottled up inside—who knew just what it was—and needed to let out whatever it was slowly. He made a few notes on the pad of paper placed before him and then dismissed the girls for the day.

The next afternoon as Emma sat on the hard plastic chair during group, she wished the counselor would wrap up their afternoon meeting so they could hurry to the dining hall. Her stomach growled as she half listened to what Bert was saying.

"Due to the low AWOL count on campus, the cottage parents and I have decided to reward Grant cottage, as well as all the other cottages, with a dance this Saturday night," Bert said.

As Emma watched, the girls began to jump up and down in their seats, and shout in excitement.

Leaning toward her roommate, Emma asked Claire, "What? What did he say?"

Grinning, and grabbing Emma by the shoulders, Claire gave her a playful shake and said, "A dance. We get to have a dance this Saturday night!"

A dance. Was that allowed, Emma wondered.

A few days later, Emma was dressed in her cutest top and jeans as she walked with her group to the Rec Hall. The Rec Hall was a large one-story brick building. It had a large foyer with couches and chairs off to the side and a hallway that wrapped around the main room. In a secluded section of the hallway, there was office space, a hair salon and a craft area. The main room was the focal point of the building with a ceiling as high as a gymnasium. There were three sections to the main room. One end of the room had a stage where a large jukebox sat. The center of the room had a large space for dancing, and off to the side of the dance floor there were small tables and chairs sprinkled about. On the opposite side of the room, up three steps, were two pool tables and foosball tables.

Emma sat with a couple of girls from her cottage, Michelle and Megan, and sipped on red punch, and nibbled on sugar cookies as she listened to music pound out of the jukebox. They pointed out their boyfriends from Bennett cottage, playing pool on the upper landing. A few minutes later, Michelle gestured the boys over. Emma estimated Michelle's boyfriend to be about six foot three as she looked up at him, and the two boys that had walked over with him were around six feet tall. After introductions, Michelle and Megan walked out of the hall with their boyfriends, leaving Emma alone with a boy named Tanner, another boy from Bennett cottage.

Ugh, Emma thought. She had no idea what to say to the boy seated across from her. He seemed to be just as quiet as she was, but he *did* smile a lot she noticed, as she smiled back. Emma checked out Tanner, seated casually, too casually, across the small table from her. His legs were sprawled under and to the side of the table, and one of his arms were slung casually over his thigh. Every so often, he would run a hand through his long hair, pulling it back off his face. Perhaps he should tie that black mane back in a ponytail, Emma considered.

Conversation non-existent, Emma asked, "So Tanner, how long have you been at the home?"

"Oh, about a year," he responded easily.

Wow, that was a long time, Emma thought. "Are you still working through the program?" she asked.

"I'm done," he said with a silly grin.

"Well then why are you *here*?" she asked curiously. If she were done, she would have been long gone.

Tanner shrugged his shoulders, and said, "It's not so bad here."

Not so bad here? Who was this guy, Emma wondered.

"Nah," he said with a smile, and a flip of his hair. "The counselors, the guys, and even the cottage dads are all cool. Could be worse. Yuh know?"

Emma absorbed what Tanner had said. Could be worse. Yeah…she supposed. Life could be much worse and had been for her. He had a point. Maybe this ultra casual guy was more with it than he seemed, she considered, as she stared across the table at him. His complexion was flawless. The black stubble on his chin matched his flowing black hair that reached to the collar of the unbuttoned shirt layered over a colored printed t-shirt. She stared at his straight white teeth, and light brown eyes with sprinkles of gold around the outer edge.

"You wanna dance?" he asked.

"Sure," Emma answered.

Emma allowed Tanner to take her in his arms, pull her close, and snuggle his chin into her hair. Snuggling her cheek into his collarbone, Emma relaxed knowing she didn't have to worry about Tanner putting the moves on her, not with twelve cottage parent's eyes glued to her back. She was able to enjoy the moment without fear of being groped or *anything*. It was nice to be held, she thought, as she closed her eyes. They swayed to the music of the slow song, and the next.

The evening passed quickly, and as the lights flickered, one of the cottage parents called out, "Five minutes!" into the microphone on the stage. Tanner led Emma out of the hall and they were pulled into the crowd of other couples, led by many of the guys from his cottage.

The teens walked toward a private section of the hall, but not too far away from everyone that she was afraid. It was as if he sensed her timidity, and that if he didn't move slowly, and gently, she would bolt like a skittish animal. With one hand at the base of her spine, and the other resting gently beneath her hair at the nape of her neck, Tanner looked down into

Emma's eyes, his expression soft and sweet. Emma looked up into his eyes, extended her arm, and grasped his shoulder gently and closed her eyes. Their lips touched—gently—softly—for a moment.

"Let's go!" Emma heard Tanner's cottage parent shout behind them, a good distance away.

Pulling away, Emma looked up into Tanner's eyes as he smiled down at her.

Softly he asked, "Would you go with me, Emma? Just see me?"

Surprised, Emma paused for a moment. She didn't want to hurt his feelings, and in a whisper said, "We just met, Tanner. Can we wait a bit? Get to know each other first?"

Grinning, he took her hand in his, and said, "Yeah. Sure."

They walked toward the entryway as the same cottage parent that had made the *let's go* announcement whistled. Emma suspected this was a routine for the cottage parents. They gave their boys just enough time to do exactly what Tanner and Emma had done…feel like they were normal teenagers. Emma did feel like a normal teen as she walked with her group back to her cottage, a small smile curving her lips. She noticed all the girls were quiet with similar smiles, and darned if the nerdiest girl in the cottage didn't have a hickey. Well, Emma thought, that'll be a Bring-Up. Sure hope it was worth it and by the look on Erin's face, it had been.

October
Dear Audrey,

I told my life story the other day to the group and last week I was given four problems to work through.

We had an AWOL the other day. We were on our way to the dining hall and Megan, just out of the blue, started running for the cornfield. Three of us in the group started running after her. I was out in front and they shouted to stop when I got to the edge of the field. She turned around and came back because there was a machine in the field. They didn't count it as an official AWOL, so it didn't count against our days.

I met a boy at the dance the other night. His name's Tanner. He asked me to go with him. I thought it was kind of fast, considering we had just met so I told him we should get to know each other first. He's real cute, with hair almost to his collar. He has a cute smile and smiles a lot and he's quiet like me. He is sweet.

Well, I'm going to have to go for now. It's almost 10:00.
Tell everyone I said hi!

Love,
Em

December
Superintendent Progress Notes – Emma

Since Emma's transfer to Grant cottage in October, she has had a difficult time adjusting to her new peer group. Even though she was well received by a rather positive and mature group, she wanted to remain as un-involved and isolated as possible. Staff and peers have since spent considerable amounts of time reassuring Emma that she will benefit most from her placement by becoming involved with her peers and showing problems rather than isolating herself and attempting to keep every comment and behavior in check just to rush through the program.

Emma told her life story to her peer group, and was assigned four problems. While telling her life story, Emma was matter of fact about most events of her life revealing few feelings about her disappointing placements with family. She was hostile towards her father, and stated that in general most authority figures have been a disappointment to her.

The major problem that Emma has shown thus far in placement has been her low self-image. She constantly puts herself down and quickly gives up tasks when frustrated. Her expectations for herself are very high. If she receives a B on an assignment, she belittles herself for not making an A. Her peer group and staff work with her daily reinforcing her positives.

The school reports that she is cooperative and usually earns the maximum daily points; however, as mentioned above, she is highly critical of less than perfect performance.

Emma requires considerable encouragement to initiate participation in sports and other recreation activities. Because of mandatory participation in volleyball, she has discovered she is quite good and can now even take pride in her performance.

CHAPTER TWENTY SEVEN

The Christmas season arrived at Grant cottage with a blanket of snow and a ten-foot blue spruce. The tree had been delivered to the cottage along with a box of old Christmas decorations, pulled out of storage. One blustery afternoon as the girls sipped hot chocolate, they decorated the tree with red and gold shiny ornaments, and other odds and ends that had been fashioned into ornaments by residents of years past. It was the biggest Christmas tree Emma had ever seen before, at least inside of any of the homes where she had lived. She stood back and admired the tree shimmering with tinsel. There was just one thing missing…her sisters, she thought, with a heavy sigh.

Emma's cottage mates had told her that all the cottages had their own sponsors from the community, and each Christmas they visited the children for an afternoon. The Sunday before Christmas, three elderly couples arrived at the cottage bearing gifts of cookies and candy canes. The cottage mother on duty had led the couples on a tour of Grant cottage and now they were seated in the common area, where the Christmas tree sparkled in front of the large window overlooking the winter field, empty now but for a layer of white fluffy snow. The three elderly couples were sprinkled about the common room as the girls sang Christmas Carols they had practiced during the last month, in honor of their visit.

Once the performance part of the afternoon was over, the girls knelt on the floor in front of the elderly people, displaying their best manners, as if they were all the oldest of friends. It felt weird to Emma, almost as if she were a pet. She couldn't wait until they left because her face was getting sore from all the fake smiling. Emma knew the sweet looking, smiling adults sitting in her cottage were there out of the kindness of their hearts, but it still felt so weird to her.

Over Christmas break, visits with family were arranged for most of the girls from Grant cottage. A visit was arranged for Emma to spend an entire week with her sister Amy, Aunt Carey, and Uncle Stan, at their two-story white farmhouse in the country, ten minutes from the home. Emma's Aunt Carey fascinated her. She was the only woman in her family that Emma knew, that wore pretty dresses and worked in an office. During her younger years, her aunt Carey had served in the military; to Emma, her aunt was courageous and beautiful...*normal.* When Emma thought about her aunt's life, it gave her hope that perhaps everything would work out for her too. Emma reasoned that just because she had been born to an abusive father and a mother that had abandoned her—passed from foster home to foster home—it didn't mean life was going to remain as it was. She had an aunt that was doing just fine. Why couldn't she have that kind of life one day, she wondered. Amy had been living with their aunt and uncle for a while, commuting to the nearby high school in the city, and it had been decided that once Emma had completed the program at the home, she would move in with her aunt too. Emma was getting another chance to live with one of her sisters, this time Amy.

Emma was nervous about the visit to see her sister Amy over the holiday. Amy was having a little trouble adjusting to her new surroundings at their aunt's house, just as Emma had at first at the children's home. It had been a few too many changes in the last year and a half for the girls, and most not good. For months, Emma had been going off campus for visits with her sister, a unique privilege. Finally, she was able to spend time with her sister, trying to capture the remnants of their childhoods before it was gone. It had been two years since they had left their dad's house and so much had happened in that time. Amy was a junior in high school and Emma a sophomore, and by the time Emma moved into the spare bedroom at her aunt's house, Amy would have one last year of high school before she moved onto whatever was next for her. But nothing had turned out right, and even now, it didn't feel right. Had it been too much time—was it too late to try to recapture the childhoods that had been stripped from them? Emma agonized over this question, fearing it was too late to rebuild what had been broken, not wanting it to be so.

January
Superintendent's Progress Notes- Emma

In spite of a difficult adjustment to her new peer group, Emma has begun to make progress in developing a more positive self-concept and trusting attitude toward authority figures. A major factor in her development has been her friendship with one of the stronger and more positive peers in her group. Emma has been increasingly confrontive to peers who behave inappropriately, and is more vocal in group meetings and mini-meetings. In December, Emma was awarded one of her problems and is presently requesting meetings on her authority problem. Emma appears committed to making positive changes in her life, even though she is often filled with self-doubt that she is not making changes or that the program is not helping her.

Cottage life staff report Emma is cooperative and has never been involved in any major acting-out incident. On several occasions, Emma and her roommate have received the cleanest room award for her cottage. Emma's standards in cleanliness and personal grooming are high, and she is often the most objective when judging her peer group in these areas.

Emma does well in school, and usually earns the maximum number of points possible. The semester has just started, and Emma's grades will be forwarded.

Emma's health is good. She recently was seen by an ear specialist who is in the process of testing to determine if the hearing in Emma's left ear can be improved.

Emma enjoys most recreational activities, especially the socials where she can spend time with her on-grounds boyfriend. During Christmas, Emma went Caroling with Grant cottage and attended the Christmas program at the local planetarium.

Emma was very anxious about her Christmas vacation. She was confident that she would not show any major problems, but was very concerned about her older sister. Emma also sees growing problems between the sister and their aunt. Emma was hopeful that during Christmas vacation she would be able to help with the situation. Unfortunately, she was unable to resolve the situation.

❧ CHAPTER TWENTY EIGHT ❧

March,
Dear Audrey,

*H*i! How have you been? Me…Great! Guess what, I got my last
problem awarded on Monday. I made it through the program in six
months after all. I thought I could do it three months but you know
what…it started off rocky, but it turned out to be a pretty good six months.

*Being awarded my last problem was the best birthday present. I am now
sixteen. Next…I need to find a place to live then I'm up for future plans, then
pre-staffing, then home visits…then the group's opinion, then staffing, and
then finally, I'm done. I'm happy, but I'm worried about where I'll live.*

*I don't really want to live with my aunt…Amy and I are having prob-
lems again. I have visited her school, and I hate it. I'm so afraid it won't work
out if I move in with my aunt, and I'm afraid of moving into a traditional
foster home where I don't know anyone, 'cause none of them have worked out
so far, except for your home.*

*Maybe I'll see about some semi-independent living. I don't know. I just
want everything to work out this time and I want to be happy. Could you give
me some suggestions? I could sure use some guidance. Amy's been getting into
some trouble and I'm trying to steer clear of trouble, but I think she needs me
and that's why I feel pulled to live with her. Maybe I can help her.*

*Good for you for joining an exercise class. I exercise every morning and
at night. I have lost weight and inches. You really feel good after awhile.*

Bye for now.
Love ya,

Em

March
Superintendent's Progress Notes- Emma

Emma is making steady progress through the program. It is anticipated that Emma will be at the future plans stage of the program by the end of the school year. Emma has recently expressed an interest in discussing a placement other than with her aunt. She has not specified a particular location nor type of placement.

Low self-image was, and, periodically still is, her major problem. During her discussion she focused on parental rejection, and the movement from placement to placement as factors which inhibited the development of a more positive self-image. Acceptance by the group and a determination to have a happier future were given as reasons for developing a more positive attitude about herself and her placement at the home.

Emma continues to be involved with her group in mini-meetings and with giving appropriate Bring-Ups to peers. She is aware of the changing relationships and priorites within the group, and often alerts staff to developing problems. In group meetings, she is not as verbal as several of her peers, but she has definite opinions about the progress of her peers on their problems and has the courage to make unpopular decisions when necessary.

Following further testing on Emma's left ear, her condition was diagnosed as moderate to severe hearing loss.

Emma participates in most of the varied activities offered at the home. She especially enjoys the co-ed socials where she can spend time with her on-grounds boyfriend. Emma has exhibited appropriate behavior with her boyfriend and makes an effort to keep this relationship secondary to her interest in her peer group.

Emma continues to visit with her aunt and sister almost weekly. She has detached herself somewhat from her sister's problems, and appears to feel less responsible for her behavior.

CHAPTER TWENTY NINE

Emma hadn't met her goal of working through the program in three months, but she had made it through in six months, faster than any teen at the home, and now that she had graduated from the program, she was allowed to take summer classes off campus. She and Beth, one of her cottage mates, were the only two children at the home attending classes off campus. Since it was summer, the girls were only allowed to take two classes, and they chose a basic speech class and the classroom portion of Drivers Ed. Emma had been pleasantly surprised when she walked into her speech classroom on the first day of the summer session. There were only a handful of other teens seated in her speech classroom. Emma had been sweating the speech class, thankful for the small size. It was tough enough to talk during group at the home, but talking in front of strangers at a strange school would have been *brutal*. Each morning, as the other girls lounged around the cottage enjoying their summer break, Emma and Beth were driven to the local high school by one of the campus staff.

The last few months had been good ones for Emma. She loved her teachers, cottage mothers, cottage mates, and had a great boyfriend. She no longer felt that she needed to explain why she didn't act how people thought a foster kid should act. At the home, Emma was allowed to be herself, dorky, goofy, or even if she were having a bad day, that was okay too. One of the toughest parts of the program had been allowing others to know her, and showing emotion, especially if she were sad or angry. For much of her life, Emma had been made to feel everything about her was all wrong, from the way she looked, ran, talked, stood, and even how she felt about things.

Emma was in the final stage of the program, the stage where she had to find a permanent placement outside the home, the next stop, and hopefully the last. Arrangements had been made for Emma to live with Amy at her Aunt Carey's house, but the plan seemed to be unraveling. Emma visited with her sister on most weekends now, and she was getting the distinct feeling Amy wouldn't be there much longer.

Amy had hooked up with an old boyfriend who lived a few towns over, about an hour away. Emma knew Amy hated her new school, and she wasn't thrilled with it either. It was even larger than the last school that Emma had attended.

Emma had a feeling Amy was going to run again, which meant Emma had a decision to make. As much as she loved her aunt, the desire to live in her home had more to do with Amy. She so badly wanted to be with her sister, to be the sisters she had always dreamed they could be, but she was finally seeing that just wasn't going to happen. It had been a dream—one she had focused on for a long time—one she was going to have to let go. That meant she was back to square one, right where she had been when she had arrived at the home...home-less. Where was she going to go, she wondered. She couldn't live with Audrey her last foster mother, because she had only been a temporary licensed placement, and besides that, she had given up her license and was no longer a foster mother. Emma had gotten much better at sharing her feelings, her fears, concerns, and even what made her happy, but this was big, her fear of having nowhere to go, so she put on a happy face and tried not to think about it, and hoped it would work itself out.

Not only was Emma allowed off campus for summer school, but she was also given the privilege of having a summer job on campus. She had been given several job options to choose from, and she had chosen to work at the Rec Hall. It wasn't a glamorous job. She was janitor, but it suited her just fine. It was a job where she could move around and get a little exercise. Typically, during the day, the hall was empty except for the two staff members that kept to themselves in their offices. Alone, Emma was able to crank up the jukebox and get lost in her thoughts. As a resident of the home, Emma still had to follow a schedule, and account for her movement around campus. The cottage mothers needed to know where she was going, and proof of her work schedule, but now Emma was no longer required to walk with her group to all locations around campus. Many afternoons, after spending hours sweeping and mopping the Rec Hall, instead of making the long trek back to Grant cottage, Emma would opt to meet her cottage mates at the dining hall. The freedom of walking unescorted to the Rec Hall, to the dining hall, and to her cottage, with the warm summer breeze caressing Emma's skin was sheer heaven. The sense of freedom was invigorating and Emma took the privilege very seriously. She wasn't about to screw up a good thing, or disappoint the people that had helped her so much.

One night as Emma sat at the table in the common room, the cottage mother on duty, Mrs. Michaels, asked her to meet with her in her office. Mrs. Michaels was the most soft-spoken, gentle, and sensitive of all the cottage mothers, and Emma's favorite. While Emma appreciated all of her cottage mothers, Mrs. Michaels was different. As a small child and even growing up, Emma had been very sensitive, brought easily to tears by the many hurtful things in her life. Sensitivity and tears had been an undesirable quality to her father. He had tried to toughen Emma up by beating the sensitivity out of her. Emma had grown to hate her tender heart, but found she could do nothing to harden it, at least not for very long. Mrs. Michael's gentle nature helped Emma to realize that everyone was different and it was okay to be who you were, even if it meant a more tender heart than some.

"What's up?" Emma asked with a smile, as she followed Mrs. Michaels into the small room the cottage mothers used as a bedroom and office space.

"Hey, Em," Mrs. Michaels said, returning Emma's smile. Sighing she said, "Em, why don't you sit down for a minute."

Emma sat down on the orange plastic chair placed next to the door, the one used by the girls in the cottage during private meetings with the cottage mothers. Curiously, Emma looked at Mrs. Michaels, and noticed her slumped shoulders and forced smile. It was obvious to Emma that whatever was on Mrs. Michael's mind was making her uncomfortable.

"Em," Mrs. Michaels said in a soft voice. "I received a call from your caseworker a little while ago. Your sister, Amy, has run away."

Emma stared at Mrs. Michaels. She was stunned by what she had just heard. Amy—ran away—again. It was quiet in the small room as Mrs. Michaels gave Emma time to digest the news.

Emma's eyes scanned the small room, glanced at the twin bed crammed into one corner with a small nightstand placed nearby, then back to the small wooden desk cluttered with papers and the small lamp casting a golden glow onto Mrs. Michael's face. As Emma examined the contents of the room, and as the initial shock that her sister had run away wore off, she realized that she had been expecting Amy to run. She had been waiting for the announcement.

"Where is she?" Emma asked quietly.

"One day while your aunt was at work, Amy's boyfriend drove to the house and she left with him. It seems as if they had it planned, because she took some of her things with her. They are staying at his parent's house about an hour away. Since she is seventeen now, her caseworker gave her a choice to stay with him or go back to your aunt's house."

"And…her choice was to stay with her boyfriend," Emma stated, as she looked down at her folded hands.

"Yes," Mrs. Michaels answered quietly.

"So," 'Emma sighed, "where does that leave me?"

"I'm sure you can still go live with your aunt," Mrs. Michaels said in an encouraging voice.

Knowing she hadn't wanted to give her such sad news, Emma looked up at her cottage mother and offered her a small smile. But the smile on her lips was in contrast to her haunted, green eyes, as Emma said, "I don't know what to do. I really wanted to go there because of *Amy*. I know there is nowhere else for me to go. My caseworker already told me that." Tucking one foot beneath her, Emma continued thoughtfully, "There just *aren't* enough foster homes. That's why they are sending so many kids here *now*." Sighing, Emma said, "There's just no place for me."

"I'm so sorry, Em," Mrs. Michaels said.

Standing up, Emma said unconvincingly, "I know. It's okay. Something will come up." She knew her cottage mother was concerned about her, and didn't want to worry her, but she *was* scared. What was she going to do, she wondered. She had been so close to belonging somewhere. *So close.*

Emma walked back to the table in the common room and grabbed the letter she had been writing to her sister, Amy. Angrily, she crumpled it into a ball and tossed it in the small metal trash can, and then walked to the sitting room and sunk into the soft couch, thinking.

The next day, deep in thought about Amy, Emma leaned over and wiped off one the tables at the Rec Hall. She knew she had to come to terms with the newest disappointment in her life. Maybe she could just stay at the home, she reasoned. Many of the kids had lived there for years. She was going to be a junior in high school this fall, so really it would just be for two more years. It wouldn't be so bad. Tanner had been right; it really wasn't that bad at the home. Actually, she had grown to love her cottage, her room, the dining hall, cottage mothers, her cottage mates, the dances, and the structure…*all of it*. Her cottage mates had become the fill in sisters she had always wanted. She stood up with the wet rag in her hand and stared across the room, a small smile playing on her lips, and thought, life at the cottage was funny at times, as some of the silliness of the past year flitted across her mind—and it was safe, she reflected.

"Emma!" Sandy, one of the girls from Illinois cottage shouted, as she ran across the large room. "Did you hear?"

Shaking her head, Emma wondered why the short brunette, with the dimple in her chin was running toward her. *Not only that, she wondered with a frown, but where was the rest of her group?*

"No. What's up?" Emma asked absently.

Emma rested one of her hands on the back of a chair and waited for the exciting news that she realized most likely had nothing to do with her. She just happened to be in the right place at the right time to get the gossip scoop.

"Tanner," Sandy blurted.

When Emma heard her boyfriend's name, she let go of the chair and leaned toward the girl, and asked, "What about Tanner?"

"He's gone," Sandy said. "He ran. He ran with one of the girls from my cottage. You know, Mellissa. Well they are both from down south. The same town. They just ran. They're AWOL."

Emma tried to appear calm, a calm she was not feeling. Her stomach was in knots over the news, and she felt hot tears sting her eyes.

"No. I hadn't heard that," Emma said quietly.

"They left early this morning. Tanner called the home and was allowed to talk to the cottage dad on duty. He was calling from his sister's house, which is where he's staying now," Sandy said in a rush.

Leaning toward Emma, Sandy said under her breath, "He was allowed to talk to some of the guys from his cottage when he called, and he told them they had sex, Tanner and Mellissa. You know, the girl he ran with."

Emma felt as if she had been slapped, as her mind sought the faces and names of the girls from Illinois cottage. She knew who the girl was—she was a nice girl. Emma didn't even get to have the satisfaction of hating her.

"I got to get back to my group!" Sandy shouted, and ran out of the hall.

Emma stared after her, the imagined image of Tanner and Mellissa having sex imprinted on her mind. How could he do that to her, she agonized, as she flopped onto the black cushioned chair. How could he leave her, and how could he have *sex* with that girl? In all the time they had been hanging out over the last year, they had never even gotten close to having sex. Not that she had ever intended to have sex with him, Emma thought, as she rested her forehead on her hand.

Since Tanner had graduated from the program, long before Emma, he hadn't needed to be escorted on campus grounds. He had a job on campus too, at the dining hall, just a few minutes from the Rec Hall. Emma thought about the last time she had seen Tanner—just a few days ago. She had been cleaning the Rec Hall when he had called her name from across the large recreation room. Surprised, she had looked up and had seen him motioning to her from the landing by the foosball tables. Looking around to make sure no one saw them, she had run up the stairs, and then they had tucked away in a corner on the landing, behind a small partition near the door that she had never noticed before, away from curious eyes. She had reached up and touched his freshly cut, much shorter black hair, soft to her fingers. His eyes had sparkled as he grinned down at her. Feeling guilty and fearing she'd be caught, she had briefly pressed her lips to his warm, wet ones. His body had felt lean and hard as he pressed into her—a few stolen moments—their last.

Tanner had been a gentle and kind boy. She had felt safe with him. Other kids at the home snuck away and had sex during dances—one couple had been caught in the act by a cottage parent. *That* had been ugly, but Tanner had never tried to do that with her, she thought, because he cared about and respected her.

Emma slumped her shoulders, leaned over the table and thought, Tanner had completed the program months ago and had decided to stay at the home for her. He *had* somewhere to go—she knew that—not like her. As far as Mellissa, the sex girl, Emma knew it wasn't as if she and Tanner were married or even a *real* boyfriend and girlfriend. How could they be? They had stolen moments together shared while she worked at the Rec Hall and the few moments they had when hidden within the shielding circle made by her cottage mates on the way to school, tucked away from cottage parents eyes—a stolen kiss—that and the silly letters they wrote to each other. Why *shouldn't* he have sex with the first girl—literally—that he ran across? Emma scooted the heavy metal and black cushioned chair back, and grabbing the oversized dust mop, began the time-consuming task of sweeping the entire hall, as her thoughts wandered.

A few hours later, as Emma walked back to Grant cottage, she kept her eyes down, staring at the broken sidewalk beneath her feet as kids from other cottages walked passed. By now, Emma knew the AWOL news about Tanner had spread across campus—knew that the news of Mellissa and Tanner having sex was, in some kids' minds, even more interesting than the fact that they had run. Emma felt the eyes of the kids from the cottages burning into her as she walked passed them and knew they were talking about her and Tanner.

Days later, deep in thought, during the afternoon group session, Emma caught only a few words here and there as the other girls discussed various issues they were having. Tanner was weighing on Emma's mind, just as much as Amy was—both of them had run—both of them—gone. She was having a difficult time accepting that two very important people in her life had left her.

Emma noticed the room had become quiet, and red faced with embarrassment, wondered if someone had just directed a question at her, but while deep in thought she hadn't noticed. Not lifting her head, she scanned the room. Realizing no one was looking in her direction, she lifted her head and looked at the faces in the room, wondering if something was wrong.

Touching Claire's arm, Emma whispered, "What did he say?" meaning the cottage counselor.

With a serious expression, Claire whispered back, "They are closing the school!"

Emma sat back in her chair and stared at her roommate, her mouth hanging open in surprise; certain she hadn't heard her correctly.

"Why!?" Emma heard Michelle demand.

"They are just going to *kick us out*?" Jena asked in a shrill voice.

She *had* heard right, Emma realized. They were closing the home—her home.

"What are they going to do with all of us? Are they opening a new school? Just where are we going?!" Corey panicked.

"The state has been discussing this issue for months. It's funding. There have been many budget cuts, and well, this school is one of them. The idea is that foster homes will be more beneficial for all of you. You will all be placed either back home with your families, or with foster families," the counselor explained.

"But there are no foster homes," Emma said on a soft breath.

She knew there wasn't a home for her—no foster home—no family placement. She couldn't even imagine what was next for her, and many of the other kids at the home. There was no place to put everyone, and as she looked around the room at the faces of her cottage mates, and the counselor, she suspected many of them were thinking the same thing. In the last two months, kids had been flooding into the home because they had nowhere to go. *Had the state lost its mind, she wondered.*

The closure would affect hundreds of people, not just the children living safe within the walls of the cottages. When the last door of the home was closed and locked, over one hundred children would be moved onto foster homes, back to their abusive families, detention centers, or forced to live on their own. The adults at the children's home would be impacted too. Cottage parents, dining hall staff, and teachers, would all have to find new jobs.

Over the weeks that followed the school closure announcement, the children at the home, and even the cottage parents became quiet, each processing what the change would mean to their future. Many of the children considered all they had been taught during their time at the home, things such as, never accept abuse, or neglect, and to take a stand against wrongs done to them. The news of the school closure became a disruption. Instead of working through the program, healing from the various abuses, the children, counselor's and cottage parents instead focused on where all the children would be placed, as quickly as possible to meet the fast approaching school closure deadline.

For many of the children, the home had been their haven, their sanctuary from abuse and now they were being thrust back into the world, with little preparation and in many cases, with no knowledge of their destination. They were safe within the walls of the school, and not knowing what awaited them off campus in the real world, had them wondering, what could they do to stop the school from closing. Distracted by their own problems, the cottage parents didn't see the secret meetings, and notes being tucked into outstretched hands as cottage groups passed one another on their way to the dining hall. Notes were shuffled back and forth between the cottages, all asking the same questions, *what can we do to stop this?*

What could they do, Emma wondered as she tucked a note a girl from Wood cottage had shoved into her hand moments earlier. The girl hadn't said anything to Emma. Unsmiling, the young girl with black hair had thrust her hand toward Emma, and as Emma reached out her hand to accept the white scrap of paper, she had known, even before she unfolded the small piece of paper, that it would be one of the hundreds of notes being passed around campus. Since Emma was one of the few children allowed to roam the grounds unescorted, she had become a connector, receiving and sending notes to and from the cottages. She knew what all the cottages were thinking and feeling—their anger, their fear, and their hope. What could they do, Emma wondered. They were just kids. No one listened to them. No one heard. No one had ever wanted to hear.

CHAPTER THIRTY

"Come on Emma! What else can we do? We can't just let them kick us out without a fight. This is our home!"

Emma stood in the afternoon sun at the edge of the dining hall with two boys from Bennett cottage, one girl from Wood, and two girls from Illinois cottage. One of the girls from Illinois cottage was insisting that they get as many kids from the home together, and run away in protest of closing the home. Emma was in agreement with them. She didn't want the home to close either. She was stressing about where she was going to go next, but running away seemed like an awful lot of work. If they did run, where would they go, she considered. How could they possibly coordinate such a massive project through scribbled notes passed hand to hand in passing? She just didn't think it was possible.

"Talk to the girls in your cottage," the six foot five, seventeen-year-old black boy said, as he looked down at Emma. "Get as many as you can to promise to run. We'll all meet again to decide when to leave."

Emma looked up at Jarod. He had been one of Tanner's friends, before he had run away.

"Okay. I'll talk to the girls tonight," Emma promised.

Emma walked around the corner of the building to the doors of the dining hall to meet her cottage mates for dinner. She had just finished her shift at the Rec Hall, cleaning the place spotless. Since Emma had graduated from the program, it had set her apart from many of the other kids, proving she was responsible, and mature.

As she sat down at her assigned table with her tray of food, she wondered, just how responsible would it be if she ran? Then she thought, but why do all the right things if it turned out wrong anyway.

She looked up from her tray and looked at the kids in each section of the dining hall, all the familiar faces, all with grim expressions. This was their home, and for many, this was all they had, and now and it was being ripped from them. Emma was tired of being jerked from home to home. The crappy homes she had lived in, she'd had to fight her way out of, and the good ones were never permanent. She was tired. As Emma walked with her group back to their cottage after dinner, she whispered to them to meet her in the TV room later that night, because she needed to talk to them about something.

"How about after the movie this weekend?" Beth asked. "A lot of us will already be off campus, downtown. A few of us at a time can just kind of walk away. During the movie, some of us—a few at a time—can say we have to go to the bathroom, but never come back."

"That's a great idea!" Corey agreed.

"So you guys are in…? Emma asked uncertainly.

"Yeah," the group chorused.

Emma raised her eyebrows at how easily the girls had agreed to go AWOL. Not long ago, one of their main goals as a cottage had been to go as many days as possible without any AWOLs. They were given special privileges for reaching their cottage non-AWOL goals, and now they were clamoring to run away …*together!*

It was decided. Emma was to meet with the kids from the other cottages to let them know the plan. Saturday—during the movie matinee at the movie theatre downtown—whoever was running needed to find a way downtown. It didn't sound like much of a plan to Emma. Where were they going? How long were they staying gone, and how in the world was a large group of twenty to sixty kids going to pass unnoticed through the center of town?

It seemed hotter than usual in the Rec Hall Saturday morning as Emma mopped up an area of the floor. Sweat trickled between her shoulder blades as she rolled the heavy bucket of water into the storage closet.

Pressing her hands to the small of her back, she leaned back trying to relieve the ache. Brushing her sweat dampened hair off her face, Emma walked down the hall, wondering if the air conditioning was out. Emma pulled her hair back in her hands, and held it off her neck. She was thankful she had worn a sleeveless top and shorts. Emma tugged the wrinkles out of her beige top then looked down at her navy blue terry cloth shorts thinking she needed to change before the movie.

Slowly she walked back to the cottage, in no hurry to be inside the cottage walls. According to the watch on her wrist, she had plenty of time to shower and change into a different pair of shorts and top before the movie. As Emma walked, she looked around at what had been her home for almost a year—at the gym where she had learned to swim. Smiling, she thought about all the hours she had practiced to get her form down. When she had begun her first swim class, she hadn't known how to swim a single stroke.

During the winter, the superintendent of the school had allowed gymnastic instructors to come on campus to teach a gymnastic series to the children. Emma had learned the uneven bars, loving the freedom of flipping round and round, competing only with herself. She had learned routines on the balance beam and had taken quite a few tumbles on the horse, never able to get her legs into position, mostly flopping to the ground in a heap. She had practiced for hours with her volleyball team in the gym, surprised at how accurate her serves were.

She glanced over at the school she had attended during the school session, thinking about how hard she had worked to make up all her freshman credits her sophomore year, then she had moved on and worked through her sophomore year. Allowed to work at her own pace, Emma had managed to catch up to her sophomore class. If she kept up her current academic pace, Emma would be able to graduate on schedule with her class during her senior year.

There were no cars—no kids walking—no one as Emma continued her peaceful walk. She wasn't afraid that some stranger or even someone she knew would approach her and try to hurt her. There weren't even any dogs allowed to roam loose on campus.

Approaching the Y-shaped cottage, Emma stopped. She stared at the building, her home—*this was her home*. She didn't want to go anywhere else. The sixteen-year-old girl, golden brown hair blowing in the breeze, stood and reflected on life. She knew life was meant to be hard, but should it be *so* hard—so often—and at such a young age?

A lavender colored butterfly caught Emma's eye. She smiled as she watched it flit by, more of a flutter she considered than a flit, and as the breeze kicked up, she closed her eyes for a moment. She allowed the moment to wash over her—the breeze cooling her sweaty body—as she lifted her face up toward the sky.

"There's Emma!" she heard as she stepped into the cottage, the door still propped open in her hand. Now what, she wondered.

"Emma," Mrs. Hays said. "Girl, we got to get going."

"I need to jump in the shower real quick, and then change," Emma said.

"Girl. You don't have time for that. We need to be up at that bus in five," Mrs. Hays insisted.

As Emma stood in the hall, her cottage mates came running down the hall toward her.

You have got to be kidding, Emma thought. She tugged at her top, feeling sticky and grimy. If they planned to run tonight, they could all just forget about her, because after the movie, she had every intention of riding back on the bus, taking a nice long shower and changing her clothes!

"Fine," Emma sighed.

A half hour later, sitting in the dark cool movie theater, Emma sighed and sunk deeper into her seat. As she stared at the action on the screen, she dug her hand into the warm, buttery popcorn. She had worked most of the morning, since breakfast, and she was tired. This was the first opportunity she'd had to sit and relax all day.

As Emma tried to enjoy the movie, a comedy about two guys in jail, her thoughts wandered. None of the girls from the cottage had mentioned running as they had ridden over to the movie theatre on the bus, and no one had approached her earlier in the day at the Rec Hall about it either. Just as well she thought, as she crunched her popcorn.

CHAPTER THIRTY ONE

The evening sun was surprisingly bright as Emma and her cottage mates, still laughing over the silly movie, stepped outside. Shielding her eyes, Emma looked up at the position of the sun, and then over to the bus parked across the street. Emma prepared to step off the curb into the street when Beth grabbed her by her arm, and yelled, "Come on!"

Emma turned her head toward Beth, knowing it was time—they were running. Out of the corner of her eye, Emma saw kids from the various cottages standing across the street and wondered how they had gotten away from campus without anyone knowing.

"Now!" Beth shouted, and ran across the street.

As Emma sprinted across the road, skirting oncoming traffic, she thought, *I wish I'd had time for a shower and to change my clothes!*

As Emma ran down the sidewalk, she found herself surrounded by kids from the home. She glanced around her as a tall, lanky, black boy ran passed her on her left. Kids from all cottages were represented, boys, girls, tall, short, chubby, thin, Black, White and Hispanic. They ran as a group of at least fifty, Emma estimated. As they left the downtown area, the largest part of the group veered left toward a neighborhood, as many smaller groups took off in other directions.

Emma heard a siren behind her, and the group burst forward, sprinting around a corner to the left of a yard, in front of a one-story house lined with large bushes. Hearing a man's voice shout, Emma snapped her head up and looked toward the house as a man emerged from between the bushes with a shotgun in his hand. Heart pounding, Emma bolted across the yard and flinched as she heard the boom of a shotgun. The group of kids scattered, fast.

She was winded, but kept running as the group became smaller with each passing block. Soon it was just Emma, Beth, Megan's boyfriend Heath, and Trey, a boy from Sherman cottage. Megan wasn't running with the group. Her family had signed her up for a survival program in Canada for a month. Right now, Emma suspected her friend had no idea they were closing the school, and that soon she would have to go back home to her nightmare.

The small group slowed to a walk, the boys leading the way.

Emma let out a long, tired sigh. "Beth, do you have any idea where we are going?" Emma asked.

"Let's just go with it," Beth said. "We'll just see where we end up. It's not like we have anything better going on back at the cottage."

It was dark now and Emma was hungry, thirsty, tired, and cold. She rubbed her bare arms and looked around. They were on the edge of town, no more houses; instead, trees, tall grass, and fields surrounded them. They ran across the abandoned road and stumbled through tall weeds beyond the line of trees and into a clearing. The small group of kids walked up a slight hill, and started following train tracks. They followed the tracks until Beth finally stopped and leaned forward with her hands on her knees.

Emma, her legs feeling like rubber, stopped and stood beside Beth, as she called out in a raspy voice, "Heath!"

Emma watched the two boys as they continued walking down the tracks.

"Heath!" she cried out again.

Emma liked Heath. She knew he was a good guy. He was another one of the kids at the home she couldn't figure out. What event, she wondered, had brought him to the home? Clean cut as any of the snooty boys she had known at her last high school, he reminded her of one of the science geeks, or student council president types. He wasn't a t-shirt kind of guy—cute, in a conservative haircut, soft blue eyes, and a nice build kind of way. Much taller than Emma, Heath was about the same height as Beth, almost six foot. Heath was the kind of boy Emma dreamed about dating. He was kind, sweet, respectful, and safe. The kind of boy she knew would never hurt her—would never be interested in her. She didn't know why that was, maybe because she wasn't pretty enough, bubbly enough, smart enough, just not anything enough she supposed. Trey, the boy walking beside Heath, was most definitely *not* the student council president type. He didn't bother with collared shirts, instead opted to wear t-shirts that enhanced his well-developed chest and abs. He was one of those boys that knew he looked good, and knew girls noticed him. Trey was not the keeper kind and yet another type of boy she would never attract.

The boys stopped, turned, and looked back at the girls. Heath began walking toward them with Trey following close behind. A light in the distance threw their faces into shadow as Emma watched them approach.

"Heath," Beth panted. "I'm tired. I need to stop."

Beth was standing upright now, her hands resting loosely on her hips.

Heath shook his head in understanding, and said, "Okay. We can hang out here. It's as good a place as any."

There were two sets of tracks; the one they were standing on had boxcars sitting nearby and the one running parallel, was empty. The two sets of tracks were surrounded on either side by trees, isolated from the view of passing cars. It was the consensus of the four kids that no one would think to look for them on or near railroad tracks, so they decided it was to be the night's hang out.

"Let's sit down," Heath suggested softly.

Thankful to be off her feet, Emma looked across at Heath's friend and thought; he sure didn't have a lot to say. What was the big plan for the night, she wondered, ready to head back to the cottage to shower and eat. The popcorn she had eaten at the theatre had worn off about an hour ago.

Rocks dug into Emma's butt as she shifted, trying to get comfortable. As the four teens sat in a circle, close enough to touch, they talked about their pasts, their hopes for their futures, and where they thought they might end up next.

Looking into Beth's eyes, Heath asked, "Where do you think you'll end up?"

Smiling, the blonde said, "I suppose I'll end up back home. I'm pretty much done with the program anyway. It won't be so bad. I'll just stay away from my old crowd, you know and stay out of trouble."

"What about you?" Beth asked, as she looked intently into his eyes.

"Same I suppose," Heath responded.

"What about you, Trey? Where are you going after you leave the school?" Beth asked.

Trey looked down at his hands holding a couple of small rocks and shook them as if they were a set of dice. "Oh," he said, "I'll probably end up where they wanted to send me all along, in jail or a detention center."

He looked up, looked at each of the kids in the circle.

"I'm one of the kids that have no place to go," Trey said wryly. "This place saved me, but now I guess there's just no saving me. I haven't been what you'd call the perfect kid. I grew up in a rough neighborhood and did what I had to, you know, to survive. I stole some stuff."

Looking back down at his hands, Trey threw the rocks onto the wood of the tracks.

His voice so soft, Emma had to lean closer to hear him.

"I don't want to be locked up," Trey said quietly. "It scares me." He looked up, embarrassed, and continued, "I'm not a *bad* kid—not like some." Looking back down at the tracks, he said with a sigh, "I'm afraid of what they'll do to me in there."

Emma watched the boy sitting next to her, and felt the fear flowing off him. She thought she had it bad—nowhere to go—but realized things could be so much worse for her. She could be Trey—locked up for who knew how long.

Each of the kids sitting on the tracks—pouring out their souls—knew that to be sent to a detention center or jail, was often the beginning of a life's journey that ended with a life sentence in prison or death at the hands of some very scary person.

Looking uncomfortable, Trey asked gruffly, "What about you Emma? Where are you going after you leave the home?"

Emma looked up, smiled, and said, "I don't know where I'm going. I have nowhere to go—no family—no foster home—nowhere to go," her voice trailed away. "The home was at least somewhere—somewhere safe away from all the bad stuff, you know?" she said, as she looked up into each of her companions faces.

Beth, Heath, and Trey shook their heads. Yes. They knew what Emma meant. They each were well aware of the many bad things that could happen to a girl and even a boy outside the walls of the home.

Oh shit, Emma thought. To add to her misery, now she had to pee.

"Guys," she said with a grimace. "I have to pee."

"Me too!" Beth said. "I've been in agony for the last half hour."

"Come on," Heath said. "You girls go that way," he said, pointing down the train tracks toward the boxcar. "Trey and I'll go this way. Meet you back here. Okay?"

"Okay," the girls chimed.

Rising unsteadily to her feet, Emma walked beside Beth down the tracks.

As they walked side by side down the tracks, Beth asked softly, "So what do you think of Trey?"

"Kind of sad, isn't it?" Emma replied thoughtfully. "That he's going to be sent to jail or something. I thought I had it bad."

"No, Emma," Beth whispered. "Not like that. I mean—do you like him, you know—*like* him."

Comprehension struck Emma. *Like him. What the hell?* She didn't even *know* him, she thought in surprise.

Stopping on the tracks, Emma said, "Beth, I don't even *know* him. I can't *like* someone I don't even know."

"Well I want to hang out with Heath. You *know*," Beth said, as she looked back toward the boys now walking into a group of trees. "While we're having fun, why don't you and Trey have a little fun too?" she suggested.

Emma looked up at her friend, the girl she had looked up to, respected, and admired for the past year. Beth had a girl-next-door look about her, and it was then Emma realized, she couldn't always judge someone by the way they looked. Emma looked back toward the dark group of trees where the boys had disappeared, just in time to see them walking back toward the tracks, their faces illuminated by a light set high up on a post.

Where Heath was light, with blonde hair, blue eyes and pale skin, Trey was dark, with hair so black it blurred with the night sky, and brown eyes the color of chocolate, and muscled skin a shade darker than Heath's fair complexion. She watched them walk, one with a boyish charm, as if he were trying to win some type of school election, and the other swaggering as if he were looking for a fight—one warm and inviting—the other cool and aloof. Turning, Emma walked toward the trees to find a place to relieve the intense pressure in her bladder.

Hidden from prying eyes behind a blanket of trees and tall grass, Emma squatted and said, "Beth, our best friend is *dating* Heath. He's Megan's boyfriend, remember?" Emma hissed.

Squatting nearby, Beth insisted, "Well she's not here. She'll never know."

As far as Emma was concerned, the subject was closed. Beth could *not* have sex with their best friend's boyfriend. The very idea was, well, just awful. Emma did not intend to have sex with someone she didn't even know. Besides, her last sexual experience was still a raw memory. Pulling up her shorts, Emma thought about Mark—remembering the searing pain of sex with him, and then the pain of discovering she had meant nothing to him—she had been nothing but a sex bet.

The girls walked quietly back toward the boys.

Sitting back down on the tracks, Emma thought she had made Beth see reason, so she was surprised when Beth and Heath stood up and began walking down the tracks together toward the boxcar.

Unbelievable, Emma thought, as she stared after them.

Trey had the forethought to wear a jacket, as had many of the other kids that had run away—but not Emma. It was a crisp Indiana night, and now, as Emma watched, Trey spread his jacket over the tracks, near Emma. Sitting down on the jacket, Trey extended his hand out toward Emma.

"Come here," he said softly. "Come lay down next to me."

As she looked at him suspiciously, still extending his hand toward her, he said, "Nothing more. I know you're tired." He cocked his head, and said gently, "It's okay."

Exhausted, Emma went to him, with no intention of having sex with him or *anyone* that night. If she were going to have sex, Emma thought, it would be when she wanted, not just because some boy felt she should.

Trey and Emma lay back, the jacket softening the sharpness of the rocks beneath them, providing a barrier between their bodies and the wooden slats. Trey's warm body curled next to Emma, his arm draped loosely over her waist, and exhausted, the teens fell asleep.

CHAPTER THIRTY TWO

When Emma woke the next morning, Trey was still holding her close. As she lay curled on her side, she watched as the sun glistened between the swaying leaves of the trees. Uncomfortable, needing to pee, slowly Emma sat up. Twisting her body, she looked back at Trey and saw his eyes looking up at her.

Scrambling to her feet, Emma quickly walked down the train tracks to the same spot she and Beth had visited the night before and pulled her shorts down, squatted, and sighed in relief. Looking around for something to wipe herself with, Emma thought, it was at times like these she hated being a girl—no toilet paper, she thought, rolling her eyes—and nowhere to wash her hands. She walked back through the tall grass and trees to Trey, sitting on the tracks.

As Emma approached Trey, she looked around and wondered where Beth and Heath were.

"Have you seen Beth and Heath yet?" she asked.

Standing, Trey shook his jacket and said casually, "They left during the middle of the night while you were sleeping."

Shocked, Emma said, "*What*? You have got to be kidding."

So that was it for Beth, Emma thought. She had just wanted to run-away so she could fuck some guy, then back to campus she went. Disgusted, Emma shook her head, rolled her eyes, leaned on one leg, and placed a hand on her hip.

"Do you want to go back?" Trey asked.

Looking down at the tracks, Emma wondered, what *did* she want, and who really *cared* what she wanted. All she could think about lately was where she was going to go once the home closed. Why had she tried all these years, she wondered angrily.

"No," she said shortly. Looking up, she said bitterly, "I'm not ready to go back. *To what?*" Emma probed his eyes, seeing within the chocolate colored depths that he was as lost and scared as she was. She knew it—sensed it in him.

She ran her hand through her hair and looked up at the trees—the sun peeked through the leaves—and allowed her mind to continue its bitter journey. What had the foster mother said when she had been a little girl, *God has a plan for you.* That's what she had said as Emma had hidden away, hidden from her daddy who had come to take her home, the man that had beaten her, and done bad the things. *God has a plan for you, the foster mother had said.*

"Come on," Trey said, as he held out his hand. "I'll go back to my cottage to get us something to eat and get you some clothes." Looking her up and down, he said, "I think I can find something of mine that will fit you—baggy, but it will fit. Come on. Let's hide you away."

Looking at his chest, then down at his hips, Emma doubted that he owned any article of clothing that would fit her, her eyes lingering on his surprisingly narrow waist. She took his strong hand in hers and together they walked down the tracks toward the boxcar, the one that had been occupied by Beth and Heath for a few hours the night before.

Trey gave her a boost up into the old rust colored boxcar, and then climbed up after her. There were doors on both sides of the car, allowing light into the empty space. After he made sure she was safe, Trey jumped back down to the ground.

Squinting in the bright sunlight, Trey looked up at Emma as she looked down from the boxcar at him. "I won't be gone long," he assured her.

Emma crossed her arms over her chest and watched as Trey disappeared through the trees. She was afraid of being alone, in the middle of nowhere—alone inside of an abandoned boxcar. As Emma rubbed her shoulders, she walked across the uneven wooden flooring of the boxcar to the other side and looked out toward a group of trees, fear making it impossible to relax, but not scared enough to go back to the home. Hands on her hips, with nervous energy, Emma paced the length of the car and hoped Trey would be back soon, not only out of fear, but she was starving.

Pacing back and forth, Emma became lost in her thoughts, thinking how strange life was. Just yesterday after watching the movie at the theatre with her cottage mates, she had been anxious to get back on the bus, wanting nothing more than to get back to her cottage, run a cool shower, and then later, read a book or watch TV. Now, here she was, pacing in a boxcar, angry with the adults for fucking up her life again—a shower was the *last* thing on her mind.

Stopping in the middle of the boxcar, Emma stared out at the trees and thought, life changed so fast—without warning, and way too often, and typically, not in good ways. Why couldn't she be like other kids, the lucky ones that had homes, that were bored silly because nothing ever changed in their life, every day was the same as the last, the knowing all the days in the future would be like all of the yesterdays.

Walking over to the edge of the boxcar, Emma sat down and swung her legs over the edge, wondering if she had done something wrong to make God hate her. Was there even a God, she speculated as she squinted up at the cloudless sky?

An hour passed as Emma sat on the edge of the boxcar, the sun warming her skin as she watched two white butterflies flutter in a dance, onto where ever it was butterflies flew on warm summer mornings. As the sun warmed her, Emma lay back on the wooden floor and allowed her thoughts to wander—why *do* the things that happen in life…*happen*. Why are some children loved—held—wanted, while others—like her…went through life trying so hard to belong. Emma heard a whistle and sat up. She watched as Trey walked through the trees, and walked toward her carrying two small white plastic sacks.

Hiking a leg up, Trey climbed up into the boxcar and sat down next to Emma. Opening one of the bags, he handed her a pair of white jeans, and t-shirt.

"I'm pretty sure this will fit you," he said, as he looked at her. "The jeans might hang a little low on your hips, but I think it will work."

Surprised that he had brought her something to wear, wondering how he had managed to pull it off; Emma looked into his eyes, grinned, and asked, "How in the world did you manage to grab this?" holding the jeans and shirt in her hands. "You just *walked* into your cottage—just walked in? Was anyone there?"

Looking down at the ground, at least four feet below, Trey said, "All the guys were there, *and* my cottage dad. I walked into the cottage, walked right by everyone to my room, changed my clothes, and then found something that would fit you. While I was changing, all the guys crowded around me, including the cottage dad, Mr. Sanders. Everyone was talking and yelling at once. They told me I couldn't go back out. And I asked…why not? I asked them, what they were going to do to keep me there. Then, I went to the kitchen and made a couple of sandwiches," he said, and handed Emma the other sack. "As I was walking out the door, things got a little rough. Mr. Sanders grabbed me and a window got broken—I'll be paying for that," Trey said looking out toward the trees.

Emma looked at Trey, and tried to picture what he had just experienced—friends he had known for at least a year—and Mr. Sanders—Emma knew him, and knew all the guys on campus loved him. He was one of the coolest cottage dads at the home. She knew Trey respected him, just as everyone else did. Trey and Mr. Sanders had gotten into a physical fight, she suspected. How else could a window have gotten broken? Getting into a fight with a cottage dad was *not* a good idea, especially if a detention center was a future consideration—this was not going to look good and Emma knew Trey knew that. She realized she wasn't the only kid at the home that was scared about their future, as she continued to look at Trey.

"So—you made me a sandwich?" Emma asked.

Looking at her with a small smile, Trey said, "Yeah."

"Are you hungry?"she asked. Standing up, she said, "Come on. Let's go sit inside in the shade."

Leaning against the back wall of the car, Emma tore into her sandwich as Trey sat next to her and took a bite out of his. As she chewed, she considered—good sandwich—thick slices of meat and cheese between wheat bread. Trey had thrown apples, several bottles of water, and a handful of napkins into the plastic sack along with the sandwiches.

"How many kids went back?" Emma asked.

His arm propped on his knee, Trey answered, "All of them."

Looking at him in surprise Emma asked, "*Seriously*, we're the only ones out?"

Looking at her, he said, "Yeah."

Emma said with a scowl, "What was the point? Why did any of them run? Did we *even* make a point or was it just a fun night out for everyone so they could *fuck* each other?"

Smiling, Trey grabbed his bottle of water and answered quietly, "I don't know," then took a gulp.

"Why don't *you* go back?" she asked angrily. "You know, I *get* that some of the kids at the home have somewhere to go after they close the place down, and I'm happy for them. But some of us have nowhere to go. I," she said pointing to her chest, "have nowhere to go! Oh my God! I am so fucking tired of people fucking with my life. I am *not* a game for some asshole adult to take out of a box whenever they are bored!"

Tears of anger burned Emma's eyes.

"Emma, I know," Trey said, turning toward her. "I'm one of the seriously fucked kids—remember?"

Shaking her head in acknowledgment, Emma apologized, "I'm sorry. I didn't mean to yell at you."

Trey jumped to his feet and held out his hand, and said with a small smile, "Come on. We don't have to worry about it today."

Allowing him to pull her to her feet she asked, "Where are we going?"

"Let's just go walk for awhile—just be free," Trey said, with a shrug of his muscular shoulders.

Smiling up at him, Emma said, "Okay!" Then looking down at the clothes he had brought for her, she said, "Just let me change real quick."

Trey jumped down from the boxcar and allowed Emma a few moments alone to change out of her grimy shorts and t-shirt. She pulled the t-shirt he had brought for her over her head, and smiled as she looked down thinking it looked more like a nightshirt than a shirt. She wiggled into his white colored jeans and thought, he was right. They hung low on her hips, but they weren't falling off. At least she felt clean, she thought, thankfully.

In no hurry, with no destination in mind, the two teens walked for hours as the hot summer sun beat down on them. Trying not to draw attention, they kept to the outskirts of town, not realizing their physical contrasts drew curious glances, the young girl with long golden brown hair, and deep green eyes, skin more fair than was usual for summer, smiling up at the boy with jet black colored hair, naturally bronzed skin, and chocolate brown eyes. As they walked, they shared the stories of their pasts, about their families, friends—their journeys so far.

Eventually, nothing else to do, and nowhere else to go, they walked back to the boxcar, their home for now. Trey stripped his t-shirt off and placed it on the rough wood floor next to his jacket softening the hard, rough surface of the boxcar floor. They lay on their sides, facing each other, and shared more about what had brought them to the home—to the boxcar. Trey was from Chicago, a world away to Emma—where a rite of passage was being beaten as an initiation into the brotherhood of gangs—where brutality meant survival. Emma's story didn't involve gangs, but it was still a life of survival.

Miles away from the home—sheltered from the sweltering heat of the sun, Emma lay beneath Trey's warm, muscled hard body, her legs tangled with his. She ran her fingers up his smooth back feeling the muscles ripple as he reached his hand to brush the hair from her damp forehead. She gazed into the depths of his eyes as he pressed his sweaty body against hers. Kindred spirits in fear and pain, Emma and Trey bared their bodies and souls on the wooden floor of the boxcar.

For a few days, Emma allowed herself to open a door, just a crack, to feel something other than fear and pain. She shoved aside the agony of being thrown away yet again—like nothing more than unwanted garbage, and the fear of what was waiting for her in her future.

A week later, Emma and Trey sat on the edge of the boxcar, their legs swinging over the edge. They knew they couldn't live in the boxcar—couldn't remain their forever. There would come a point when they had to go back—had to face their lives—and that time was now. Emma wanted to walk back to her cottage when her cottage mates were away to avoid questions. She didn't want to talk to anyone. She needed to be alone. The most likely time would be during lunch when all kids on campus were at the dining hall. Looking down at their watches, they estimated that they had an hour until they needed to begin walking back and after a long, lingering goodbye, they began their walk to the home. Trey's cottage was first. They stopped down the road, out of sight of his cottage, and with nervous smiles, they parted. As Emma walked to her cottage, a five-minute walk, it seemed as if the home was already deserted. It was so quiet.

Emma pulled open the door to her cottage, knowing as she did so that the security system would beep an announcement. As Emma walked down the short hallway, she expected to see the cottage mother on duty rounding the corner from the longer hallway to greet the unannounced visitor. When no one met her in the hallway, Emma kept walking, rounding the corner toward the longer hallway. As she walked down the long hallway, she saw Mrs. Michaels walk out of her office, and the expressions that washed across her face—shock—worry—then tears. Mrs. Michaels held open her arms, ready to comfort the scared teen.

Emma knew she smelled awful, there was a limit to the stink one could wash off in a gas station bathroom. With tears of her own running down her cheeks, she walked into the shelter and safety of her favorite cottage mothers arms.

"Are you alright? Did anyone hurt you?" Mrs. Michaels asked, brushing away the tears streaming down her cheeks.

"I'm okay, "Emma assured her.

"You had us worried sick," Mrs. Michaels said, as she walked Emma to her bedroom.

"I'm sorry," Emma said," and meant it. She had never meant to hurt or worry anyone. She just needed someone to hear, to care, to understand that the kids at the home mattered, that *she* mattered and throwing her away wasn't right. Having a place to be, *mattered.*

"Don't you worry about it. You get showered. I'm going to call the dining hall and have them send the girls back to the cottage," Mrs. Michaels said.

Emma looked up with a worried expression.

"No, Emma. No one's mad at you. When the police couldn't find you, we all thought something bad had happened to you." With fresh tears in her eyes, Mrs. Michaels said, "The girls are just going to be so happy you are safe."

The girls, cottage mother, and even the cottage counselor knew there was no point in issuing Emma Bring-Ups or re-assigning her problems, or even putting her in the Quiet Room to punish her. They were closing the school. She had no home. They understood. All they could do was to reassure the sixteen-year-old that it would all work out—when even they didn't know what would happen to her.

CHAPTER THIRTY THREE

Over the next month, Emma felt little pieces of her fall away, as one by one, the girls she had spent the last year, walking to school, eating with, pouring out hopes, dreams and nightmares with, packed their bags and moved on, either to their old lives or somewhere new. Emma still had no home lined up, had no idea what lie in wait for her outside the grounds of the home.

With each goodbye, each tear shed, sobbing as the girls clutched each other, Emma began to withdraw. The pain was unbearable. A year had been spent teaching Emma to open her heart, to let others in to love her and to love back. Now as her cottage mates were ripped away from her, not gradually, but in a mad rush to meet the states deadline for the closure of the campus, Emma recoiled from the world, vowing never to allow anyone in again.

"Emma," Mrs. Hays said, knocking on her bedroom door. The old rule which stated the girls couldn't be in their bedrooms during the day had been eliminated when more than half of the girls had been transferred out of the home.

Lying on her side on her bed, Emma stared blankly out her window. She had her own room now, almost able to have her pick of rooms, since most of the girls had moved away.

"Emma, I need to talk to you. You know the foster mom that brought you to the home last year—Audrey?" Mrs. Hays asked.

"Yeah," Emma said in a muffled voice. Of course, she knew Audrey. *All* the cottage mother's knew Audrey. Emma had written Audrey almost every night while she had been living at the home. The cottage mothers all knew that because they read every incoming and outgoing letter the kids wrote.

"She is going to come pick you up tomorrow. You need to pack your things tonight," Mrs. Hays said.

Turning her head toward her cottage mother, Emma opened her mouth to protest but nothing came out. She had been dreading this day for months, and now it was here. She wouldn't leave, she thought. If they wanted her to leave, she wasn't going to make it easy on them. They would have to use force to remove her. They would have to *carry* her out, she thought, and turned back toward the window.

"I'm not packing!" she said angrily. "I'm not leaving. There are still kids here. I have nowhere to go!" Turning back toward Mrs. Hays, she hissed, "I have nowhere to go."

"Emma, you *have* to pack. You can't stay here. This place is going to be locked up in a few weeks," Mrs. Hays pleaded.

Crying now, Emma said, "What about the other kids that are still here that have nowhere to go? I don't see you kicking them out!"

"They can't stay here either. Oh, Emma. I know this really sucks. I am so sorry," Mrs. Hays said.

The cottage mother laid her hand on Emma's shoulder to comfort her, but knew there was nothing she could say that would make what was happening any better. What could she say to a child that had been beaten down so many times by life—and now it was happening again. How many times, Mrs. Hays wondered as she walked out of the bedroom, could a child get back up and try again.

Rough fabric from the orange and brown couch in the common room scratched Emma's tear stained cheek. She clung to the couch as the few remaining girls at the cottage tried to rip her from it. Audrey had arrived over two hours ago to take Emma away from the home; from there she was to be taken to a temporary foster home until a permanent placement became available.

Emma lay sobbing on the couch as Audrey, kneeling beside her, begged her to please go pack her things. Mrs. Simpson, the cottage mother on duty, had given Audrey a black garbage bag and now Audrey was trying to coax Emma to pack her things into it so she could take her away. Mrs. Simpson was part of the skeleton crew of cottage parents, all that was left of the adults that had cared for the kids. Most of the other cottage parents had found other jobs, and had left Emma to.

"Emma, please," Audrey begged. "I'll help you pack your things if you want."

"No," Emma wailed. "I'm not leaving. You can't make me go back out there. You are *insane* if you think I'm going back out into that fucking world where people do horrible things. Leave me alone!" she screamed.

Emma cried, exhausted, and thought, *if they think I am going to walk, willingly, out of the glass door of this cottage, out into the fucked up world they call society, they are insane!*

Corey knelt down by Emma's face and wiped her cheek, and with tears of her own, said, "Emma you have to go. We all do."

"I can't," Emma, wept. "I can't go back out there, to whatever is out there. I just can't do it again."

Corey leaned over, wrapped her arms around Emma, and cried with her, as the two other remaining cottage mates came over and held Emma too, creating an emotional barrier from the world. They all cried together for a while as Audrey and Mrs. Simpson stood back with tears in their eyes, and watched the girls comfort one another.

In defeat, Emma rolled off the couch; her eyes almost swollen shut from hours of crying, and held out her hand for the garbage bag. Slowly, she walked to her bedroom, and not caring anymore, dumped everything that belonged to her into the mouth of the black garbage bag. She was numb—heard a buzzing in her ears—her motions automatic, as she drug the bag behind her.

Audrey took the garbage bag from Emma, noticing the dark circles under her eyes and swollen face. The girl Audrey looked at was a ghost of the girl she had seen just months ago. Then, Emma had glowed, so excited about her future and all she had accomplished—but that had been before the announcement of the school closure.

Patiently, Audrey waited by the door as Emma sobbed her goodbyes.

As Audrey drove off campus grounds, Emma looked back at her home, the place where she had been loved, accepted, and safe. Only after the grounds of the home had slipped out of her sight, did she turn around in her seat. Emma stared straight ahead through the windshield of the car. She didn't blink. She was numb. She didn't care anymore. Exhausted, she leaned her head against the passenger side window and closed her eyes, shutting out the world. A tear trickled down her cheek as she wondered, *what next...*

❧ ACKNOWLEDGEMENTS ❧

A heartfelt thanks to my family and friends, for their dedication to this project, and to me, and for the countless hours of reading drafts and assisting with the editing process. Without your faith and belief in me, this book would not be what it is.

* * *

One thing no one can take from you is your dreams...

ABOUT THE AUTHOR

After over twenty years in the business world, Carol Knuth is now focusing her time advising various organizations regarding at-risk children. When not advising or spending time with her family she writes about societal issues. Knuth has an interest in the topic of at-risk children because of her own childhood spent in foster homes.

To find out what happens next in the life of Emma, look for the next book in the series, fall of 2013.

www.ingramcontent.com/pod-product-compliance
Lightning Source LLC
Chambersburg PA
CBHW071314250626
47159CB00004B/1419